stories for my sister

stories for my sister

Elizabeth Aurelie Duvivier

SOLIDEN

Providence
2019

© 2019 Elizabeth Duvivier

All rights reserved. No part of this book may be used or reproduced in any manner whatsoever without written permission from the author.

elizabethduvivier.com

Cover art "Jusqu'à ce que la mort nous sépare" by Dominique Fortin

ISBN 978-1-7330324-0-7

Designed by Elizabeth Leeper

Typeset in Sabon and Canto Pen

This is a work of fiction. Names, characters, places, and incidents are the products of the author's imagination or are used fictitiously. Any resemblance to actual events, locales, or persons, living or dead, is entirely coincidental.

Printed in the U.S.A. by a family-owned business that recycles, uses soy and vegetable oil inks, and works with suppliers that share its environmental commitment.

SOLIDEN

Providence

2019

*for my mother, Barbara, who taught me to read
my father, Jean, who made up fantastical stories at bedtime
my sisters and brothers, Christine, Michele, John and Marc,
who have always been my shelter in the storm*

contents

1. iterations
2. no help at all
3. the holy grail
4. sex, lies, and the divine feminine
5. unconventional for the win
6. wherein Bea learns about the third chakra
7. more lies
8. the day of the morphine did not go as planned
9. a forever home

acknowledgments

~~To Bea~~

To Bea

I will forgive you
if you give me
Blue cotton candy

—not love,
Mona

I do not know which to prefer,

The beauty of inflections

Or the beauty of innuendoes,

The blackbird whistling,

Or just after.

—Wallace Stevens

iterations

That day in January, no more rose flowers. Spidery yellow witch hazel crowded the door when Bea came home from school. Her mother sat on the sofa in front of the window with sunshine spilling everywhere, over her shoulders, down to her knees, across the floor. Layers of her fluffy, white robe rippled like foam across the blue cushions. An angel with the baby Jesus on her knees. Her mother laughed and reached for a cigarette.

"No honey," she said. "Not baby Jesus. This is your sister, Mona. Here, you can hold her."

Her mother's name was Janet and sometimes she scared Bea because she moved quickly and used words that Bea didn't understand.

Janet pushed a pillow behind Bea's back and set the baby into her lap.

"Isn't she pretty?" said Janet.

Bea looked down at the baby. It was sleeping like a kitten, but with no fur and no tail. The ears tiny, tender and pink. Bea traced her fingers in circles over the smooth head, over the round belly. The baby seemed to like this.

The doorbell rang. People brought gifts and food like it was a birthday and Thanksgiving all at once.

"Do you know who you are?" the woman with the soft voice asked as she set a pink box wrapped with pink ribbons onto a stack of white blankets that hadn't been there when Bea left for school that morning. The woman with the soft voice had slept in Janet's bed and made breakfast for Bea while Janet was at the hospital.

"You're the big sister," she told Bea.

"I am the big sister," Bea whispered to the baby.

The baby's belly lifted up and down as it breathed. Bea tried to breathe in and out at the same time as the baby. They stayed like that for a long time. Then, without warning, her mother came and took the baby away. Bea sat on the blue sofa, her feet not reaching the floor, and felt the weight and warmth missing from her lap. The emptiness became an ache. She wished her mother would let her hold the baby again.

• ❖ •

Bea stands in the doorway to her sister's apartment. She flips the light switch. Overhead is a light fixture the size of a hubbard squash. It is beautiful with intricate designs hammered into the silver, like filigree, that break the light into sparkling bits that bounce off the ceiling and walls. Bea tries to remember if Mona had ever traveled to Morocco. No, she decides. Mona would think it is too chaotic, too messy. Plus, she never traveled anywhere you needed to get shots.

A dish for keys and a basket for mail sit on the table below the front hall mirror, both are empty. Facing the mirror is a lavish clay mask with the eye holes rimmed in white. The mask unnerves Bea; it adds to her growing unease.

She inches down the hallway to where it empties into an expansive living room, dining room, kitchen complex. There are floor to ceiling windows outfitted with white wooden shutters that block the morning sun; only the thinnest halo of light seeps around the edges.

Bea pauses in front of the fireplace that has an arrangement of birch twigs on the hearth. She is struck by how fake it is. No doubt Mona chose the birch for its pretty, ruffled bark, but if the idea is to have a fire ready for a one-match start, two sticks of kindling is not going to cut it. Bea wants to grab some hornbeam from the stack in the corner, toss in a few pinecones, or ball up some newspaper to get it set right; she knows how to make a great fire.

Instead, Bea sits at the edge of the white sofa and looks around the room. She remembers the dollhouse that Mona would play with for hours. Nothing fancy—not gingerbread or Victorian; simply a big wooden box cut up into smaller boxes on two levels with a slanted roof that could lift off. If Bea tried to play, too—moving the rocking chair closer to the bed—Mona would squall, "don't touch."

Bea looks down and sees that she has tracked bits of straw and dried manure across the carpet. Trying not to make any more of a mess, she takes off her boots and pads back down the hallway to leave them by the front door.

Why would anyone want to live somewhere it looks like nobody lives?

Her feet on the cold tile send a jolt up her spine. What if she is in the wrong place? Maybe this isn't Mona's apartment and she is in someone else's home. What would she say if they walked in and found her here, barefoot? She is caught between the urge to grab her wellies and run back to the truck and the force that she needs to find something to prove she is in the right place.

The last thing Mona ate was chocolate cake with coconut whipped cream and fresh raspberries. Bea fed it to her from a cereal bowl in teaspoon sized bites. She could tell that even though Mona didn't have the strength to feed herself, her mind was active enough to be bothered by the bowl. Bea had bought three of them at a yard sale for a dollar. She knew they weren't anything valuable, but she liked the turquoise color.

"There's a box," Mona said, her tongue soft, waiting for the next spoonful. "In the back of the tall kitchen cupboard, the one with the butler pantry doors, underneath the basket of votives."

Bea creeps into the kitchen. Hand-painted ceramic, Mona had said. An impulsive purchase, she kept meaning to get rid of them, but never did.

"I want you to have them. They're perfect for cake with raspberries."

Bea can't tell if the discomfort in her belly is from poking around in someone else's kitchen cabinets, or a stab of guilt for thinking how typical of Mona to wrap a gift with an insult.

She finds the plates stored neatly in their original box under a basket of candles and exhales in relief. This is the place.

No longer tentative, Bea explores the apartment. When she steps into a walk-in closet the size of a tractor shed, she knows she is in Mona's world. *No wonder she went nuts at my place.*

How could anyone need so many shoes? It made no sense. Racks and racks of shoes. Most of them look like they had never been worn. Clothes on wooden hangers are sorted by color, season and god knows what other micro levels of organization. A matching pair of pink Italian suitcases sit shoulder to shoulder near the entrance of the closet, as if ready to go on a moment's notice.

On a small shelf by the full-length mirror, a private spot and yet something you would look at every single day, is a framed photograph. Bea is in the center wearing a black graduation gown still fully zipped, the mortarboard tipping awkwardly despite copious bobby pins. It was a hot day in May. Her forehead is shiny, her hair curling wildly in the heat. The look on her face is surprise: a wide, can't-believe-it-is-true smile as if she had unpeeled a candy bar to find a golden ticket. Janet, on her right, has uncharacteristically moved her sunglasses to the top of her head so that, for once, you can see her eyes, except she is gazing not at the camera, but up at Bea with pride. On her left is an impossibly young Mona dressed as if she were thirty-five years old; her hair carefully coiffed and sprayed, every strand perfectly in place, utterly unaffected by the heat. Mona wears a sleeveless sheath with blue cornflowers scattered across it that are so large it almost looks like an impressionist painting. The dress fits her body precisely without an inch to spare. She looks happy and confident, as if the whole world were waiting for her, as if she were the one graduating.

Bea slides down to the floor to sit with the framed photograph in her lap. She is finding it hard to breathe. Her chest crushes in on her like when she swims out too far into the lake and can't touch the bottom.

Her fingers burrow into her pocket for the beads, the secret way of feeling safe that Nana taught her. Repeating the words over and over with eyes closed, seeing the words, melting between the words, the words sing on repeat until she is in a place of light, ease and safety. She can breathe again.

The beads always bring her back to Pennsylvania. Nana's house.

Nana gave her the beads the summer after Mona was born.

Janet passes Mona around the living room. She is so pretty and all the aunties want to hold her, but she starts to scream so Janet hands her to Bea. The baby quiets. Janet seems proud, not embarrassed.

"They're very close," she says.

"Why doesn't Bea call you Mommy?" asks one of the aunties.

Janet shrugs. "Sometimes she does."

"Doesn't it bother you—that she calls you by your name?"

Janet shakes her head. "I like it. It makes me laugh."

It's nighttime. Bea sits up. She hears angry shouting from downstairs.

Her grandfather's voice. Her mother's voice. Then both voices banging together which makes her chest hurt. And then, Nana is there. Sitting on the edge of the bed. Nana doesn't seem angry, she seems sad. Her smell is Bea's most favorite smell in the whole world. Gently, she unfurls Bea's fingers from where they grip the bedspread and presses a small necklace of brown beads into her hands.

"These are for you," she says. "Keep them just for you. Don't let your mother see."

Bea remembers giving Janet rocks she found and how her mother had tossed them out the kitchen door where they landed on the ground. *Those need to stay outside.* The beads are like little dirt colored stones.

"She won't want them," Bea tells Nana.

"Don't let her see them or she might take them away."

Bea feels the stomach sick rise up in her chest. She doesn't want to get in trouble. This feels like lying. She loves the beads. She doesn't want them to get thrown out the kitchen door. The shouting is still loud.

"Oh, Beatrice, dearest. I didn't mean to scare you. Here, let me show you how they help." From her pocket, Nana lifts out a long length of black beads that make slick clicking sounds as she drapes them between her hands. She pulls and settles the necklace as if she is setting up for cat's cradle.

Warm light glows from the hallway and helps her to see Nana's face, the cheeks soft and fallen forward. Nana's fingers have nails so clean Bea can see each edge where the pink becomes white. The skin on Nana's hands has small and big brown shapes the way potatoes do and so many lines, some so tiny they disappear into the folds of her skin. Underneath the skin are greeny blue veins twisting and crossing over bones and knuckles and then, at the tips of her fingers, the nails that glisten like rosebuds.

At the breakfast table, Bea eats oatmeal with blueberries and maple syrup from a bowl the color of robin's eggs. Nana pours a long stream of coffee into her teacup from a silver canister that is plugged into the wall. Bea knows not to touch it because it is hot. Her grandfather stands beside Nana with a little stick in one hand and a grater in the other.

"A bit of spice for the sweetest lass," he says. He shaves a sprinkle of dust into her coffee and she smiles up at him.

Love, thinks Bea.

"Cinnamon," he says to Bea. She watches as he shaves a sprinkle onto her oatmeal. Nana smiles into Bea's eyes as she lifts the teacup to her lips and drinks deeply.

The next time they go to Pennsylvania, Nana is gone. Mona is four. Aunt Ruby and Aunt Rose want the girls to change their clothes. The aunties do not like the dresses that Janet has chosen. Mona starts to cry. She loves her yellow dress.

The night before the funeral, people crowd into the house. In the kitchen. In the hallways. Perfume and shiny shoes like it is a grown-up party. Men and women press against the wall, lifting their glasses up over her head, as Bea worms through. Everyone is laughing. The nuns sit on the hall steps, laughing. Their black shoes poke out from under pigeon colored skirts. Bea pulls on Janet's arm.

"Mom, why is everyone laughing?"

Janet's dress is black. Her throat is hidden behind a stack of pearl necklaces. Her lipstick is not as red as it usually is.

"Oh, bunny," Janet says, pulling her attention away from the group for a minute to look down at Bea. "This isn't happy laughing," she explains.

Bea stands next to Nana who is lying on her back. White hair brushed smooth. Her smell is gone. Under her hands the black beads are coiled against her belly.

They were back in California when Janet saw the brown beads for the first time.

"Where did you get these?" Janet demanded, as if Bea had taken a packet of gumdrops and left the store without paying for it. Janet reached out to take the beads but Bea sprang forward with a fierceness she had never felt before, her voice deep like grandfather thunder.

"Don't," is all she said, but it was enough.

Her mother stopped.

"You don't know what they are," she said finally. "When you want to know what they are, come ask me."

Bea never did.

Bea pulls the truck to a stop and shuts the engine off. The drive back to the sugarbush felt endless. Her exhaustion is so deep she cannot imagine ever getting behind the wheel again and yet, in a few hours, she will.

In the passenger seat, the box of plates looks unchanged, every bit as secure and happy for the road trip as when she strapped the seatbelt across it. Bea imagines how bored it must have been, buried away in that dark closet for so long and now, look at all it has to gaze upon. She tosses the keys onto the dash. Her body and the door both creak loudly as she swings herself out of the cab. She walks over to where the meadow meets the drive and drops to her knees, then rolls over to sprawl like a snow angel in the fragrant grass.

There is a moment of exquisite peace where the only sounds are insects throbbing. It is broken by the sound of dogs barking wildly to welcome her home. They land like a storm around her. Licking her face, her hands. Overexcited, one of them steps on her belly, hard.

"Ow. Stop. Go lay down."

They settle close by her side.

Bea stretches her arms wide and buries her fingers in their fur. Peace returns. The earth warm under her back, the sun melting the bones in her face. A breeze ripples over them. She smells honeysuckle and sweet pea. Her eyes open. The maple leaves are no longer small bundles of promise. Masses of bright green skins are fully open, fresh and taut against the blue sky. They sway on the breeze. Only the trunks and the largest branches of the sugarbush are visible.

Bea pulls herself up to standing with her eyes still on the leaves. The dogs get up, too. They wait for her next move. She is waiting for the words to come. The same question has been on repeat for days now. What were the right words? What should she have said?

She heads over to the pigs and sees Giusita is on the other side of the fence deadheading roses. Bea likes how Giusita didn't rush down to the truck when she arrived. Giusita doesn't need Bea to tell her all about New York, what Mona's apartment was like, what she found. Bea likes this young woman's wise, gentle ways. It has been so easy having the two of them, Giusita and her boyfriend Diogo, live here.

Giusita looks up from under the pile of hair that is pinned to the crown of her head and calls out to Bea to stop her from feeding the pigs.

"Hey sweetie, you don't have to do that. You need to take it easy."

Diogo turns, a roll of deer fencing on one shoulder to look at Giusita. When he sees she is not talking to him, he continues walking out to the vegetable gardens.

"Bea," Giusita calls out again. "A letter came for you. I put it on your bed."

Bea waves, then unlatches the gate and steps into the pen. She begins to bucket out slop for the pigs. Giusita sits back on her calves, the wellies soft and compliant. She watches Bea for a moment, swipes at her brow with the back of her forearm then resumes popping the dry blossoms off so that the bud underneath can grow.

In the pen, the pigs are playful in their bumps and nudges. Bea no longer worries about being knocked off her feet. There is an easy confidence in her body as she works through the dance of bucket out, bucket back, unwinding the heavy hose to gush water into their tubs. Carlton, the big one, shakes his head when water comes near his ears and Bea wishes for the hundredth time that she was an artist who could capture how exquisite the soft pink inner oval contrasts the outer flap, especially when it is flecked with mud.

Using both arms, she loops the hose back onto its curved hook. She remembers how this once felt raw and awkward with a constant underground stream of fear that she was doing it wrong.

Bea looks back. The pigs are safe and fed. She can feel the ribs of straw under her feet and smell the wet mud. The new shed roof gleams silver in the sun. The sky utterly empty of clouds after last week's storm. Her boots make a sucking sound as she exits the pen. She walks over to where Giusita is now staking the peonies.

"Hey," says Bea.

Giusita looks up.

"Will you help me? I am going to drive down to my mom's tonight and want to bring her some flowers. Like, in a bouquet, but a nice one."

"You're driving to Providence. Tonight." Giusita is trying not to look shocked. "Are you sure that's a good idea? I mean, you just did that long ass round trip to Manhattan. Even your truck probably needs a break."

Bea puts her hands into opposite armpits and rocks back on her heels. She knows it sounds crazy. She doesn't have the energy to explain.

Giusita stands up.

"Sure. Of course. Here, take these," she hands Bea a bucket and clippers. "There's a whole patch of lupines out there," she gestures to the meadow. "Go grab a bunch of those. Meet me over at the shed."

Bea swings the bucket in one hand as she walks away.

"Bea," Giusita calls after her. "How about some of those?"

She points to the roses sprawling over the split rail fence. Bea nods.

"Sure. That would be great. Yes, thank you."

The dogs lead the way into the field that stretches out below the sugarbush. As they walk, Bea looks up the hill to where, just two weeks ago, Mona sat on a chaise lounge in the shade of the biggest maple tree. She stops walking and looks down at her hands; she rubs them clean on her jeans.

The words have rolled in.

Next time.

She takes a deep breath and exhales. Finally, the release.

That's what she should have said.

Next time, Mona. Next time, we'll be friends.

A cluster of chickens, their bodies soft and golden in the late afternoon light are busy digging. "Next time," Bea tells them, but they don't even look up as she walks by.

no help at all

She lied to me. Bea comes to the door and taps on the window. I don't roll it down. I don't take off my sunglasses. The tears burst out. Can I never get anything right? How did this happen? I don't understand. This is the last place I would ever be.

All I asked was to be out of the hospital, somewhere nobody could see me. Strangers, fine. Nurses, doctors, fine. That's their job. They're used to it. But I don't want my friends coming by. Nobody from the office. God. That would be death. I just need my own space. I thought maybe she would find a nice place in France or Switzerland for me. Or Devon. Devon is lovely this time of year. Though it can be rainy, but what the hell. I didn't specify. I did not line item weather. Something charming, I said. Hardly a tall order. Simple is fine. I didn't expect extravagance from Bea but standards were implied: an ensuite bathroom, Italian linens, maybe a stone terrace with a pergola that looks out onto a winery or an olive grove.

Instead, this dump. *Putain.* Her shitbox of a pickup truck should have clued me in. It is filthy, streaked with mud, central casting for Mad Max. But I made it through, willing myself to keep it together because I believed they were taking me somewhere good, somewhere beautiful, and then we pull up to this.

When we stopped, I figured someone needed to get out for a pee, but then when I saw people walking up the rough, grassy drive, I thought, oh, it must be a bigger problem like a flat tire or to check the map. Never did I think this was it. This squalid, *chiottes* of a place in the middle of nowhere. No fucking where.

One of the guys carries me in. He doesn't look that big but he is strong. I feel like a paper doll in his arms. He bumps my ankle into the wall as we go down the goddamned narrow hallway. I can't say anything because the sobbing hasn't stopped and the whack on my foot feels like what this whole day has been about. Careless. Stupid. People.

I was so desperate to get out of that place before anybody got it in their heads to visit. I should've asked more questions, but dear god, who puts a hospital bed into the same room they have been keeping dirt and bugs?

"We have to wait until after the last frost to put them in the ground," Bea explains with a gesture toward the flats of seedlings by the window. "But I can move them if they bother you."

As if that was all that stood between me and perfect happiness.

As if that could fix anything.

He sets me down on the bed. Him. Two nurses. Bea. I want to scream for everyone to get out. I can't breathe for how crowded it is in here. The guy just stands there, like he can't figure out for himself that his job is done.

"Go," I dismiss him, but my voice is a fucking whimper. I am cracking up.

I just don't know how this could've happened. I give clear directions but leave the execution to someone else and I end up here? Everything is tight and itchy. My belly aches and throbs. Nausea floods through my whole body from the edges of my skull to the soles of my feet. Every part of me wants to throw up.

"My pajamas." The sobbing is breaking all my words up.

"Okay honey," Bea's fingers are gentle on my shoulder but I shout like I've been burned.

"Don't touch me."

The nurses get involved.

"Monique," says the fat one in a nurse-y voice that means you have to do what I say. "We will have to touch you if we're going to get you into your pajamas."

The three of them work as a team to get me out of the Chanel tweed that I grabbed the second it came off the runway last September. Spring/Summer 1993. I knew I was sick. I knew I probably wouldn't get a chance to wear it but I wanted everything in that collection. Maybe I'm exhausted from this morning's battle with that *espece de merde* nurse who insisted I would rather leave the hospital wearing something comfortable like sweatpants. *Putain.* This gorgeous suit, the exact shade of ripe cantaloupe, is the only good thing in this room. They slip the skirt down my legs. I love the short skirt. The little patch pockets on the jacket, the texture of its weave, the shimmer of the lining, how every edge is bordered with trim the very palest shade of strawberry. I just love it so much.

"Hang it up. Right away."

The other nurse, the one with the bleached Bon Jovi mullet, is useless.

"No. The pink ones and the robe."

How can no one understand? I got the Oscar de la Renta camisole and shortie set in Montevideo last summer. It was on display in the hotel boutique and I bought it mostly for the matching robe which has the most perfect three-quarter length sleeves. They tip me forward to get my arms into the robe and I sit back, letting them wrap the silky comfort close around me.

That was my last big trip. Funny how you don't know when you're doing something for the last time.

It was supposed to be a working holiday, but I could hardly get any work done. It wasn't just pain after eating. When I went to lie down, that hurt, too. I thought maybe I had mono and the front desk sent up a doctor when I called down for help. He was a small man. Very nice shoes. He took my pulse and put his hand on my brow. His eyes were kind but I didn't understand them. It looked like he felt sorry for me.

"You need to get home," he said. He knew in that moment, but he didn't tell me. He gave me a small brown glass bottle. There was some kind of oil mix in it, something that smelled mysterious and old like I imagine frankincense and myrrh might. Earthy. Dark. Like it was dug out of a cave. I was to rub it on the soles of my feet.

"It will help you on the journey," he said, his English, not so great.

I still have the bottle though it's empty now. I keep it next to me on the little wicker table she's got set up in here. Sometimes I unscrew the cap and breathe it in. I've come to love the scent. It helps me remember how soft his skin was, so smooth and tanned, cool to the touch. He wore a beautiful vintage watch on his wrist. It was silver.

I breathe it in now and it takes me back to that spectacular, sumptuous room with that incredible balcony. The white and yellow linens with the pale blue fringed throw across the foot of the bed. The sheets and duvet cover were Yves Delorme. How the bathtub was so deep and when you sank into it, you could look across the bedroom to the sea. Louvered doors split wide. That living, breathing blue coming in and out of view as the white curtains danced like seven veils in the breeze.

I open my eyes.

And I was worried about visitors to the hospital. Feral cats wouldn't sit on that armchair. If that door in the wall is a closet it couldn't fit a winter coat. Slapped right in front of me, directly across the foot of the bed is a bureau so old you can see layers of paint breaking through as if battery acid had been poured down the sides.

I feel the sadness roll up and since no one is here, I don't fight the tears.

Why would anyone live like this if they didn't have to?

An antique, sure. Vetted with a documented provenance. But shabby, beaten down junk that you find at a yard sale or on the side of the road. You bring that into your home? Who does that?

"Hey," says Bea. She has come in so quietly I didn't see she was there.

"I need a tissue."

She sets a box next to me on the bed. These must be from some factory where old hippies sit around turning worn out shoes into doormats.

"I could file my nails on this."

She comes back with two linen handkerchiefs and puts the box of tissues on the floor. The handkerchiefs are linen and edged with some grandmother or maiden aunt's hand stitching, god knows where she found these. At least they are soft, and clean.

"I need to be at my place," I say once the sobbing has slowed. "No one will know I'm there so I don't have to worry about visitors."

"Honey," says Bea. "It's…we're here now."

"Manhattan." Oh, that sweet word.

Manhattan. Manhattan. Manhattan.

"You said quiet and away from the city."

"I didn't say crappy junk shop on the side of the road."

Bea says, "I'm sorry. I'm so sorry."

"I don't care if you're sorry. I'm sorry I asked you for help. Just get me out of here. Get me out of here."

Fuck, there are black streaks on the handkerchiefs. I must have mascara all over my face.

The fat nurse comes in on little clog feet. "Do you want some pain meds?"

"Yes." I slam my head back. The nausea is so constant I almost don't even notice anymore but pain is flaring even in places I had forgotten about.

"Bring in a goddamn TV," I say to Bea. When she doesn't answer, I open my eyes to look at her. "You have a television."

I remember one time at a party overhearing a woman talk about how at the end of her labor she began making animal sounds and didn't even realize it was her. It was beyond any recognizable animals, she said. It was primordial.

"Sounds like someone is dying in here," says a voice from the doorway. Raspy. A caramel stuck at the back of her throat voice, like Blythe Danner, but this woman could not look less like an actress. Not a nurse. Hard to put into a category, though. Kind of New England wasp meets hippie chick meets top shelf litigator.

"This is Ellen," says Bea, weaseling toward the door. "I'll be back. I gotta get some mowing done before it rains."

"Looks sunny to me," I say.

Ellen shrugs. "Give it a day." She holds up a deck of cards in one hand, a cribbage board in the other.

She cannot be serious. Oh my god. The hell. I am in hell.

"I have zero interest in playing a stupid fucking game," I say in my coldest, this-meeting-is-over voice.

Ellen deals out two piles of cards then sets the deck down and flips the top card. I have an overwhelming urge to sweep it all to the floor in a magnificent Katherine Hepburn huff, but my left arm is on the morphine drip and it could make an awkward mess if I reach across with my right hand. I don't want to do it if I can't do it right. So I sit. Trapped. Ellen leans back in her chair as if we were at a camp in the Adirondacks, drinking whiskey from tin cups and waiting for the marshmallows to brown. She smells like lemon and mint. The cord on her glasses is so cruddy and old I can see where the white elastic shows through.

"Don't they sell eyeglass cords this far north?"

Ellen looks straight into my eyes. She wears no makeup. Her eyes are fringed with thick black lashes and I am surprised by how pretty they are. She taps the deck to indicate it's my turn and says, "Funny. Your sister has such lovely manners. I just assumed it was a family trait."

I flip a card. Four, eleven, twenty-one, thirty-one.

"Thirty-one for two," Ellen moves my peg two hops.

Just winning that little bit is the first good thing I have felt in so long, but I am not going to give her the satisfaction of seeing that.

· · ·

Some people might think pain is the worst part of being sick, but it's not. If you can keep busy, if you can get your mind immersed in work, you won't really feel too terrible until you are falling into bed but by that time you've spent every last bit of energy and sleep crushes you like a bug. When you are too sick to work and you stupidly stupid stupid stupidly call your sister who is barely tethered to this earth by some *connerie* of an alfalfa farm you will know true misery: lying in bed with nothing to distract you from your thoughts.

Lying in bed on a Saturday morning used to be one of my most favorite indulgences. I would make a french press of hot coffee so that I didn't have to change out of my pajamas to go down to the bodega. Then, with the big bolster behind my back, all the files I was working on spread across the duvet and my favorite pens at the ready, everything felt delicious. It felt like the biggest luxury to be able to work from home with no knocks at the door or phones to answer and to savor how beautiful my sheets were, something that I barely noticed during the week.

Best of all, I would get so much work done in those long mornings that stretched into the early afternoon. At some point, around three or four, I would venture out to get some food, maybe soup from the Vietnamese place in the East Village and, depending on the weather, I might bring my camera and walk about as the daylight ended. I would capture whatever I could before it got too dark. Sometimes along the river. Sometimes I'd get on a bus and let it take me around and then get on the same line to bring me back. When I had my camera, I felt safe, it was like a protection from speculation about why I would be walking along alone. And, when I was taking pictures, I lost all track of time. If I started too late on a Saturday, I might try Sunday morning with an early walkabout before starting my Sunday routine which was focused on body care: facial, manicure, pedicure, waxing, laundry and setting out my outfits for the week.

And then, Monday, when everyone was dragging about, hungover, slow, scrambled, my collar was crisp, my earrings perfect, and I was ready for bear. The office was a terrible place to get work done because of all the interruptions. I never understood how anyone could get ahead without working from home. Of course the late hours after most everyone had left is when you saw the people who were really gonna make a move. In the mix were straight up workaholics who weren't so much about getting ahead as not heading home to whatever was waiting for them there. Staying late was how I met Clary Endicott.

Clary had crippling anxiety that she masked with bright red lipstick and an approach to work that would make a Russian stevedore weak in the knees. Not since Marie-Thérèse had I met someone who put such heat and precision behind every decision. When I joined Norman Ashby, I was twenty-five and Clary was thirty-two. She landed an internship with them the summer before her senior year in college and never left.

I had wrangled my way into a junior, entry-level position at Norman Ashby. This was far below what I had should have been offered, but concessions are part of the game if you're gonna work at the company everybody is dying to work for. Clary was one of only three women on the executive staff and the youngest director on the team.

She was the Art Director.

Her perfume was unfamiliar. Base notes in sandalwood and a hint of jasmine was all I could pick up, but I knew who she was as she stood next to my desk. It was the Siaconset photograph that drew her in. I knew the rule of thumb was to have nothing personal on your desk, but it operated like a touchstone for me whenever I felt overwhelmed. Plus, there was nothing sentimental about the photograph which is probably why I was okay having it on my desk. I took that photograph at Eddie's beach house. The weekend Janet met Antoine. The last time I was ever there.

"Yours?" asked Clary, pointing to the photograph.

I nodded and looked down at her feet. She was wearing a Norma Kamali top, Calvin Klein jeans and was barefoot.

"I save my feet for when it's important," she said as I looked down at the burgundy pedicure that matched her fingernails. There were red marks where her shoes had pinched and pressed all day. I nodded. All she needed was to put those heels back on and she could head straight to the clubs. No one else at work dressed like this but she was the Art Director.

"May I?" She asked after she had already picked up the frame to look at the photo more closely. She turned it and read the back.

"Nantucket." She sounded surprised. I'll never pass as a preppy.

I nodded again.

She set it back on the desk.

"Nice," she reached out her hand. "Monique. I'm Clary."

I smiled, relying on what Marie-Thérèse had taught me that when you don't know what to say always best not to say it.

"Have you got anything to drink?"

I looked at the can of Diet Coke I had bought at the vending machine as a treat for working late. It was no longer cold.

"It's almost half gone but—"

"Not soda. A drink. No whiskey? No vodka?"

I had no idea that was what she was scrounging around for.

"Oh, yeah. No, sorry."

"That's fine. Next time, though—I like Dewars."

She sashayed up through the aisle between the empty desks and stopped at the door to an office that still had its lights on. I could hear her voice cooing a friendly hello and a bark of a laugh in response. The office door closed.

Of course, it wasn't long before I learned that Clary was super territorial about anything to do with creativity, so I was careful to not let her know how I felt about taking photos. Our time together was usually after seven at night when the corridors were quiet except for the cleaners pushing their carts through and running the occasional vacuum. We would sit in Clary's office. Cognac colored leather sofa, Moroccan wedding blanket tossed over the back that was always sliding off, an entire wall filled with images torn from magazines, books, photographs all taped or thumb-tacked into place. Her desk was a single slab of lucite. Nothing like a normal office, she was the art director, after all. Someone I respected and admired. Someone who was everything I wanted to be.

Because I was under the umbrella of sales and she was under marketing, our work life kept us in parallel lanes. During the day we were in different meetings and rarely crossed paths. It was at night that we got to hang out. Clary was the same age as Bea, but her polar opposite. I can count on one hand the times I ever saw Bea express anything close to anger; Clary would snap into a rage if her sandwich arrived with the wrong cheese on it. I never understood the furnace of anger that seemed to be lodged in her chest always ready to spill over at the slightest infraction until she told me that her mother committed suicide when Clary was nine years old.

"Totally selfish," said Clary. She and her three older sisters were sent off to boarding school, but not all the same place. School vacations meant being stuck at the family home with a dad who had no idea what to do with four daughters and drank vodka at dinner while the girls ate SpaghettiOs.

"One Christmas he got us all matching Laura Ashley nightgowns," Clary said. "It was like he had no idea who we were."

"Didn't you have an aunt or—"

"Oh sure," Clary said. "My mom had two sisters who were crazier than she was. One of them had nine cats. Nine! The whole place smelled like the stairs down to the subway. Cat piss everywhere. I couldn't even walk in the door without gagging. My dad had an older brother but that was way before I was born. He was killed in the war before his twenty-first birthday. His younger sister, my aunt Tansy, was nice enough, but she got married and moved to California. She was the smart one. She got out."

"What about your sisters? Were you close with them?"

"You close with your sister?" Clary spun it back to me. I had to think for a minute.

"She was a lot older than me. We didn't like the same things." Clary got up to walk down the hall to the bathroom.

"So you know what it's like," she said, as she walked out.

In some ways, I felt like Bea and I were close, but Clary was right, we weren't, not really. Not once we moved from L.A. to Wellesley, anyway. I was in second grade and she was off to high school. I almost never saw her. She was always over at some neighbor's house. If she was home, and I told her how nobody wanted to be friends with me, she'd roll her eyes or say something like, who cares what other people think? She was useless. She'd do what she wanted and people would let her. If she walked into high school with a bird's nest on her head, people would think it was cool. It was so unfair. She never even tried. Everything came so easily to her.

Janet is the one who understood. When I really needed a pair of Frye boots, or the jeans that all the popular girls were wearing, she always helped me get them. She knew what a difference it could make if you had the right clothes. It was Janet who fed me books and taught me how to style my hair and practice make-up at her vanity. She taught me what she loved about oils and perfumes. It was Janet who stood on the other side of the bathroom door coaching me through using a tampon for the first time so I didn't have to be that girl who was still using pads. Poor Clary, I thought as she came back into the office. You can survive if your sister doesn't think you're good enough to hang out with, but what could be harder than going through life without a mom?

After that night of reveal, which was brought on by Clary drinking better than half the bourbon that I had given her, I knew enough to let Clary know that her secret was safe with me, that she could trust me to understand. The next morning, I made a point of getting in early so I could leave a small framed photograph of tulips with a note that said, "Albert Camus wrote what doesn't kill you makes you stronger but then he went and drove his car into a tree so, there's that."

She never acknowledged the gift, but I knew I'd hit the bullseye. From that moment on, Clary was my greatest champion. It was Clary who pulled me out of the office and brought me to her favorite bar when I got passed over for the promotion to manager and they gave it to that stupid joker who had only came on six months earlier. There was no way he was more qualified than I was.

She ordered me a margarita.

"Try it," she said.

I took a sip. It was like a salty lemonade.

"It's good," I said, not really liking it. I wished she had left me alone so I could go home and crawl under the covers.

"Look Monique, you don't have an MBA. That's the issue. They can use that as their reason even though we both know it's because you're a girl and he has a penis, but once you have the MBA, they don't have as much room to be skanky."

Up until that point, I had been sailing. I was made for business. Nobody called me bossy, they said I was motivated and decisive. I was rewarded again and again for my fanatical attention to detail. This was the first time I had hit a wall and it wasn't just any wall. I knew Clary was right. Without an MBA, I would never be considered for upper management no matter how talented or skilled I was.

"But you don't have an MBA," I said.

"They don't expect creatives to have a background in business."

"How in the hell am I going to get an MBA?" The idea was overwhelming. My weekly schedule had not one inch for anything more to be added and I wasn't going to stop working to get that degree because who knows if I would lose my place.

It was Clary who told me about the executive MBA program at Columbia where you could get your degree while keeping your job. Once I started the classes, there was no more time for lying in bed to work on accounts or walks with my camera. I don't know the last time I touched my camera, but it must have been before I took on that MBA which was worse than any albatross, it was a fucking boa constrictor. Sometimes I would go into a bathroom stall with my notecards just to get fifteen minutes of studying in. Every inch of my week was work, getting ready for work, studying, writing papers or going to class. I got good grades even when I skipped classes because most of what they were teaching me I already knew; I'd been running a business since I was a teenager. So much time and energy wasted on a goddamned piece of paper that means exactly nothing.

The hardest part was making time for Clary. We still had our time together at the office, but I would watch the clock knowing exactly how many hours I would need to work after I got home. Finally, I just told her I had to go home at night so she started coming to my office to eat her lunch while I worked and pretended to listen to whatever she was talking about.

Of course, Clary knew exactly how the game was played and had lined me up for a win. The moment HR knew I was getting an MBA, a promotion rolled in that had me reporting to the VP of sales. Now I was making money and doing the really fun travel. No more Chicago and Dallas, I was off to London, Madrid, Milan. I loved sending postcards to Clary, whose job never called for travel. When I landed back at JFK, the first person I would call was Clary. When she came in to my office for lunch, I would hand over the gifts I had picked up for her, as if they were no big deal when, in fact, I was consumed with finding the perfect thing for her that would show her how smart I was, what good taste I had and how much I loved her.

For the first time in my life, I had a friend. I had a best friend.

. . .

"You're awake." It's Bea. I didn't realize she was in the room.

"It's so dark at night."

"No streetlights," she says. "I could get the wheelchair if you want to go out and we could look at the stars."

Sacré bleu. It has to be three in the morning. I forgot what it was like to be around her. Always saying the strangest things as if they were perfectly normal. With so little light everything is fuzzy, but I am in that terrible state of awakeness where I know there's no chance of falling back asleep. I can smell everything. I can feel how the sheets are bunched up and sweaty under my legs.

I remember the first time I was violently ill. Janet held my forehead as I bent my head into the toilet. I was shaking and crying. Shivering and sweating. I was terrified of throwing up again.

"Mommy, I'm so sick," I sobbed, collapsing into her lap.

"I know, baby. You have the flu. It's miserable." She carried me into the room I shared with Bea and put me into clean underwear then tucked me into bed with a blanket tight around me.

"I have to go to work," she said.

"No," I begged her to stay. I needed her hand on my forehead.

"It's gonna be okay. Bea is here. She's going to take care of you. I'll be home as soon as I can, baby. I promise."

I was home from school for three days and Bea stayed with me the whole time. She taught me how to make a friendship bracelet like she and Setsuko wore. She gave me sips of ginger ale and would only let me eat one half of a saltine cracker at a time. We played Tic-Tac-Toe on every piece of paper Bea could find. She sat by my side, just like this. Only we weren't in the dark. Only I got better exactly as Janet said I would. On the fourth day, she gave me a bath and washed my hair. I sat at the table in the kitchen and ate a grilled cheese sandwich which was the most delicious thing I had ever eaten in my life. I couldn't believe how good I felt. It was like I had never been sick at all.

I roll my head toward Bea. I can't see her, but I know she is there.

"Tell me a story," I say.

Bea adjusts herself in the armchair. The dogs are by her feet, I can hear them snoring. I think there's probably a reason hospitals don't allow dogs, but I don't say anything. This hour of night has such a different feeling than the rest of the day. In the dark I can feel how tired I am, how weak.

She turns on the reading light.

Her eyes close and she tips her chin toward the ceiling. This is how she always begins. She explained it to me once. She has to think of a place to start. Was she always that pretty or is it that she has finally found a way to style her hair that suits her? Maybe it's all that gardening she is doing getting her tanned and toned.

She opens her eyes and smiles at me.

"It was a sunny January day. All around the castle, masses of witch hazel bushes had been left to grow wild, big as trees, and the walls were now covered in a thicket of yellow blooms. People were crowding the gates. They'd been waiting for days, looking to the sky and then, that morning, as the bells began ringing out across the fields, they dropped their rakes and scythes and hurried to see if the prophecy was about to come true. The excited murmurs broke out into cheers and shouts as the flag was raised. Yes. It was a girl. The warrior princess had come."

People were terrified of Marie-Thérèse. It wasn't simply that she was tall or that she rarely smiled, Marie-Thérèse had exquisite taste and if yours was anything less than excellent she let you know in a way that could be indelibly printed onto your soul.

"Darling, if you hang that mirror in the foyer, people will think they are arriving for a seance." And the client, a not-yet fortyish woman with professionally colored hair and diamonds for days would protest, "but it belonged to my grandmother."

"Wonderful," Marie-Thérèse would say, closing the discussion, "bury it wherever you put her."

I loved Marie-Thérèse. Not love like in a Harlequin Romance, no. My love for Marie-Thérèse was fierce, protective, predative. If she had asked me to pledge undying loyalty with my blood, I would have.

Of course, had I ever suggested such a thing, she would have sniffed at her wrist and then waved me off saying something like "Desi darling, please audition for your Mayan ritual elsewhere and bring me those swatches of Fortuny I left on the front table."

She only called me Desi when we were alone. It was her pet name for me. To everyone else, I was Monique. One of the best results of moving to Montreal was getting that upgrade in my name, but when Marie-Thérèse read over the employee form she had me fill out, she looked up as if someone had just offered her a bowl of sugared almonds.

"Desdemona?" She rolled the name across the desk.

"Oh. Truly. I must meet your mother some day. Desdemona. How utterly fabulous."

And then, that sound for yes, a lips together inward tug of the mouth quiet grunt which I later learned was rare. Far more common was her clipped, *non*.

She put the sheet down and returned her attention to the open folder of photos, magazine clippings and graph paper she had been working on before I walked in.

"Go and bring me that roll of blue chintz by the door and find the wallpaper samples I need. The box will be postmarked San Francisco."

And that's how I began working for Marie-Thérèse.

At first, I was a little scared by how much I didn't know and felt confused by everything. As impeccable as the front of the boutique was, the backroom, where I spent most of my time in those early weeks, was *un vrai bordel*.

A rack of cubbies, unsecured to the wall and ever threatening to topple over, was stuffed with fabric samples, bags of curtain rings, drawer pulls. Files brimming with scribbles and receipts piled on top of the file cabinet whose drawers were already filled with wheels of trim, thick plaids, skinny lace, velvets and brocade and silk, so many colors and textures it was overwhelming and exhilarating. Tables, buried under a jumble of boxes and drapery, were only discovered when my leg unexpectedly connected with a sharp corner. There were heavy bolts of fabric propped against the wall which needed to be moved constantly because they were always in the wrong place and if an upholstery bolt landed on your foot, that was the worst.

At night, I would pull my knees up to my chest and examine the bruises, some so large, like baby eggplants, that lasted for weeks, but I didn't mind. They were my battle wounds, like Odysseus and the wild boar. Of course, it was a good thing that they were not permanent as Marie-Thérèse once caught sight of my legs as we were unloading her car after a client visit.

"Really darling," she said, "don't you think poplin trousers would have been the better choice this morning?"

But not long after that she seemed to acknowledge that there was an issue and gave me permission to clean the back room.

"Nothing can be thrown away," she said. "If it is back there, then

I have already decided it must be kept."

One hundred dollars cash to get what I needed, but I got to keep the change. It was my first real assignment for her and I was elated, consumed or, as Janet would say, obsessed.

The day I brought her back to show how I had reconfigured the space will always be one of the most shining moments of my life. Marie-Thérèse stood in the doorway and gazed around slowly. She was pleased, but even more than that, she was surprised.

Taking a cue from something I observed she would often do, I had painted one wall a French blue and then stencilled a series of white fleur-de-lys across the top. I had made the storage units decorative in their own right. My idea to put fresh paint on fruit crates that I picked up for free from behind the grocer and attach them to the wall was something she hadn't seen before. The way I had created a pallet of flat rails overhead to keep the bolts of fabric off the floor but still visible and accessible was something I had seen in the carpenter's shop when I was there picking up a couple of end tables Marie-Thérèse had ordered. As I had stood waiting, I saw how they stored lumber, but I didn't tell her where I got my ideas. I just let her look around at the bowls of buttons sorted by size and material, the drawer pulls held by pins on a discarded piece of carpet that I tacked to the wall, each one sitting in a neat row so that you could grab the one you wanted and then return it to its spot. The way the file cabinet drawers slid out easily, no more jamming and sticking, to reveal alphabetized client folders with color-coded tabs.

As she looked around, her lips were pursed and she made three short grunts of yes. She smiled.

T'es débrouillarde, Desi. Cela me plaît, beaucoup.

And then, the phone rang and she went out to answer it.

She only called me Desi when she was in a mood to be playful or when I had truly exceeded her expectations, something I tried to do every single day. Her praise, as innocuous as "well done, Desi" following her inspection of how I had organized and displayed her picks for an upcoming client meeting would have me smiling for hours. I wouldn't be able to stop. I would be waiting for the metro and realize people were looking at me because I was smiling at nothing, like an idiot.

Her words of appreciation were like a perfect white stone you might find on the beach, simple beauty, and yet, you knew enough to collect them. I prized the ones she gave me in French most highly.

The backroom renovation had taken me eleven days and I had spent fifty-two dollars. That next Tuesday, after school, on my way to Marie-Thérèse's shop, I stopped at the Laurentian. I had seen the name on receipts and decided it must be the best if it was what Marie-Thérèse used. My first ever bank account in my own name and the deposit was for forty-eight dollars and ninety-three cents. When I stepped out into the September sunshine, crisp and clear, I felt like a millionaire.

Oddly, Antoine was the one who expressed concern that I was working so much.

It was because of Antoine that I had ever met Marie-Thérèse. She would commission pieces from him now and again. That summer, I had stopped joining Janet and Antoine at the table for dinner. I had stopped getting dressed. I only got out of bed to use the bathroom. I could hear them fighting about it in the kitchen. Antoine was very concerned. Janet said it was good to see me taking it easy for once.

"That kid is not taking it easy," Antoine's voice had urgency in it. "She's depressed. What kind of mother are you?"

I held my breath and strained my ears to hear. When my mother got angry her eyes became a green so clear and sharp they could use your words like flint and set you on fire, but as I waited for her response, I realized she was different with Antoine. Somehow they never sparked into the kind of spitting fury she'd had with Eddie. It was as if she just didn't care enough to fight with him.

"Well Tony," she drawled. "I'm not sure. Could you please go and bring me the Manual on Motherhood? There's got to be a copy on the bookshelf somewhere. I'll have to check the categories. It's been a while so I can't quite remember if I am the kind of mother who believes in her children's autonomy or the kind who wants to suffocate them with her pedagogy."

"How about you let go some of that brainiac smarter-than-everyone-else bullshit and see what's bothering her?"

"She has made it quite clear that she wants to be left alone."

The next day I woke up to find Janet in my room, my closet door open, rifling through my skirts. My effort to get her to stop was pointless. She started the shower for me and was waiting with a towel when I stepped out.

"Mom," I said, annoyed, but also kind of loving her in the bathroom with me. It was a small space and she was so pretty and wearing one of the outfits I had helped her pick out.

"God, you're thin," she said, rubbing my arms and shoulders.

Antoine was waiting for us in his orange Westfalia. I shared the back with a stack of canvases until we dropped Janet at one of her Westmount ladies and then rode shotgun as we headed down to Old Port. It wasn't often that I had to ride around in his traveling studio bus, but it always embarrassed me when I did. I didn't like knowing that anyone looking at us might think I was a hippie, too.

Never could I have imagined Antoine would know a place like MT GALLANT with its simple gold plate address plaque and a vitrine that, on that day, was filled with dozens of birdcages, all different sizes, all in varying shades of blue or gold, except for the smallest one hanging in the center which was painted a deep red, the color of ripe cherries. Some of the cages hung from ribbons, some were perched on stools, each one was set with a tiny room, like you would make for a dollhouse, but there was nothing childish about it. It was enchanting and clever and I could have stayed on the street staring at it forever, but Antoine was calling for me to get the door. His arms were full of canvases. I held the door open as he walked through.

If I was surprised that he knew of such a place, I was stunned to see him be welcomed in as if he were an old friend by an immaculately groomed woman who was wearing a Halston dress and Elsa Peretti earrings.

I stood by the door while Antoine and Marie-Thérèse talked, drank espresso and she examined his paintings. Never had I been in a place like this. A space dedicated to making things beautiful.

Each small detail carefully attended to. There was the most wonderful scent. Later, I learned that it was Marie-Thérèse's signature perfume based in neroli and vetiver, but even in that moment, not knowing what it was, I knew it was everything I ever wanted.

C'est qui la petite créature, là?

La gosse de ma petite amie.

She didn't think I knew how to speak French.

Je ne suis pas une gosse. I shot back.

This made her look at me more closely, but then they resumed wrapping up their business. When they came to the door and exchanged *bisous*, Marie-Thérèse looked down at me from where she towered on three-inch heels.

"Keep your fire, girl. You'll need it."

The next day I went back without telling Antoine or Janet where I was going. I walked in and marched up to where she sat at her desk and told her I wanted to work for her.

"And what makes you think I need anyone to work for me?"

"You might not need it, but everyone does better when they get help."

She tapped the eraser of her pencil against one cheek. She was waiting for something better.

"Yesterday, my mom had to drag me out of bed because I wished I'd never been born."

"*Et, alors?*"

"And then—and then. I would live in that window if I could."

"*Oh là là, la drame!* My little *courgette*," she looked back down at her work. "You should know I am quite indifferent to Tolstoy. I much prefer Dumas."

I was not sure what she was saying but she hadn't said no.

"Please. I will work hard."

The phone rang. She gestured for me to sit and wait. I pretended to not be listening as she chatted with some hotel person that wanted her to come and renovate their lobby. It was a long call and I forced myself not to fidget. Janet hated when I was fidgety. I heard her digging around in drawers and pulling out some paper.

Marie-Thérèse snapped her fingers, the phone cradled under one ear to make me look at her. She handed me the paper and a pen and pointed to a table. It was an employment form asking for name, address, etc.

• • •

Antoine's objections began in late January when I had long stopped being able to find fresh blossoms to put in small vases for Marie-Thérèse and her client meetings. It was Bea who had shown me how to make an arrangement with just a few flowers and how you could find them for free. All you needed was to have some damp paper towels, plastic baggy, and scissors. Of course with Bea, we'd be gathering weeds that nobody cared about; wildflowers that grew up around lots or by the side of the road.

I wasn't gathering weeds. I was just using Bea's technique down the alleys of Mile End where people had gardens and could spare a few blossoms here and there.

Sometimes my timing would be way off and there was actually someone in their garden, or on the stoop, and I would have to ask for permission. I would play up my age and say oh, it's for a school project, may I take one or two, they really are the prettiest in all of Montreal. This was how I could afford to bring in small thoughtful bouquets to Marie-Thérèse.

Going on the hunt was the best part. I loved finding just the right elements. A few times, I even clipped a bit of flowering branch from fruit trees, mostly apple or Japanese cherry. Pear trees were rare, but I found two growing behind the liquor store next to what once must have been someone's house.

Although I could sense that Marie Therese appreciated them, she never said anything directly. And then, right before she left on Christmas holiday, when we were about to close the shop for two weeks, I knew she had noticed those little bouquets and that they had made a difference.

When we moved to Montreal, holidays were no longer a big deal like they had been in Wellesley. Eddie loved decorating for anything that was a celebration or a holiday but he was especially crazy about Christmas. All the ornaments were wrapped in tissue and stored in two big trunk-like baskets that had worn leather handles. Eddie would ho ho ho as he came down the stairs from the attic with the baskets. The tree would be set by the front window of the living room and as he unwrapped each ornament, Eddie would tell me where it came from. The German glass ones from his grandmother's mother, those I couldn't touch. He squealed the loudest when he found little wooden airplanes and birds and an oddly shaped Santa that he had made in kindergarten.

Janet didn't seem to want to get involved, so I would help him string swags of balsam across the mantle and around the entries to the living and dining rooms. It wasn't that Janet didn't like holidays or that she ever forgot my birthday, it was more that she didn't see the point of putting so much effort into something that was going to be over the next day.

Christmas in Montreal meant giving Janet a list of things I wanted but then never getting them. She might find something sort of like what I had asked for but mostly her gifts were stuff she found at second-hand stores or cast-offs from her Westmount ladies, as if I couldn't tell the difference.

But Marie-Thérèse. Marie-Thérèse.

That first December, she had presents for me that she had chosen and purchased just for me. Bought especially for me. New. Still in their original packages.

The shop was going to be closed for the holidays, from December fifteenth until January fifth. Marie-Thérèse had been getting more and more excited as the time drew near because she was headed to the Bahamas. I was getting more and more depressed.

That afternoon, we had just finished putting shipping labels onto the gift boxes that Marie-Thérèse sent to each of her clients when livraison showed up to cart them all away. They were luxury packages expertly stuffed with chocolates, bespoke jams, a bottle of port and, of course, sugared almonds. Each package had a handwritten note from Marie-Thérèse and was wrapped in gilt paper. It had taken days to get them assembled, made and finished so when the last package went out the door, we both exhaled and fell back into our chairs.

Ca y est, she said. Happy. Satisfied.

Oui, I replied. Tired.

Marie-Thérèse got up and went into the back room. She came out with two beautifully wrapped boxes in her hands. I sat up, terrified. Did I make a mistake? Were those supposed to be in one of the client boxes?

She had a funny smile on her lips.

"*Viens,*" she said, inviting me to join her on the divan. She set the packages onto the glass coffee table in front of us, then picked up the larger one and handed it to me.

"Merry Christmas," she said.

The wrapping was so beautiful I didn't want to undo anything, but I knew better than to say such a thing. Inside was a box from Tiffany's.

I did let out a sigh, then. I couldn't help it.

"Tiffany's?"

A midnight blue velvet pouch that held a silver frame.

"For one of your photographs," said Marie-Thérèse. "You need to have them on display. And now, this. A bit early for your birthday, but since I won't see you until after, I thought it would be better to give it to you now. Come on, hurry up, I'll miss my flight if you go any slower."

It felt like I was up on the ceiling looking down at me opening a second box, a birthday present, she must know because I put it down on that employment form but still, she remembered my date of birth? And she got me a present?

The box was small. Inside, a Gucci bifold wallet in the most sumptuous leather. I'd never had a real wallet before.

Walking home, I decided not to take the metro. I needed miles and miles to let all the feelings settle. It started to snow. I unbuttoned my coat and tucked my packages against my chest so they wouldn't get wet. The streetlights glowed golden, illuminating the drifting flakes. It was as if I was floating. As if it wasn't the least bit cold outside.

After that, I was always on the lookout for holly bushes, evergreen, juniper—anything that I could clip without someone noticing. I was just wondering how hard it would be to make a small wreath when my report card became the topic of conversation.

"This kid is getting straight A's," Antoine said as he checked the pasta then began cutting the baguette, loading the pieces into a basket that he put on the table right in front of Janet. She was reading one of her books and pushed the bread toward the center of the table so that it partially covered the official blue paper.

Antoine set the bowl of pasta down and ladled puttanesca over top. He undid the apron he had tied around his waist and sat, each of us on a different side of the table.

"Jeannette, are you listening to me?" he asked as he poured red wine into her glass.

She marked her place and put the book on the floor by her feet.

"Bon appetit," she smiled at me. "Yes baby," she said to Antoine. "I heard you. I'm taking Mona out to celebrate this weekend."

"Monique," I said, putting a scoop of the red sauce next to my salad. "And I am working this weekend."

"That's my point. You are way too smart to be working so much. You need to focus on your studies. You are seriously smart. Stop filling your plate with rabbit food. Why aren't you eating my pasta?"

"She's already getting straight A's, Tony. What more do you want?"

They began an argument as if I wasn't sitting there. As if I wasn't the one to make choices about my life.

"I might be a photographer."

"What's that?" Janet's voice was still a bit sharp from fighting with Antoine.

"A photographer. Marie-Thérèse says I have real talent."

"And did your guru Marie-Thérèse happen to mention you can't make a living doing that?"

Antoine whipped around to look at her from where he stood at the sink. It looked as if he was going to say something, but then turned back to washing dishes.

"What do you mean?"

"I mean, of course you have loads of talent. You have so many talents. And if you enjoy photography then don't stop. Keep it as a hobby."

I could feel the hard ball in my throat. It was hot and telling me better not try to say anything because she will always win, but I couldn't help it.

"Mom, photography is an art."

"Exactly. It is an art. And like all the arts, there is no money in it. That's all I am saying. Don't look at me like that, Mona."

"Monique."

"I'd be a pretty lousy mother if I didn't help you find your way in this world. Do you think those mansions in Westmount belong to any artists? You want to be in the position to buy art, sweetie. That's what you want. And you will. You are going to be very successful. I have no doubt."

Antoine walked away from the sink, water still running, grabbed his jacket and slammed out the front door. Janet got up and turned off the tap.

"Temperamental and no money."

"What about you? You have no money." I wanted to slap her.

She looked at me. I watched as she waited for the pain of what I just said to pass through her. She dug out a cigarette. Her hands trembled, just a bit.

She took a drag, then on a deep exhale, picked a bit of tobacco from her lip.

"That's right. I have no money. And you hate everything about me. Is this the life you want? Jesus, Mary and Joseph. You have the most expensive taste of anyone I know. Be logical, Mona. Use that good head of yours. Get the money first, then do whatever you want."

I pushed away from the table. My stomach felt heavy and sharp at the same time.

"I want to go to bed."

She waved her cigarette at me in dismissal.

I shut my door, pushed my bureau in front of it and dropped into bed. I pressed my face into the pillow as deeply as I could.

· · ·

I can hear them in the kitchen. Do they think I can't hear them? Do they think I am sleeping? Do they think because my body looks like this that I am any different on the inside? My chest is so sore. My head. My feet. God, my belly is on fire.

I need a bell. Why are they not helping me?

"What happened?" The mean one stands in the doorway looking down at the broken dish. I don't know what possessed her to become a nurse; she hates cleaning up messes.

"Ginny," she calls. "We need a dustpan and brush." While she waits for the other one to come and clean up what she is perfectly capable of cleaning up and paid to do, she tries to joke with me.

"Good thing you aren't walking around barefoot."

If I could land a vase of flowers in her face, I would.

"Get Bea," is all I say.

If she knew she was stupid I wouldn't mind so much, but it is her bloated sense of power and authority that makes me insane. She always makes the other one do all the crap she doesn't want to do. And, what's most annoying is that she really thinks people like her, that she is likable or funny, or something. I am so close to telling her what she is really about, but it's like complaining to a waitress, don't do it because you don't know what she will put in your food back in the kitchen before serving it to you with a smile. Although really, what's the worst she can do to me at this point?

Nursey number two begins picking up the shards and putting them into the waste can. She is on her knees to reach under the bed to get the bits that went flying.

Number one comes back with Bea on her heels and the dogs. Suddenly my room is a circus.

"They're muddy," I say to Bea as the dogs push around to the other side of the bed sniffing everywhere. "Their tails are gonna knock something over."

Bitch nurse makes a sound and I know exactly what she means by it.

Bea whistles, low and short, the dogs come to her. She strokes each of them with a long, deep caress from head to neck then says, outside. And they go.

The nurses are always glad when Bea comes in because it means they can go back to sit their fat asses down in the kitchen and get paid to eat potato chips and fight with each other. The only thing they don't fight about is how much they hate me.

"I need a bell and those two have to go," I tell Bea as she tries to make me more comfortable. There's dirt under her fingernails. The lines of sweat down her neck are gritty with dust.

"A bell? To ring for us?"

"How else am I supposed to get help? Those two stupid cows are in some endless audition for Jerry Springer—"

"Hey," Bea tries to interrupt.

"Don't hey me. You're off in some pigsty somewhere and I'm stuck listening to their white trash yowling about whoever the hell Jenny and Cubby and Mikey D and their stupid kids are. I don't even know these people and I have to listen to this dumpster drama."

"You know they can hear you."

I shout as loud as I can. "They should be able to hear me. I'm the fucking patient."

How can I be so sweaty? Why am I always so itchy? Where are the beautiful people? What did I ever do to be sentenced to this hole with so much ugliness and stupidity around me?

Bea is putting cool cloths onto the soles of my feet. How much longer. How many more hours? I can see that it hurts her to see me sobbing. I'm just all water and pain.

Bea comes back with the other nurse. They get me on the drip.

I keep thinking they should load it up, put me down like an old dog, but there's something weirdly alive about the pain and somehow, I'm not ready to go. What am I waiting for? There's no miracle ahead. The doctors showed me everything. I made them show me every x-ray and every test result before I called Bea. There's no miracle for me. So what am I waiting for? Why don't I just tell them to—

And there it is. Every time. The morphine kicks in and I'm just that little bit okay.

"Is there a book I could read to you?" Bea asks. "A magazine?"

The very idea of a magazine, the promises for glossy hair shampoo and lipstick sexy pouts, is an insult to me now. It's as if they exist in another dimension, another planet. And books? There's no book I could possibly listen to.

God, the shouting in the kitchen is back on. Bea closes the door.

Putain. "They should not be assigned together."

"Well," says Bea, "not a lot of hospice workers in this area."

"What is their problem?"

Bea tries to explain. "Oh, some kind of thing where Paulette's sister broke up Ginny's brother's marriage. Paulette's sister Jenny was married to Cubby and they were friends with Mikey and Dee, Ginny's brother and sister-in-law. And then, Jenny left Cubby to be with Mikey. Dee went batshit not only because she lost her husband but because she thought Jenny was her friend."

"Stop. Oh my god. Stop. Who cares? I'm sorry I asked. *Putain.* Just get them replaced."

"Honey…"

"Don't." I turn away. I know what she is going to say, some putrid mewling excuse about how there really isn't anyone else. Blah blah blah. Fucking excuses.

"Not everyone is an old soul like you," says Bea.

She moves the cool cloths gently, up my ankles, down my calves and shins. It is soothing, sort of.

That miserable, hot summer, Janet put a pot of cold water with ice cubes next to my bed. Like most of the apartments on his street, Antoine's place had no air conditioning. The apartment technically belonged to his parents but they lived in Vancouver now and never used it. Janet had put dishtowels into the pot so one could be soaking and getting cold while the other one was on my head or my chest. This was how we were able to get some sleep. So hot. Too hot to be indoors. Too hot to be outdoors.

Janet and I sat on the stoop eating popsicles at ten in the morning.

The neighborhood had lots of Hasidic Jews. On Saturdays I would watch as the men with their black hats and long beards would push the strollers while their mob of kids followed along. The mothers were not with them and I asked my mom if Saturday was their day off. I don't know if I have ever seen Janet laugh so hard.

It was still early in the morning and I was already dying in a halter tank and shorts. Bare legs, bare arms, bare feet and I could barely stand it. My mom was in a sundress with skinny straps and I knew she wasn't wearing anything else underneath.

I watched a girl across the street. She couldn't be much older than Bea though it was hard to tell because she was wearing a wig and the most god awful ugly clothes. Long skirt, long sleeves. The girl, I guess woman, as she was obviously the mother of those three kids she was wrangling, was wearing heavy black shoes and stockings. Stockings.

I watched the kids play. All the girls were more subdued. Also in long skirts, though they didn't have to wear wigs, yet. The boys were screeching, screaming at the top of the lungs just because they could, absolutely no curbing their behavior. Totally allowed to do whatever they wanted. The girls followed the mother inside. The boys continued to make my ears hurt.

"Mom, why would anyone stay? Why doesn't she run away?"

Janet licked at the drips. The popsicle fell apart and she caught a piece. Filled her mouth. Sucked off the last drips from the wooden sticks then tossed it into the trash can on the other side of the wrought iron fence. She wiped her fingers on the tops of her sandals.

"Well, you know, not everyone can handle freedom. Someone once told me that people who are here for the first time, really young souls, choose to come into super strict religious environments because the rules help them cope. Otherwise, life can be utterly overwhelming. Some people are more comfortable with restraints on them."

She stood up and tugged the skirt of her sundress away from the back of her thighs.

"It is too hot for this devil's child. Let's go to the library and sit in the air conditioning, *d'accord*?"

We walked down the street and paused at the red light.

"Mom, am I an old soul?"

Janet stroked my cheek and pulled me in by the shoulder for a squeeze.

"I don't know honey. You look like a pretty young girl to me."

"Oh my god stop," I said, pushing her away. "It's too hot."

• • •

Bea strokes the cool cloths down the inside of my arms, along my ribs, she is super gentle over my distended, Jonah the whale belly.

"Is it true young souls want lots of religion and rules?" I ask her.

"Who told you that?"

"Janet."

Bea laughs. Not so much at me, but at anyone who would ever listen seriously to anything Janet ever said.

"Have you ever met an old soul?" Bea asks me.

My heart sends up the old ache. I hadn't thought about it in so long, but I guess that's what you do when you're dying. All the deepest regrets walk into the room. A procession of judgement. Each one more piercing. No escape from how I did everything wrong. How whatever I touch turns to barbed wire. How I just couldn't get anything right.

Patrick. I can see every detail. I can feel him. Not as clearly as I once could, but I can still see him rolling over to look at me, his torso, how good he smelled, walking down Boulevard Raspail avoiding puddles, his scarf tied like a true Parisian.

It was November in Paris. I had spent the week before in Brussels for endless meetings and dinners with lecherous men whose hair should have been white but was stained black with hair dye that might as well have been shoe polish. Men in Italian suits and too much cologne. Each of them assuming I'd go up to their room with them. But I was savvy, thanks to Marie-Thérèse, and always had Michel show up around the time they were clearing plates and putting out cheese or dessert. Michel would settle in by my side and that kept the handsy men at bay. Those dinners often didn't end until one or two in the morning and I barely got a few hours of sleep each night, but end result was that New York was happy when I called in Wednesday, noon their time, for reports. They'd gotten the account.

I was relieved and exhausted. Like I'd just run a marathon, but without any of the cheering crowds to welcome me over the finish line. I ended the call and lay back onto the hotel room bed. They expected me to win. They were not thrilled or surprised. And, they had not *le moindre d'idee* what I had to do, all I had to go through, to land that account. Italians are notoriously difficult to negotiate with for a reason; it's handling live eels, extremely charming eels, *bien entendu*, but they've had centuries to hone their skill and I'm making it up as I go along.

But I did it. Back in New York they were celebrating and there I was in a stale hotel room at six p.m. on a Wednesday in Brussels. I couldn't sleep or eat. I'd done neither with any regularity in the past three weeks, maybe longer, and now all I wanted was to go outside but it was dark, too late. Didn't want to go to a bar by myself. Michel was off with his boyfriend. I was alone and it felt unbearable.

I checked the train schedule. Called the front desk for a cab. Yes, I would be checking out tonight. Quickly packed my suitcases. Was just finishing with the cosmetic case when the bellboy knocked at the door. Perfect timing. He wheeled everything away on a brass trolley.

The elevator dropped me gently into the lobby where my bags were already in the cab waiting for me. How I loved the flow of well-executed actions, one into the next and yet, my decision to go to Paris, totally spontaneous.

I had no idea things would be wrapped Wednesday night, why not. Brussels was dreary. Easy enough to change my flights. Plus, four days in Paris. What a total reward that would be. My heart began to lift with excitement and light. I gave the concierge my best smile. I was making this happen. I was this woman signing the bill and walking across the red carpet in my Donna Karan suit and Bruno Magli pumps. With men watching me and holding doors for me and driving me to the station. I was the woman I always dreamed I would be.

In the darkness of the train, I finally let myself feel the depth of exhaustion. Only two more exams when I got home and I would have the MBA. That, added to this most recent account meant I would get the promotion for sure. An executive director before I turned thirty. Well, sure, technically, it might be official in late January when I'll already be thirty, but good enough. And nobody on my team had ever seen so young an executive director.

I felt lightheaded when the cab pulled up in front of Lutetia. The valets hurried to get my bags and escorted me up the steps into the lobby. The exact room I had requested was waiting for me. I didn't care if it cost more than my roundtrip flight. This was my reward. I ordered up room service and fell asleep before it arrived.

Next day. Woke up feeling like a genius. Opened the windows to gaze down on the prettiest city ever there was. Even on a chilly gray November morning, its beauty runs deep. Thursday. In Paris. I began by walking along the Seine until the shops opened. The last time I was here on business, the people I was with insisted we stay on the Right Bank. The whole week was very George V and the Champs, almost as original as what you'd find *chez une taxidermiste*, Marie-Thérèse would have said.

But on my own, the smaller boutiques, side streets like Vavin that dropped down to the Luxembourg gardens, the winding lanes of le Marais where I always got turned around, shops that only sold tea, or only sold Italian paper and calligraphy nibs, or only sold chocolates, that was what thrilled me in Paris. Everything had its perfect place.

Ducked in for a midday movie at Bonaparte cinema because it started to rain and I didn't want to go back to change my shoes. When I came out, the rain had stopped so I walked up to a *papeterie* I remembered at Place de Dôme to get a new pen. And that's where I met him. In a space barely big enough for the three of us. Him, me and the woman behind the counter. I was getting the pen because I had decided to order in room service and was planning on sendin Clary a postcard from Lutetia. Maybe take a bath.

None of that happened. I must have bought a pen but I don't remember if I did. All I remember is him. His pants were chinos, the color of Autumn, not brown not gold. He wore a charcoal zipper sweater like Mr. Rogers that I would have totally mocked except it looked wonderful on him. A scarf striped with school colors that was clearly sentimental since it was long overdue to be tossed, but again, somehow the way he wore it implied he knew he should throw it away but didn't care.

We circled each other without saying anything. Each peering into the glass displays of pens. He was watching me, I could feel it.

"You're American," he said, not rudely, not a judgement like most Parisians would, but as a hello.

Canadienne, I said. Not true, but always better in France.

"I've never been to Montreal," he said. "Do you know it?"

We exited the shop at the same time. He held the door for me and nodded his chin toward the cafe directly across from us.

"Care to join me for a coffee?"

I was surprised to realize I was feeling relaxed, open for adventure. I had just closed that deal, didn't I? This was my reward, wasn't it? Besides, my hotel was right down the street. I could always head straight there after an espresso.

"Sure," I said. Everything light and fresh after the rain. The sky was

November blue heading to darkness even though it couldn't be much later than four pm. As we crossed the street and settled into the cafe, I could feel it. Paris had cast its spell. I was smiling more, laughing more.

"What is it about this city?" I asked him. Maybe he knew the answer to the mystery.

"It's the immersion," he said. "Total immersion into beauty. What you hear is beautiful, the language, the church bells. What you smell is so good, the bread, the food, the perfumes. And all around you the architecture, the avenues and the shops—everything you see has cohesion and," he paused, "beauty."

He was so close I could see the bumps on his neck from razor burn. I couldn't believe I had sat with five men for hours this week and felt not the least bit of intimidation and in this moment, I was a bubble shaking on the air, one touch and I would shatter into nothing.

He was American. From Michigan. Thirty-two. His mother was French. He had an apartment around the corner on rue Léopold-Robert.

"Patrick," he put out his hand. I shook it.

"Monique." I told him that I grew up in Montreal. Currently in New York.

"Are you a photographer?" He pointed at my camera.

"Private detective," I said.

"Oh, that's too bad. There's an exhibit of Eugene Atget over at the

Musée d'Orsay. It stays open late tonight."

"I go off duty in," I took his wrist and checked his watch. "Oh, look at that. I went off-duty at five. I'm all yours."

. . .

Bea's voice brings me back to the dark room. To the cool cloths.

"Did you think of someone?"

"What?"

"An old soul—have you ever met one?"

"Maybe—there was this guy I met once, Patrick."

"Why do you think he was an old soul?"

"I don't know, he seemed happy. Like that everything was okay and there wasn't anything to worry about."

"What happened to him?"

Am I weeping? Is this weeping?

"I don't know. I don't know."

. . .

How do I ruin everything? Oh my god, oh my god. I ruin everything. One memory crashes into the next and I am back in the car with Janet crossing the Tappan Zee. It hadn't hit me until that moment that I had no idea what was ahead. I wasn't thinking straight. I should never have let Janet talk me into this. We had no plan. I couldn't live in New York. This was a terrible idea. My whole body was in panic. We needed to go back to Montreal, now. Immediately.

"Listen to me," Janet did not like to drive. She was always more sharp when trying to navigate cars and trucks. She pulled into the far right lane and settled into one steady speed, letting the faster cars pass.

"You are not the one at fault here. You did not do anything wrong."

But I did. I kept replaying it all in my head, over and over. Marie-Thérèse didn't mean to hurt me. She didn't use me as a fall guy like Janet said. Marie-Thérèse always said she wanted to meet Janet but the first and last time she ever did was when Janet stormed in there with the Furies screaming by her side.

Marie-Thérèse was on the sofa with a client next to her. They said nothing, frozen as Janet slashed into Marie-Thérèse, piercing in her word choice, a diamond tip slicing steel to ribbons. Her anger was so fierce it held both women down; they were each in a posture of not daring to breathe in case things got worse. There was no telling if Janet would get physical should they stand or try to respond. The things she said to Marie-Thérèse. Who just sat there. Stunned. She looked over at me once where I was pressed into the doorjamb but we were like strangers. Did she believe I believed what Janet was saying? Did she believe I thought she had thrown me under the bus to get free of a client who was threatening a lawsuit? Janet had forced me to come. There were bruises on my arm for days after. She was incensed. Oh, god, the things she said. I didn't believe Marie-Thérèse would ever have done such a thing. She couldn't have. But when she looked at me, I knew. Janet was right. And that, that was hideously worse. My lungs, heart, belly, bellybutton, all of it turned to lead. As if I had swallowed a cannonball.

I put my head down into my lap. I wanted to throw up.

"Listen to me," Janet repeated. "You are too good for Montreal. It's not big enough for you. Auntie Annie is so excited you are coming. It's a fresh start. New beginning."

"But I don't know anyone," I moaned.

"Of course you do. Auntie Annie adores you and she is going to help you start a new life. Better than ever. New York is the place everyone wants to live. There isn't a girl in the world who wouldn't trade places with you. You'll see. This will be the best thing that ever happened to you."

She fumbled in her purse but then put both hands back on the wheel.

"Can you light me a cigarette, sweetie?"

I dug one out. Lit it. Held it out to her.

"Thank you, baby."

I stared out across the bridge. A body of water they call it. I wanted to jump into its arms. I wanted to burrow in deeply to its blanket of blue and have it hold me close.

the holy grail

Like every great love story, Bea had nearly given up when she found it. Ellen, her realtor, partial to batik tops and blue jeans, whose unkempt hair was streaked with white and reached nearly to her waist, had been a perfect fit because she was unruffled by Bea's rejection of place after place as they combed through old farms across Addison County. Ellen was so chill, so definitively yankee with the cultivated practice to never register surprise or reaction. Sometimes Bea wondered if Ellen even cared if she bought something. Maybe Ellen just liked being a realtor so she could drive around and look at houses.

But Bea had had enough. She was getting tired and discouraged. Where once there had been a bright, shimmering vision of a small homestead in a big meadow, now there were dark clouds of doubt and mocking voices that questioned her every decision. Why did she even come back to Vermont? What was she thinking that there could be a place that fit with her vision, her needs, her budget, a place she could burrow into and make her own? Ellen had shown her lots of perfectly good places. Why weren't any of them right? What was wrong with her? Did she have the same perfectionism disease as Mona and was only discovering it now?

And then, most unexpectedly, on a Sunday morning in August when their destination was an open house in Cornwall, they passed a sign on the side of the road, FOR SALE 82 ACRES. Bea insisted Ellen turn in and check it out. What they found at the top of the hilly drive was an overgrown meadow swelling like a wide and yellow river around a cluster of sap houses that rolled out to meet a deep woods fronted by a long row of maple trees.

When Bea, only moments after stepping out from the passenger seat, leaned across the hood of the white VW Rabbit and scrawled a big YES across the dusty windshield, a sound of air popped out of the realtor's lungs, her body unable to conceal the surprise. Ellen lowered her chin so that her eyes were fully exposed over the red plastic bifocals anchored behind her ears by croakies that might once have been blue. She wanted to make sure she was reading correctly. There wasn't even a house on the property, just a few wooden sugar shacks with weary metal roofs rusting in the August sun.

Ellen shut off the engine.

Bea crossed the dirt drive and waded into the expanse of tall fescue that swayed with buttercups, swathes of rudbeckia, echinacea, white daisies and wild phlox, her fingertips drifting behind. She snaked toward a giant maple that had to be well over two hundred years old.

Ellen let her glasses drop to her sternum and leaned into the driver's side door. She watched as Bea approached the tree as one might enter a temple.

Someone has taken the time to do a deep clean on Mona's room. Bea hopes it was one of the nurses, but figures it was probably Giusita. The curtains have been washed and dried. The floors smell lemony. Pill bottles that are normally a scattered mess across the night table are lined up neatly in front of the water pitcher. A few stems of sweet peas, pink, yellow and white, curl over a small jelly jar.

Bea sits in the chair and watches Mona snore.

When Mona was a baby, Bea would sit with her for hours. She loved to watch her on the blanket, shaking out her chubby legs, trying to get her fist around things, to her mouth. Bea would rub her belly and Mona would squeal or coo or fart which made Bea laugh. She loved everything Mona did. She loved to find ways to comfort her and keep her happy. But that time her mom went out. *I just have to get some cigarettes, I'll be right back.*

She didn't come back for a really long time. Mona started to cry and cry. Bea couldn't get her to stop crying. Then, she started to smell so bad Bea couldn't hold her anymore. She remembered how her mom would say she sometimes she just needs to sleep and close the door and let her cry. So Bea put her in the crib and closed the door but was still singing to Mona on the other side, sitting on the floor, crying and singing and the baby is screaming.

When Janet came home, she was angry.

"What are you doing on the floor?"

"I sang and sang and sang. She won't stop crying."

Janet went into the bedroom and made a loud sound.

"Oh my god, why didn't you change her diaper? My god. This baby needs a diaper change."

After that, Janet made sure Bea knew how to change a diaper.

Ray must've been gone by then. Bea's memory of him are all before Mona arrived. When he was there, everything was better. Janet's friends stayed away. No more loud nights in the kitchen where Bea had to sleep with tissues stuffed in her ears or walk out in the morning to find bottles all over. Ashtrays spilling. Someone asleep on the couch.

Bea always knew when Ray was coming back because she'd come in the door from school and Janet would be scrubbing walls and the house smelled like furniture polish and detergent. Rugs shaken and hung out on the line in the backyard. So much fuss and fury and energy to get things right. Janet would be sharp with Bea to clean up her room. Make things nice, she would say.

It was the only time Bea saw Janet pull out the ironing board. Dish towels folded in a stack on the table next to her, freshly laundered and pressed.

Ray was the opposite of frenzy. He melted into the house as if he had never left. Easy. Smiling.

"Hey Queen Bea," he would say to her in his deep voice when she came home from school to find him sprawled on the sofa next to her mom.

He would hold out his arms and she would crawl onto his lap. The three of them, just like that. Janet would tell him how Bea was the smartest kid in class and the teacher said she was going to grow up to be famous. Bea knew none of this was true, but she didn't mind. She almost didn't want to breathe, afraid she would break the spell of how it felt to have his arms around her and her mom telling stories of everything that had and hadn't happened while he was away.

Ray would take her for walks, especially early in the morning before Janet got out of bed. He showed her the light on the leaves, how it edged the buildings. They stepped into a world of softness and stillness, where you could see more and smell more clearly. A world under the world that was always there if you moved quietly enough and didn't disturb. Just watched.

When he stopped to take his camera into his hands, he would hand the lens cap to her. She would hold it carefully the way he taught her. They would stand on the pier and breathe in the ocean. She remembers closing her eyelids against the sun, the air on her cheeks, not minding the sand inside her sneakers. Seagulls swooped, floated, circled and dove down toward the sea. Their cries a thin cut of sound against the surf's breathy exhales.

Ray didn't ever say much. He would look down. When he saw she was feeling how special it all was, he would smile. He held her hand as they walked. Both of them knew not to spoil it with words. They would walk like that until he stopped to take another photo, offering the lens cap to her safekeeping.

Some mornings they would go into town and walk down streets with all the shops not open. Rooftops with hundreds of clay fingernails all tucked one into the other. A tangle of candy wrappers causing water to pool and shimmer in the sewer grate. They could almost see themselves in the reflection of the drugstore window. Ray tall next to her, his camera at his belly. She could kind of make out her head and shoulders but it wasn't like a mirror and she couldn't ever really see herself. It made her feel very grown-up when he would take her on these walks.

When they returned, Janet would be sitting in a crisply ironed housedress, smoking, flipping through a magazine, drinking coffee. Her skin soft. Her hair smelling good.

She smiled down at Bea, was that fun? Then lifted her gaze to Ray and the light poured between them.

Bea remembered the wedding. It was in the grass. In someone's backyard. Her mother's dress had a great fluffy umbrella of a skirt with tiny white roses tumbling, white flowers on the toes of her shoes. A spray of lily of the valley tucked into her hair like a feather, like Tiger Lily.

Ray. Big wide smile, his hair glinting in the sun. He wore a vest. His shirtsleeves rolled up.

Bea's dress was pale almost the same color as the violets trapped in the ice cubes she watched float around in the punch bowl. They all went down to the pier for ice cream. Walking along the boardwalk, singing songs, Janet's musician friends leading the way until the sky got purple and red.

Bea remembers waking up in a strange house. Not bad, just strange. Being told her mother would be back to pick her up tomorrow. She got to change out of her fancy dress into the woman's son's dungarees and white t-shirt, then ran into the backyard to play, barefoot. That was a really good day. The woman made her lunch that they ate on the patio. Rice and beans, warm tortillas. She had other children. Her own children. It was like being in a family.

She slept in the room of one of the daughters who introduced Bea to each of her dolls and told her all about them. One of the dolls was a very famous actress who lived high up in the mountains with her pet tiger and only ate strawberries and chocolate. Bea did not want to leave.

Her mother laughed and Ray scooped Bea up and carried her over to the car. Bea asked who that was.

Oh, that's Adelita. She is the hairdresser of a friend of mine. We couldn't find a babysitter on such short notice.

For weeks after the wedding, Bea would beg to go stay with Adelita and her family, but she never saw them again.

They moved to Crenshaw. Setsuko, the most beautiful girl in the world, sat next to her in kindergarten circle and lived close enough for her to walk to her house. She had a friend. But the wedding and the move to Crenshaw was the end of Ray. Mona must've been very little when he left for that photo shoot.

. . .

Mona has Ray's wide smile. Her hair glitters in the sun like his did. But not today. Today her hair is matted, flat to her skull. Her cheekbones and chin pointy, sharp. Nothing Bea does is helping. Bryan, the hospice nurse, comes in. He gets her on the drip that seems to ease her discomfort somewhat. He gives Bea a look that says, *I'll stay, you go*, but Bea shakes him off. She knows Mona's moods better than anyone.

After Ray left, Janet took on more hours at work.

Bea discovered that Mona loved the vanilla pudding that came in the baby food jar, but not the creamed spinach that Janet tried to get her to eat.

"She likes carrots and peas," Bea told her mom when they went through the grocery aisle, pulling things down from the shelves and putting them into the cart.

"Stop hopping up and down."

"I'm a bunny. I eat carrots," answered Bea.

"Well stop it. I'm exhausted and you're making me crazy."

Setsuko's mother never said things like that. She would say, "would the little bunnies like some carrots?"

Setsuko and Bea would hop over to eat the carrots and cucumber slices her mother would put on the plates.

"Carrots make you strong," said Setsuko.

"Carrots are magical," said Bea. "When you eat them, you can see everything that is far far away."

"And you never get sick," added Setsuko.

At school, they opened their lunch boxes next to each other. Bea might have an apple or a banana. Setsuko would have grapes, each one carefully sliced in half. The centers empty, the seeds having been flecked out with the point of a knife. Pale green shimmer slippers. One side curved, one side perfectly flat with a little space in the middle for the feet of tiny fairies.

The grapes were in one of the small containers inside a pail that didn't seem big enough to have so many compartments, but it kept unfolding with more things to find. Shiny crackers that tasted funny, rice in a ball with a bit of something pink and pickley in the middle. Bea didn't really like how any of it tasted, but she was mesmerized by the unfolding.

Mona has woken up.

"We need to call Janet," says Bea as she holds down the button that raises the back of the bed. She rubs Mona's feet and legs with a body cream. Mona is very particular about her lotions and potions. This one is made in France and smells like vanilla and orange blossoms.

"You're so lucky to have a friend like Ellen." Mona's voice is congested. Her eyes are fixed on something far away beyond the window. Blue veins are visible at her temple and threading into her eyebrows. The neck of her nightgown is buttoned all the way up to the top like an old lady. It is as if she has become ancient overnight. A wicked spell turning a beautiful maiden into a crone.

Bea walks around to the other side of the bed so that her body blocks Mona's view of the window then reaches down and undoes the top two buttons.

"She's not my friend, she's my realtor. Mona, we need to call her."

"But you don't need a realtor anymore. You bought this place like six years ago. So she's your friend."

Bea drags the rocking chair so that she can sit directly in line with Mona's gaze.

"You can't avoid this any longer."

"She plays games with your sister. She brings pie. She thinks you are friends."

"No. It's different up here—it's more like we're neighbors."

"I don't see the difference."

"Look, Mona. Cut it out."

Slowly Mona drags her gaze away from the window and looks directly at Bea. Little Bear has snuck into the room and is pressing her body against Bea's leg. She drops her muzzle onto Bea's thigh and whimpers.

"How does she know you're crying?" asks Mona.

Bea wipes at her face with one hand and rubs Little Bear's head with the other.

Bea shrugs. "It's a dog thing."

Mona's cough is phlegmy and thick. She reaches over to the nightstand for the glass of water. She takes a few small sips, coughs again, then puts the glass back in its place.

"You think you can find her?" It's not a question. It's a challenge.

"When I get her on the phone, you will tell her. Yes?"

Mona stares out the window. Bea realizes she has just set herself up. Marcus, Janet's husband, has taken Janet on a trek for her 60th birthday. Three months across Nepal, India and Thailand.

How will I ever get Janet on the phone?

I'll ask Ellen.

Bea gets up and puts the rocker back by the window and heads to the door.

"Tell me a story," says Mona, the way someone might ask for a hug.

The bed seems to swallow her. The edges of her hair are curling from the sweat on her neck. Ray's hair did the same thing. Bea wants so much to tell Mona about her dad. There have been so many times she might have, she could have, she wanted to, but didn't. She could do it right now, in this moment, but what if it makes her jealous? What if she doesn't want to know that Bea got to spend time with him. What if it makes Mona hate her? Why tell her now?

"What kind of story?" asks Bea.

"Jesus, Bea. I don't know. Anything." Mona kicks at the sheets to get her feet free. "I have to wait another—" she checks the clock, "forty-five minutes before Bryan will give me any more. I can't sleep. Everything is itchy and tight." She slaps her hands on the bed and tosses her head from side to side. Small whines of discomfort and frustration are beginning to spiral out from her chest like bats at dusk, swooping out from under a bridge where they'd been sleeping, whirling up to the sky, gathering in number.

Bea only has a minute to come up with something before Mona's agitation flips into high gear, but nothing in the room is sparking her imagination. It's all so much sickness and bedpans and disinfectant. For some reason, she becomes fixated on Mona's distended belly. She tries to ignore it, but images of round things—pumpkins, cabbages, jiffy pop popcorn when the aluminum foil fills to bursting—is all that comes into her head. She wants to give

Mona something beautiful and soaring like the seagulls and the ocean on the pier with Ray, but can't find anywhere else to start.

"When Jesminder, the girl everyone called Minx was named Cauliflower Queen at the State Fair," Bea began, "she knew the spell had worked."

The State Fair was the only time all the families from all the farms in all the land gathered to make popcorn, sell their blue ribbon vanilla pudding and eat cotton candy. Minx loved cotton candy, but an evil woman named Prudence forced Minx to wear a hockey mask when she was out in public and it was impossible for Minx to eat cotton candy when she was wearing the hockey mask.

Everyone knew Prudence. Pardon and Prudence Parkhill lived in the little hamlet of Bigot with their children Petulance, Flatulence and dear Diligence. Prudence did not want anyone to see that Minx was prettier than her three daughters.

The day before the State Fair had been the wedding of Pardon and Prudence's poor relation, Charity Green. The Parkhills had spared every expense making sure the guests never came in the house and the only food—the nibbles as it were—was a tray of cottage cheese balls that had been rolled in pimento. Not imported pimento, naturally. There were exactly three bottles of flat soda for the twenty-seven guests in the wedding party which meant once the first toast was done, everyone's glass was empty and they had to leave.

Minx had watched the wedding reception from where she lived in the attic. Her room didn't actually have a window, but she could peer through the slats that she normally had stuffed with straw to keep the snow out during the winter months.

She saw Patrick Parkhill arrive on his beautiful blue bicycle.

Patrick wasn't like the rest of the Parkhills. He was a cousin twice removed. His mother was Bodacious Kinder of the Kinders from the hills of Affable. His father, Rebel Parkhill, had been killed before Patrick was born. In order to keep anyone from ever challenging the king again, Patrick had been cursed that on his eighteenth birthday, which would be the same day as the annual State Fair, he would be forced to marry the Cauliflower Queen.

This way, Patrick would only ever sire children who would uphold tradition, pomp and circumstance as only Parkhill girls and the maidens from Disdain were ever chosen to be Queen of the Cauliflower.

Minx loved Patrick. He was the only one who ever tried to see her eyes behind the mask. She could see how unhappy he was standing by the table as Flatulence scooped up the last of the cottage cheese balls. Tomorrow he would be married.

No, thought Minx. There has to be a way to save him.

That night, long after Charity Green and her new husband had driven away in a golf cart with a fringe of pom-pom tassels that Prudence and the girls had hot glued on to the roof—Prudence had found the pom-poms in a box of old Halloween decorations she was throwing away and thought this would be a good way to get rid of them—Minx crawled across the roof and slid down the drainpipe.

The Parkhill's lawn was entirely artificial and felt sharp under her bare feet, but she was on a mission. Clutching the magic book to her chest, she raced to the sanctuary at the back of the yard and burrowed in. The sanctuary was a few two by fours Pardon had set up for the dog they once had. The dog with no name that nobody fed or walked. He had died before Minx ever came to live with the Parkhills. In fact, when she first arrived, Prudence suggested that the lean-to might be a very good place for Minx to live. She'll have so much privacy there, said Prudence. But Pardon insisted they could do better and so Minx was sent up to the attic to live.

Minx had found the magic book under the floorboards one day when she was trying to escape. At first she was so excited because on page 37 there was a recipe for 'how to escape from an attic' but four of the ingredients were listed on page 38, which had been eaten by a mouse.

Although it was very dark after midnight, the Parkhills and their neighbors all had their floodlights blaring in case someone tried to break in and steal their television sets. Minx could easily read the book and she found exactly what she was looking for, *How to be named Cauliflower Queen.*

The next morning as Pardon parked the Parkhill's Porsche at the fairgrounds, Minx waited for Prudence or one of the girls to unstrap her from the roof of the car. But they got so caught up in the sounds of the children screaming on the rides and the sound of polka music blasting that they raced to the entrance gates and forgot all about her.

Minx started to cry. Sure, her face wouldn't get sunburned thanks to the goalie mask Prudence made her wear, but now she'll never get to the fair. She'll never get to eat cotton candy. She'll never be named Queen of the Cauliflower. She'll never save Patrick.

She heard a bike scoot to a stop on the gravel next to the Porsche. A voice called up. It was Patrick.

He undid the straps and helped her climb down from the roof.

That can't be too comfortable, he said.

You get used to it, said Minx, adjusting the mask so she could see him better.

The mask or riding on top of a car roof?

Both.

He parked his bike and they walked into the fair together. She wished she could spend the whole day with him, but she knew she needed every minute to get her spell underway.

First she needed a handful of popcorn kernels that had not popped, two tablespoons of cherry syrup and the wings of a balsa wood airplane. It didn't take her long to gather all the bits together, but she was getting hot under the mask. Nobody will notice if I take it off, she thought.

The moment the mask came off, everything changed. She looked down and saw she was wearing a blue jumpsuit and pink mary janes—her most favorite outfit in the whole world. And her mouth—she could eat! She raced over to the cotton candy man. He handed her a great big fat fluffy wand of pale blue cotton candy, for free. The magic was working, thought Minx.

The polka music stopped and a voice on the loudspeaker announced it was time to name this year's Cauliflower Queen. Everyone gathered around the stage where all the Parkhill girls and maidens from Disdain were standing in their white dresses. Each of them had a crown of flowers in their hair.

Minx looked around, but there were no flowers she could use to make a crown. She tucked one end of the cone into her ponytail so that the great puff of blue cotton candy sat high on her head. In each hand, she held a balsa airplane wing that had unpopped popcorn kernels stuck to it with cherry syrup. She opened her arms and a great breeze came under and lifted her to the stage, setting her down gently in the center.

That's the one I choose, shouted Patrick from the balcony.

Before anyone could object, he grabbed a rope that was holding the circus tent up and swung down to grab Minx under one arm. The tent came crashing down on the people and knocked over the popcorn machines. Minx could hear Prudence screaming as hot oil landed on her face.

Run, said Patrick and they raced to where he had left his bike. But instead of putting her on the back of his bike, he strapped the bike to the roof of Pardon's Porsche.

Get in. Patrick gunned the engine and they drove toward the hills of Affable.

Minx settled into the bucket seat that felt like a little bit of heaven.

"And they lived happily ever after," says Mona.

"I don't know about that. But their kids blew up the patriarchy."

"What about his mother? Did she like Minx?"

Bea doesn't know how to answer such an odd question. She comes over and helps Mona turn to one side. She props pillows behind her back, between her knees and tucks a bit of extra bedding under her belly.

Mona doesn't seem to want to talk anymore. Bryan comes in.

Bea takes the dogs for a walk. When she comes back, Mona is asleep. Bea settles into the chair with her sketchbook, but doesn't open it.

It was Ray who gave her that first sketchbook and pencil set.

Janet had some boyfriends after Ray left, but never anyone serious. As soon as she wanted them gone, she would invoke Ray, her husband who would be back soon, but things started to feel different when Bea was in sixth grade. Janet wouldn't let them walk home from school by themselves anymore. She stopped going out so much at night and had a man come to put a second lock on the front door.

One night they drove to a neighborhood Bea didn't know. Her mom ordered them both to stay in the car. They watched as she walked up to a stranger's house and knocked on the door. A woman came out and made a loud cry, then she hugged Janet. They stood like that. Both making noises. Hugging.

"Where's that baby," the woman said. She looked over her shoulder to where Bea and Mona sat like stone statues. Bea thought the woman was coming to the car to see Mona, but she opened the passenger door and took Bea's face in her hands.

Her hands were large, warm, and kind.

"Oh look at this baby. All grown up."

The woman insisted they all come inside. People were coming and going. Someone had died. A boy. He got shot. People were not as friendly to Janet and the girls as the woman was. One girl, maybe bigger than a teenager, remembered Janet and hugged her. Janet was crying. Bea had never seen her mother cry. Mona pressed in tightly next to Bea and whispered that she didn't like it here. Bea pinched Mona on the thigh to be quiet.

Outside there was lots of shouting and cars driving by. Janet sat next to the woman whose name was Bessie and held her hand. Bessie was crying and shaking her head.

When it came time for them to go, Bessie got to her feet heavily.

"It's good you came. I miss that baby. Look at her all grown up."

Then, just to Janet, but Bea heard what she said.

"You need to get out of this town."

It was a long car ride home. Janet's cigarette was shaking and she kept missing the ashtray.

"Who were those people?" asked Mona.

"Some old friends," said Janet. "Some very dear, old friends."

"Why did she think she knew who I was," asked Bea.

Janet took a few moments to answer.

"She knew you when you were a baby."

More questions from Mona, but her mother had had enough. It was dark, traffic was fast and Janet shouted for them to be quiet. She needed to concentrate.

They never talked about Janet's old friends again but on the last day of school, the very day that she and Setsuko promised to be best friends forever, Bea came home to find Janet packing suitcases.

She had met a wonderful man named Eddie. They were getting married.

"We're moving to Boston," said Janet as she made piles of things she was keeping and things she was leaving behind.

"But what if I don't like it," said Mona.

"Oh you are gonna love it," said Janet. "You're going to have your own room."

"I can't leave Setsuko," said Bea.

"She can come visit us as much as you want. You'll have two beds in your room, one for you and one for her."

Bea never saw Setsuko again. Her friend never came for a visit. Boston was a million miles away from Crenshaw.

Besides, Eddie didn't live in Boston, he lived in Wellesley.

. . .

Bea had seen her mother dance with her friends barefoot in the living room with records playing on the stereo, the coffee table moved into the kitchen so that there was room enough for all of them to move. She had never seen anything like the wedding reception at the country club where Janet and Eddie danced to 'Under the Sea' as if they were in a movie.

Janet's dress such a pale blue it was almost white. Her hair glossy and bouncing. The thick band of satin at her waist tied into a bow at her back. She held the skirt up with one hand so you could see her white pumps in quick conversation with Eddie's black shoes that had skinny black laces tied tight. Eddie's shoes gleamed as he whisked Janet around the dance floor. They made faces at each other. Pretended surprise. Her mother did that thing with her head where she turned it side to side. Eddie's tie was loose. The collar of his shirt open.

Bea heard people making comments.

Aren't they sensational?

You would think they had been dancing together for years.

Aren't they just a pair.

Beautiful, the friend agrees.

She looked at the horseshoe of people gathered around the dance floor. Some of the guests sat at the white tablecloth tables that had a small circle of white candles around glass bowls of flowers at the center. Some of the guests stood near the edge of the dance floor with a drink in their hand. All of them had their eyes on Janet and Eddie as the couple danced under the canopy of rose boughs and twinkle lights. Eddie was so light on his feet, so masterful with each dip and turn. He made it look easy, like he was having the time of his life. Janet was radiant. She loved to be the center of attention and she loved to dance.

When the music ended, Eddie swirled her to drop back into his arms. Everyone broke into applause. The next song was 'All of Me.' Eddie's mother rushed the floor and held her arms out to her son. The uncle that Bea had met at dinner last night took Janet off to dance. More couples moved onto the dance floor but no one could match Janet and Eddie.

The dance floor filled. Some guy had Mona dancing, her feet on the tops of his shoes. Everybody seemed happy.

Except for the man by the bar who wore a gray and white seersucker suit with a navy polka dot bow tie. He was watching Eddie, but he was not smiling. His shoes were white. They looked like penny loafers but with tassels. None of the other men were wearing white shoes. The man wasn't tall, but he had a very large presence. *Maybe it was because of his glasses*, thought Bea. His glasses had thick black frames that made him look like a raccoon or an angry owl.

No one seemed to notice Bea. She overheard conversations without even trying. In the ladies room, two women at the mirror powdered their cheeks and blotted lipstick as they talked.

Isn't it great that Eddie found his girl.

Took him long enough.

Worth the wait. Met her last night at the rehearsal dinner. She's darling.

She has two children.

Two. Oh my. Well, that's something.

A ready-made family.

Yes, well. Good for him.

Can't be easy growing up with Louise for a mother.

God. Can you imagine.

Some of the conversations weren't so polite.

I heard he met her in a bar.

No.

Some kind of chorus girl.

Really.

No family to speak of.

Well you could see that at the church. Did you see the ushers? They didn't know what to do. They had to make people sit on her side.

What did he expect? If you are gonna wait until you're 40, don't be surprised if all the good ones are gone.

The little girls seem nice.

Well, the little one is pretty enough. But the older one. Something's not right there.

I thought the same. Odd bird.

. . .

The morning after the wedding, Bea and Mona rode in the backseat of Louise's station wagon. The way way back was filled with suitcases and wicker hampers of food. Miss Flossy, Louise's miniature poodle ran back and forth across the front seat. Louise would try to get her to sit in her lap, but Miss Flossy didn't ever do what Louise asked. Miss Flossy liked to ride with her face out the passenger side window.

Ahead of them were Eddie and Janet. Eddie's car only had room enough for two. Eddie had put the top down for the ride to the Nantucket ferry. Bea watched the edges of Janet's scarf whip in the wind. They both wore sunglasses. Eddie had a v-neck sweater over his tennis shirt. She could see Janet talking. *She's probably still mad we are all coming with them on the honeymoon*, thought Bea. She had heard them arguing.

Eddie said it would be good to have Louise there so they could go out at night and not worry about a sitter. How about she stays with the girls at the house and watches them there, Janet had countered.

"You don't want to leave the girls, do you?" asked Eddie.

Bea didn't hear a reply. She didn't have to. She knew the answer to that.

Eddie loved to play with them on the beach. They played tic-tac-toe on a giant grid Eddie carved into the sand using shells and stones for the x and o. He would bring out wooden paddles for them to bat a ball back and forth. They would play with the ocean at their ankles so they could dive in any time it got too hot. He had a face mask and snorkel that he let them each use. He and Mona would make sand castles for hours. The two of them would go crazy adding all kinds of details like a stable for the horses and a conservatory so they could have a lemon tree in winter.

Janet and Bea would lie on the beach blanket that was under the umbrella they had to set up every morning. That is until Louise came out to the veranda and called for Janet to help her get lunch ready. It was Louise's house, but she never went swimming. Bea couldn't imagine her wearing a swimsuit. Louise never went barefoot.

Janet would stab her cigarette into the sand and run out to the water to rinse off. She might take a few minutes to bob or float on her back.

"Janet dear," Louise would call again.

Louise never called for Eddie. Except when it was time to eat. Then, the bell rang and they all went up to the outdoor shower that was under the house at the base of the steps. When they had rinsed off, combed their wet hair and changed into sundresses—bermuda shorts and a collared shirt for Eddie—Bea and Mona were allowed to head in for lunch, which would be set as if company was coming.

But there was never any company. It was just them.

Life in Wellesley was nothing like where they used to live, but Janet slipped into that world like she had never lived anywhere else.

Bea didn't know her mother could cook like other mothers, but suddenly there were dinners every night. A bowl of potato salad, platters of sliced tomatoes and a pyramid of corn on the cob with melted butter on the side. She would hand Eddie a plate of chicken parts she had marinated in a sauce and he would take it out to the charcoal grill and cook them with a white apron tied around his waist. He would call out to the Matthews next door to come and join them. The Matthews had an older boy who was off at boarding school and a girl named Madeline that everyone called Maddie who was between Mona and Bea's ages. The girls were expected to become friends, but they didn't really ever get along. Bea would go upstairs for bed and the adults would still be drinking cocktails on the patio.

Eddie bought a family car, but Janet was the one who drove it. It seemed like she was always shopping. She redecorated the kitchen and bought new tablecloths and seat cushions for the dining room. She wore pants that stopped at the ankle and little cotton shirts like the wife Laura on The Dick Van Dyke show, which was Eddie's favorite. Every week Janet went to the beautician so that her hair could look like That Girl, which was Janet's favorite.

Everyone seemed to be old friends of Eddie's. He was always inviting people over to join them for dinner. Other nights, Bea would stand in the doorway of their bedroom and watch as Janet sat at her vanity putting on earrings and applying lipstick from a gold metal tube. The room smelled like a mix of her perfume and his cologne. Eddie would pull a navy blazer from his closet.

"Better get dressed," he would say. "We're going to the Mitchells for dinner."

"I don't wanna go. Can I just stay here?"

Janet would whip around to give Bea that look.

"Go put on the green skirt I got you. And that nice blouse from Bonwits."

Mona loved getting dressed up. She would bring her brush and comb to Bea and ask her to do her hair.

"Girls," her mother would call up in her Wellesley voice. "We're waiting."

The dinner parties had the same people at them, just different houses that didn't look that different. The men stood around in the backyard smoking cigarettes, laughing, making fun of each other.

The women would fuss around the kitchen like birds chirping.

How can I help? How can I help?

Mona would wander out to the patio. Bea could hear the things men said to her.

Hey pretty lady, are you married?

Gimme a smile. No? Are you gonna break my heart?

Eddie, you're gonna need a shotgun to keep the boys off this one.

Eddie's mother and her friends visited Janet while Eddie was at work. They sat in the living room. Janet put out glass bowls of salted nuts and a plate of cheese and crackers. The women drank Seagrams mixed with ginger ale. Louise ate her maraschino cherry, but not all the women did.

Janet looked relaxed with her legs tucked to one side, ankles crossed, but Bea knew she was tensed like a mountain lion on full alert.

"Beatrice is such a lovely name. And Mona, is that short for Ramona?"

"Desdemona," Bea offered. Her mom shot her a look. *Don't tell them what they don't need to know.*

"Desdemona. How interesting."

Normally a compliment, an adjective that Janet sought out. She liked to be unusual, do the unexpected, but in this case, it meant something entirely different.

"Shakespeare," said the friend. An effort to both underscore she had gone to Bryn Mawr after all, but also to reinforce what a bad choice for a baby girl name.

"Oh, you didn't name them for the book *Beezus and Ramona?*"

Janet's cheeks flamed at the insinuation of a lack of originality.

"That came out much later," she said.

Landing in Wellesley was like visiting another country. Dorothy waking up in the land of Oz. There were nights Bea lay in bed wondering if it were all a dream. Would she wake up tomorrow back in the narrow room she shared with Mona that had aluminum foil taped over the window so the street lights wouldn't shine in at night and the carpet with blobs of pink nail polish stains from when Mona tried to paint her toes—and run down to Setsuko to tell her all about the dream she had?

No. Each morning she was already awake when the birds began to sing their thank you songs. She would slip down the dark stairs and go out onto the patio to lie back in the deck chair, watch the sky and listen to the birds.

She thought about the fight she'd had with Janet after overhearing Louise talking with Eddie. She'd burst into their bedroom where Janet was in bed reading.

"You lied. You told them my father is dead."

That was the first, maybe the only time that she ever saw anything resembling fear in Janet's face. It wasn't fear exactly, but close. Janet got up quickly and shut the door then settled herself back onto the bed with its headboard upholstered in gray and white toile fabric.

"Sit," Janet pointed to the white hobnailed bedspread.

Bea remained standing. Arms crossed. Her belly pooching over the waistband of her skirt. Traces of the iced tea she had been drinking before she overheard Eddie and his mother was bitter on her tongue.

"Look at me," commanded Janet in a low voice meant for Bea's ears only. "We are safe here. Some things need to be kept private."

"He's not dead."

"Beatrice," a rare event to hear her full name from her mother. "I appreciate you are upset, but you need to think about me and about your sister. We are all in this together."

Stand off.

Janet lit a cigarette. She seemed to be considering her options. She shook out the match and exhaled a long, thin stream of smoke.

"If you never mention this again, I will give you his name when you graduate from high school." Janet was many things but she always kept her promise.

"Promise?"

"I said I would."

"Promise."

Janet looked up. "I promise."

She set the cigarette into the ashtray and picked up her book.

Bea looked down at her mother curled like a cat into the pillows. She felt old enough to graduate tomorrow.

• • •

"Bea," Eddie was surprised to find her under a blanket on the chaise lounge. His clubs slung over one shoulder. He liked to get the earliest tee time.

"You didn't sleep out here?"

"No, just came out a few minutes ago."

"You know, if you're looking for something to do, you can use the court." He gestured to the wall of hedge on the right side of the yard that had to be three feet thick and twelve feet high.

"There's a racket and some balls in the garage. Why don't you hit a few against the backboard?"

Bea watched him back his convertible down the drive. He waved.

She found the tennis racket and a can of balls easily, but it took her a bit to find the door in the hedge because it had been painted a dark blue green so as not to stand out. That must have been a long time ago. Now the wooden door was a mass of cracks and peeling paint. There was no lock. The door pushed open easily.

She was playing a game against the backboard, trying to make the ball hit the same spot ten times in a row when she heard a voice behind her.

"Thought I heard someone batting it around out here."

Mr. Stewart was the father of the family on the other side of Eddie's house. You couldn't see their house from the patio because of the hedge. Maybe that was why Eddie never hollered across the lawn for them to come over for barbeque.

"Eddie said it'd be okay for me to use the backboard."

"Glad someone is using it. Up for a rally?" Then, without really waiting for an answer, he darted over to his back door and disappeared inside.

When he came back he was wearing all white, his sneakers white. He jogged across court lightly hitting his palm against the beam of his racket.

Mr. Stewart made her smile. He was such a happy guy. That, or he really loved tennis. When they played, Bea found she couldn't stop smiling.

On the very rare occasion where she landed a point, she would be elated. As happy as if she had won an entire match. And who knew she'd be so good at it? Somehow her ability to focus on one thing at a time helped her connect with the ball again and again.

July and August became one long summer of tennis with Mr. Stewart although Saturdays were the only morning they played. The rest of the week they played late in the day, after he walked up the hill from the train station and changed out of his jacket and tie. She would have been practicing what he'd taught her against the backboard for hours before he got home.

Sometimes his son Robert who everyone called Bo would venture out to join them and they would play two on one. Bo was one year younger than Bea. His older brother Ricky was seventeen, a junior in the high school where Bea would be going in September. If Bea and Mr. Stewart were playing when Ricky pulled up in the drive, Mr. Stewart would call out to him.

"Hey Rickster. Come play a few rounds with your old man."

But Ricky would just give a polite nod, his golden hair swinging slightly at the movement and keep walking inside. That is, if he came back to the house alone. Most of the time Ricky had a couple friends with him and usually a girl, or two.

If it was Saturday, after they finished playing Mr. Stewart would invite Bea to join them for brunch. She could say yes because it was still early enough in the morning that Janet wouldn't be up and Eddie never came back from golf until late in the day.

Brunch meant a pitcher of orange juice and thick glasses with blue rims. It meant toasted English muffins, sliced peaches, honey, marmalade and poached eggs.

"Cora makes this marmalade every January, don't you, lamb chop? Her cousin Millie sends up a crate of oranges from Florida. Every year. It's her secret recipe."

"I'm having trouble keeping up with the weeds," Mrs. Stewart replied. "I think the compost we got from the nursery wasn't clean."

"Gardens always have weeds," said Mr. Stewart.

"Yes, but they are coming in so fast. I can't seem to stay on top of it."

"Well, Jenna can help you. Won't you, puss?"

Jenna was the same age as Mona. They would be starting second grade together in September. Bea had tried to get Mona and Jenna to be friends, but they didn't play well together. Jenna said Mona was too bossy. Mona said playing with horses was dumb.

Jenna put an egg onto one muffin and then squished another on top so that the yellow squirted onto the plate.

She licked yolk from her fingertips and shook her head, no.

"I can help," said Bea.

Working alongside Mrs. Stewart in the garden, Bea saw all sorts of tiny worms and beetles, spiders and slugs. Slugs were shiny and had the most fantastic double horns. Once, she saw what she at first thought was a worm—it was not more than four inches long—but as she watched it she saw the body tapered to a tail and that it had the most perfectly shaped head with a tiny tongue that darted out. She didn't know there could be snakes so small. When it saw she was about to pick it up, the snake retracted and then tried to hurry away; it was scared of her giant hand. She only wanted to put it somewhere safe. She knew if Mrs. Stewart saw it she might jam her spade into its neck. She lifted it up in her hands that were filled with dirt and tucked it off to a safe side near the hedge where no weeding would happen. She wondered if it was a baby or full grown. Or if anyone else has ever seen one so small. She never saw such a tiny perfect snake again.

Over the course of the summer, Bea helped Mrs. Stewart weed, gather cucumbers, stake tomatoes, pinch back lettuces and make blueberry cobbler. Mrs. Stewart was always gentle but unequivocal in her approach to the right way of doing things.

"Oh no, dear. We don't wash mushrooms."

Mrs. Stewart reached across to shut off the water running into the sink where Bea had put the mushrooms into a colander. The correct way to prep mushrooms, Bea learned that fall, was to rub the dirt off with a clean cotton towel.

She tried to carry over the reverence for vegetables into Janet's kitchen. How she could lose herself into the complex beauty of purple cabbages as she sliced them into ribbons for coleslaw. But her mother wasn't having any of it.

"For god's sake. It's coleslaw, not a requiem," Janet would say as she pulled a bottle of white wine out of the refrigerator. "People are arriving. Finish that already and bring out the tray of hors d'oeuvres."

It was so easy to ignore Janet in Wellesley. Bea would just go next door where everything was different. In Mrs. Stewart's kitchen, herbs hung from the rafter in the pantry. Wire baskets held a profusion of onions, rutabagas and potatoes. Jars of all sizes, each with a strip of masking tape across the front were labeled in Mrs. Stewart's wiggly script. Oatmeal, farro, flour, rice, lentils.

Late at night, when she was alone in her room, Bea liked to do lots of sketches of Mrs. Stewart. She never showed the drawings to Mrs. Stewart because in them she looked less like a woman and more like a funny bird puttering between the garden and the kitchen.

The rough blue pants with the cuffs rolled up—they use them in Brittany to gather oysters, Mrs. Stewart told her—that she wore into the garden and then into the kitchen, with a worn red checked apron over top. The way she tucked her braid into a knot at the nape of her neck.

Bea didn't understand Mrs. Stewart. There was a distance between them that, no matter how many hours they spent in the same space, always gave an odd formality to their interactions, but Bea knew one thing. She wanted to be just like Mrs. Stewart when she grew up.

Bea asked her mom if they had childhood boxes—Bea had seen cardboard boxes in Mrs. Stewart's basement marked "childhood."

Bea held back her tears as Janet ducked her head. She could tell Janet was trying not to laugh as she pulled sheets from the dryer. How she hated her mother sometimes.

Hated her. Hated her. Hated her.

Janet kicked the dryer door shut and lifted the laundry basket with both hands. She blew air out one side of her mouth to get the hair out of her face as she headed to the bottom of the steps.

"This is your childhood. Get a box. Put something in it."

· · ·

The first time Bea went up the back stairs in the Stewart house, she went as slowly as she could to take in the family photos that lined the walls all the way up to the third floor landing. Bo was leading the way and he was impatient with her as she stopped to look at photos of baby Ricky with golden hair. The farmhouse in Maine. The Stewarts at the beach, skiing in Vermont, on canoes in a lake in New Hampshire. Mr. and Mrs. Stewart where they met at Bowdoin College, her in a long, pleated plaid skirt. Black and white photos. Wedding photos. Generations of family. All mixed in with Ricky, Bo and Jenna's school photos, little league photos, Christmas day photos. But nothing precious. No rhyme or reason. Expensively matted heirloom photographs set in thick wood next to snapshots in drugstore metal frames. All sizes. Ricky's hair was so richly golden you could see shimmers of red in it. Mrs. Stewart had red hair. Jenna was straight up strawberry blond. Only Bo had brown hair like his dad.

The narrow staircase led to the third floor. There were three rooms. Ricky's bedroom, Bo's bedroom and the bathroom. All the walls leaned in because of the eaves which made it feel like a kind of cozy, secret den.

Bo's room was smaller than Ricky's by half. It had twin beds with matching blue sailboat bedspreads and plaid cotton curtains. There were some baseball posters taped to the wall and the back of the closet door. And, more baseball stuff on his desk.

"Look at this," Bo said, handing her a baseball with signatures in blue ink on it. Bea had never held a baseball before and was surprised at how smooth it was and that the stitching was red.

"Team signed. Cincinnati Reds. It's got Gordy Coleman and Joe Nuxhall and Pete Rose."

"The Red Sox?" Bea was confused.

Bo grabbed it back from her with disgust.

"No, stupid. Where are you from anyway? Boston is the Red Sox. I just said. This is from the Cincinnati Reds."

"Why would you want it from a different city?"

Bo shook his head and made an exasperated sound of air through his lips.

"My dad grew up in Cincinnati. They're my team."

"You a baseball fan, Beatrice?"

It was Ricky. He was leaning against the doorway. It was the first time he had said her name. He said it slowly. All three syllables. She didn't know he even knew her name. She shook her head. Embarrassed. Why didn't she know more about baseball?

"Good, me neither." He smiled. And with a nod of his head he invited her over to his room. She followed him.

"Hey. She was visiting me," said Bo.

"Well, now she's visiting me," said Ricky with that loose, gentle way he spoke. He closed the door in Bo's face.

Ricky's room was soft. There were no bedframes. The two mattresses were on the floor and pushed together to make one square in the corner of the room. There was a wall of bookshelves, but no desk. Three of the lower shelves were nothing but record albums. Ricky went over to where the turntable was set up.

"Have you heard Buffalo Springfield?"

Bea shook her head.

"Oh," said Ricky, slipping a black disc out of its sleeve and handing her the album cover to look at. "I think you're gonna like this. I just got it. Have a seat."

Bea looked around then sat on a wooden chair near the door. The music came out of two speakers that sat on the floor on either side of the credenza that held the turntable.

Loud thumping and voices were coming up the stairs. Ricky looked up from where he was lighting a cigarette as the door burst open. Three guys and two girls tumbled in. Seniors and juniors. All friends of Ricky's.

Suddenly, there wasn't enough space for all of them. Bea got up to leave. She turned to say goodbye but no one was paying attention to her, so she just left.

. . .

Late September and October afternoons were still warm enough for tennis. She would come home from school, drop her books on the bed and change into shorts and navy tennis shoes. She would walk out the back door, cross the yard and push through the mottled green door into the tennis court. The door, weathered by long winters, had a patina that grew more beautiful each time she passed through it.

Lots of nights, Mr. Stewart would come in to volley with her or play a few games until it got too dark to see. Then they'd say goodnight and she would run back through the hedge, her muscles warm with blood pumping, pulling huge sucks of cold night air into her lungs, the sweat along her scalp cooling quickly. If the lights in the kitchen of Eddie's house were on and she could see Janet making dinner, she'd slow her steps to a stop. She was not yet ready to go inside. She wanted to let this feeling be all of her. Nothing hurt and everything smelled so good.

In March, when she heard an announcement at assembly about playing tennis, she went down to the gym after school. She didn't realize it was a tryout, but all those hours playing on the court next door paid off. She was as startled as anyone when she went to see if she were going to be allowed to play and found her name listed on the sheet with the girls assigned to the varsity squad.

"Varsity? As a freshman?" Eddie let out a low whistle.

"We do not whistle at the dinner table, Eddybear," said his mother.

Janet showed no reaction. Whenever Eddie's mother joined them for dinner it was as if she had a mask over her face. The only way Bea knew what was going on inside was by watching her hands.

"This is wonderful news, Beatrice dear." Eddie's mother had never said anything so warm to her before. Usually her comments toward Bea were along the lines that she needed to stand up straight, stop slouching and do something with her hair.

"Does she have tennis whites?" Eddie's mother directed the question to Janet.

"She has everything she needs," answered Janet as she refilled her wine glass.

At first, Janet got her kilty skirts and Lacoste shirts at the shops on Grove Street but even Janet blanched at how much it all cost so they began hitting the church basements and thrift shops in towns like Brookline and Newton where they wouldn't see anyone they knew and of course, Filene's Basement.

Everything changed when she joined the tennis team. Senior girls would say hello to her in the hallway; teachers were nicer, but mostly, it was just the fact that she got to play every day and she loved it. Loved the focus. Loved how it consumed her. Super simple, no team, just one on one. Learning the layers of the game, the strategy, the spin; she had never felt so fierce before. At night before bed, she would spit her toothpaste out and lift her hands above her head so that she could see the muscles in her upper arms in the mirror over the sink.

Eddie's mother insisted she get private coaching on Sundays so by the end of the season, Bea was winning most of her matches even against senior girls. When school ended, Eddie's mother wanted to sign Bea up for two weeks of tennis camp at the country club but Janet didn't see the point.

"She has a tennis court in her own backyard," she said to Eddie as she crumpled the flyer and tossed it into the kitchen trash can under the sink.

"She can ride her bike there and back if that's what's bothering you," said Eddie. "God forbid you'd have to interrupt your busy day having to shuttle her to and fro."

He held a crystal tumbler half filled with scotch in one hand and carried a black transistor radio by its leather strap in the other; he had handed the flyer to Janet on his way out to the backyard where he would lie in the hammock, sip his scotch and listen to the game until Janet called him in for dinner.

In one tight movement, Janet slammed the cast iron skillet onto the range and spun to face Eddie with a bright smile.

"Why don't you go outside, darling?" Janet slid a knife out from the wood block and cut off the head of an onion in a single stroke. "I'll talk to my daughter. It's her decision, after all."

Mona decided she wanted to play tennis, too. Janet bought her the sneakers, socks, tennis dress, hair ribbons—a new racquet, but Mona was helpless at tennis; distracted by everything, always fussing about her socks, her skirt, her headband—even the racket seemed to overwhelm her. When a stray ball hit her on the side of the head she threw her racket to the ground and stormed off in tears.

"I hate tennis," she said.

Bea was on her own. Eddie played golf, Mona played with her dollhouse and Janet curled up on the sofa with a book and rolled her eyes anytime someone suggested she take up a hobby.

As school came to a close, Bea had invitations to parties from girls who liked her now that she played tennis, but after going to a couple of them, she began to stay away. The parties were about sneaking alcohol into the punch and boys who would chase the girls around the pool then grab them. Worst was when they caught you they would give a purple herbie which meant grabbing a girl's boob and wrenching hard it before she could get away.

The only boy she liked was next door.

"I don't want to go to tennis camp at the country club," she announced as they sat for dinner with Janet and Eddie facing each other from opposite ends of the table.

"I just want to play here," said Bea, looking down at the napkin in her lap.

"Fine by me," said Janet as she took a warm roll, ripped it in half and tossed the other piece back into the bread basket.

That summer, Ricky did not come home with the Stewarts after their vacation in Maine.

"He's decided to stay with his grandparents for a while," Mrs. Stewart said.

He did not return for school in September. Or Thanksgiving. Not even Christmas. It was a long year. Bea kept a box under her bed of the things that reminded her of Ricky. She would pull them out and remember.

When Bea came home from the library with books by Whitman, Emerson, and Kerouac, Janet laughed. Then tried not to laugh when she saw how insulted Bea was.

Bea stormed up the stairs and slammed the door before tossing the books onto her bed. She hated Janet. Hated that she didn't think she was smart enough to read these books, but she was right. Much as she tried, Bea never got beyond the first few pages before the two weeks were up and she had to return them.

Then, the following September, Ricky was home. It was as if he had never left. He looked the same, but different. Not quite as skinny. His hair was shorter, but he had begun growing a beard. The best news, for Bea anyway, was that he would have to repeat his senior year. They would be at high school together one more year. And, once again, the third floor of the Stewart house became the place to hang out on weekends.

What Bea loved was the coziness of the space; the smell of incense, the candle drips she would pick off while the wax was still hot and mush it between her fingers listening to the music and conversations about things she didn't know or understand, but she knew better than to ask questions. She'd tuck into a corner. If no one else was there she might pull out her sketchbook and mess around as Ricky smoked and zoned out to Steppenwolf. She would always put it away once Ricky's friends started arriving, but once, when it was just the two of them, Ricky asked Bea to read *Carrot Girl* to him. He loved it. He laughed at the funny parts. He got quiet when Carrot Girl was lost in the badland and all her powers were useless against the cactus people.

"Lemme see it," he reached for the sketchbook. When he handed it back to her he rolled onto one side with his elbow bent so that his head was in his hand.

"You're a genius."

But they were never alone for very long. Some of his friends would spend the whole weekend and lots of his friends were girls. The one Bea loved most was Lori who had soft dark hair and the most beautiful dark eyes. She wore cotton wrap skirts with block printing, big silver hoop earrings, a turquoise ring.

When more people were there, Ricky tried to include her.

Bea shook her head no to the joint Ricky offered her. What if his parents came up the stairs and found out what was happening on the third floor? All the windows were open but still the room was full of smoke.

"You worry too much," said Ricky, lightly tapping her temple with his index finger. "My parents never come up here."

He carried the joint over to the mattresses and wiggled his way in between Lori and her friend Patty. Patty was loud, freckled and she liked to make Bea feel she didn't deserve to hang out with them.

"You're so lucky," said Patty before sucking hard on the joint. "My parents are always in my hair." Her voice was tight as she tried to hold her breath before the smoke burst out of her lungs in a fat gust.

She held the joint out to Peter, the skinny guy next to her who was the one that had brought the pot in the first place.

"Learn how to toke, would you?" Peter tried to stub down the long ember. The boys seemed irritated, fidgeting, their eyes darting over to Lori in the corner and then away again as if they didn't want anyone to notice that they could not resist looking at her. She had thick bangs and wore a sleeveless white blouse just like Linda Ronstadt on the cover of *Evergreen*. Everything looked more beautiful when Lori was in the room, but she only had eyes for Ricky and everyone knew it, especially Ricky.

"I'm so high," giggled Patty, rolling against Ricky.

Ricky nodded, smiling. There was nothing nervous or agitated about him. He was the sun king, benevolent, wise and good. Light poured through the window above his head to land in the center of the room just beyond the edges of the mattress. He gestured to Tommy, who was sitting with his back against the bookshelves, for him to toss over a paperback. Ricky motioned to Peter to flip the record which had already played that side through twice. When everything was how he wanted it, Ricky began reading.

Lori gazed up at him, drinking in every word. Patty let Peter rub her back.

There was pounding at the door.

"Go away," Tommy answered, knowing it was Bo.

Bo's voice whined from the other side.

"Bea, your mom is looking for you."

Ricky stopped reading. Everyone's eyes were on her remembering that, of course, she was not one of them. Lori was the only one who looked sympathetic. Bea's neck and ears were on fire. She got up and left the room, pulling the door closed behind her so Bo couldn't see in.

Bea wanted to go upstairs and change her clothes, she knew her mother would know what was going on if she smelled her shirt, but when she got to the foot of the stairs her mother called out for her to come into the living room. Usually, that meant Eddie's mother was visiting or neighborhood ladies were sitting at card tables playing bridge and her mother wanted Bea to bring them more ice for their drinks, always fussy, proper, formal. Not this day. Her mother was sprawled on the pale blue sofa, barefoot, eating potato chips from a bowl in her lap. On the other end of the sofa, her bare legs reaching down to tangle at the ankles with her mother's feet was a woman in a sundress whose breasts were not held back by a bra. The woman wore lipstick in a vibrant shade of red that matched the flowers on her dress.

"So this is Bea," said the woman, as if she already knew all about her.

"Darling, this is Auntie Annie. She came down from New York just to see us."

"Oh god, Jannie—are you becoming one of those New Englanders who think the world revolves around their provincial little villages. Why do they always say down—down east to everything? Ridiculous. Surely Bea knows Boston is north of New York, don't you, poppet?"

Bea didn't know what to say. Who called her mother Jannie? This was her aunt? She didn't look anything like Janet. Eating potato chips and Cheez Whiz on the living room sofa? Eddie would lose his mind if he found them doing that.

"You're right," said Auntie Annie, emptying the last of her can of Tab into the highball glass and lighting a cigarette. "She's a quiet one."

Janet shrugged, as if to say *told you.* Her mother looked totally different, like the way Bea remembered her from before Wellesley, as if everything she'd been doing since they moved here had been a costume and now she was back to her normal self. Janet held out the bowl of chips to Bea.

"Want some?" It was an invitation. Bea stepped in to the room slowly.

"Oh my, you are a tall drink of water, aren't you?" It wasn't a question.

"Are you really my aunt?" asked Bea. The women laughed.

"Annie and I grew up together," said Janet.

"And went to college together," said Auntie Annie.

"You never went to college." Bea looked at her mother.

"We started college together," Auntie Annie said smoothing her skirt over her knees as she turned onto one side and propped her head onto her hand. "Your mother says you are in love with the boy next door."

"Mom!"

The women laughed.

"Oh, darling—it's too rich."

"Is that where you were?" Janet asked.

"Yes," said Bea as meanly as she could possibly make it sound.

"Don't take that tone with me, Missy."

Auntie Annie mixed a choke with a laugh.

"Jannie! You sound like your mother."

Who was this woman talking about Nana as if she knew her? Nana with her spiderweb hands and rosebud fingernails that touched so tender, her gentle words. Who smelled so good, but it had been so long she couldn't even remember what the scent was like anymore.

"Nana is dead," said Bea.

Auntie Annie tapped her cigarette ash into the empty soda can.

"Yes, poppet. I know. I was there."

"But not at my wedding," Janet kicked Auntie Annie's foot.

"Are you going to be mad at me forever?"

Mona marched in. "Who put a suitcase on my bed?"

Auntie Annie squealed.

"Oh this is Mona—come here you darling girl. Come here." Auntie Annie sat up so that Mona could sit between them on the sofa. "Has anyone ever told you how pretty you are?"

Mona nodded, yes.

"You are just too pretty for words." She looked up at Bea.

"Your girls are beautiful," she said to Janet.

They went out to eat at Howard Johnson's. Windows down. Auntie Annie's fingers drumming the outside of the passenger door in time with the music.

"We'll have a booth," Janet said to the hostess who led them through the land of tangerine and turquoise. The air was filled with the smell of fried clams, onion rings and frankfurters.

"This is my favorite place in the whole world," Mona told Auntie Annie, pointing out all the flavors of ice cream to choose from.

They settled into the booth with Bea and Auntie Annie on the ends.

"Who's Charlie?" Auntie Anne wanted to know everything.

Charlie was the man that Bea had seen at Eddie and Janet's wedding, the one who didn't smile when they were dancing. He often pulled up the driveway and tooted the horn for Eddie. Eddie would give Janet a kiss on her cheek before running over to the passenger side and climbing into the car. Charlie would wave at Janet before backing down the drive, but she'd only smile and nod, her arms crossed over her chest.

"Eddie's best friend," Mona explained. "They grew up together just like you and Mommy."

"Well," Janet scanned the room for their waitress. She was ready to order. "They met in boarding school. Not quite the same."

"Yes, I don't imagine they have nuns terrorizing little girls at boarding school."

"You were terrorized?" asked Bea. "By nuns?"

She remembered the nuns she saw at Nana's funeral. They were all laughing and eating lemon cake. They didn't seem mean.

"How *did* we survive?" Janet said, waving for the waitress to come take their order.

Auntie Annie raised her eyebrows at Janet and twisted her shoulders as if she were flirting.

"So. Is he single?"

"Very," said Janet.

A look passed between the two women that Bea did not understand.

Auntie Annie's shoulders dropped back to normal.

"You're kidding. Oh, Janet." She exhaled her smoke away from the waitress who was standing in her turquoise checked uniform with pad and pen in hand.

"I'm having a chocolate milkshake. What's everyone else having?"

"For dinner? That's a dessert," said Mona.

"It's a special night," said Janet. "Order anything you like."

Mona's eyes almost popped out of her head.

"Why is it special?" asked Bea.

Janet made a sound of hot exasperation.

"Why do you have to be such a pill? Can't you ever accept something without always questioning it?"

To the waitress, Janet said, "a cup of chowder and a plate of onion rings, thank you." The waitress took the big menus from the two women and looked to the girls.

"I'll have a chocolate milkshake," said Mona. "And a frankfurter."

"A cup of chowder and onion rings," said Bea.

"Goddamnit, Bea," Janet whispered hard across Mona who was sitting between them. "Don't you dare spoil my night tonight."

"To drink?" the waitress asked.

"Manhattan straight up," said Janet.

Auntie Annie put up two fingers to indicate she wanted the same.

"Ginger ale," said Bea.

Mona put up two fingers to indicate she wanted the same.

The waitress walked away.

Janet lit a cigarette.

"Honestly, Jannie. I don't see the problem. So she ordered what you did."

Janet's exhale was voluminous.

"She won't eat the chowder. She's just trying to burn me."

Auntie Annie seemed to find the whole thing hilarious. She smiled at Bea.

"Are you married, Auntie Annie?" asked Mona.

"Not anymore, darling."

Janet dug two pens out of her purse and handed them to Mona.

"Here you are, baby. Why don't you and your sister play tic-tac-toe so Mommy and her friend can talk."

"I'm not a baby," said Mona as she grabbed the pens.

Bea let Mona win so she could listen as Auntie Annie asked Janet if it is hard being a mother.

"It gets easier once you give up worrying about being any good at it," answered Janet. "There are no prizes in motherhood."

• • •

Bea couldn't tell if Auntie Annie in the house had made things softer or if when Eddie came home from his weekend away watching the golf tournament with Charlie that things got sharper. All she knew was that Janet seemed to be angry about everything. Which didn't make sense. Eddie was so fun. When he came back from trips he always had presents for each of them. Not Christmas. Nobody's birthday. Presents.

A watercolor set with brushes and a palette in a wooden case for Bea. A charm bracelet for Janet that she dangled like a worm she didn't want to handle.

"How sweet," she said to Eddie, before dropping it back into its robin's egg blue box.

Mona made out like a bandit with a new Barbie plus three outfits: Bermuda Holidays, Patio Party and Fashion Shiner that came with a red vinyl raincoat lined in bright blue taffeta.

"A halter dress!" she squealed as she pulled the plastic off and set the clothes free. "Just like Auntie Annie."

"Who is Auntie Annie?" asked Eddie.

Mona froze. Her wild happiness cut dead. She looked at Janet in terror. They were not supposed to mention anything about Auntie Annie's visit.

"TV character," Janet said smoothly, standing up. "It's a cartoon show called The Jetsons. What do we say, girls, for all these nice gifts that Eddie brought us?"

"Thank you, Eddie," said Bea.

Mona jumped up and ran into his lap, hugging him with a Barbie in one hand and the Bermuda Holidays beach hat in the other.

"I love you," said Mona.

Eddie pulled her into his lap and wrapped his arms around her. He kissed her on the head. "I love you, too Monkey."

. . .

"Did you just call me Monkey?" The bed is flat as Ginny and Paulette change the sheets. Mona's nightgown is drenched and twisted around her thighs.

"Did I?" says Bea as she maneuvers Mona's arms out of the nightgown and drags it down and away from her body so she won't have to pull it over her head.

"Eddie called me Monkey."

"Yeah, I was just remembering that."

"Okay now, easy, easy," says Paulette as the nurses roll Mona to one side. The sight of her buttocks bruised dark red simply from lying there, hip bones that press so hard against the thin skin Bea can feel her own hips ache and the spine, a cord of knots, each bulge delineated. Skeleton, thinks Bea, and the word punches the air from her lungs. She bends down to stroke Mona's head but ends up kneeling next to the bed, her forehead on the bed frame.

"Sweetie, you're gonna have to move." Ginny nudges Bea out of the way with her thigh. She bathes Mona with a facecloth that she dips into a plastic bowl held in the crook of one elbow. Bea retreats back to the chair and kicks the sketchbook under it before pulling her knees into her chest as she watches her sister endure the process of getting into a fresh nightgown. Paulette smoothes the hair back with a brush so soft you would use it on an infant.

"There," says Ginny as Paulette leaves the room with the remnants of last night bundled in her arms. Ginny pushes the window open. "It's a bit overcast this morning but give it a couple hours and it's bound to change."

Mona makes no effort to rebuke Ginny's weather report. She seems resigned to the fact that another day is about to begin. Her head falls to one side.

"Have you been there all night?" she asks Bea.

"I guess, yeah."

"Well you can go now. I'm sure you have things to do."

"Not really."

"Don't you want to go walk the dogs?"

Bea looks down at the dogs that are on either side of her.

"They're fine."

After a while, Paulette comes in with a tray for Mona.

"Giusita's made a pot of coffee," she says to Bea.

"I want coffee," says Mona. Petulant.

"Not so good for your tummy, now is it?" Paulette answers.

Bea unfolds herself from the chair and hobbles a bit to the door, one foot asleep, as Paulette helps Mona with her breakfast.

Bea drinks her coffee on the porch while the dogs sniff about. She remembers the times Eddie took them to the Fireman's Fair that was held every September in front of the memorial hospital.

She knew what that big red brick building was but never gave it a thought on the night of the fair. She only ever thought about it as a hospital that one time she visited Karen Scott who had appendicitis in eleventh grade, but that was in February when everything was covered in snow. There was no connection between those long corridors smelling of sadness on that cold winter day with the wild end of summer festival that was the Fireman's Fair. It never occurred to her that there were people up there, lying in beds, the carnival lights flashing on their wall, or maybe they were near a window and could look down at the rides, smelling the funnel cake, listening to kids scream that cotton candy got in their hair. People who were sick. People who were dying. Who was it that decided having a carnival on the front lawn of a hospital was a good idea?

• • •

They walked from the parking lot over to where an entrance had been set up with plywood boards and orange neon tape. Mona hopped and swung between Eddie and Janet who held her by each hand. Her hops got bigger and more excited as they got closer and the sight of popcorn machines and stuffed animal prizes came into view. Bea followed behind. It was early in the night, not full dark sky, but dark enough to make the colored lights of the rides pop orange, blue, green, yellow, red while the parameter of the fair was roped with white lights. Bea could see the top of the Ferris wheel climbing and descending, people swinging their legs from the seats. A radio DJ was playing music on the speakers. Screams reverberated across the lawn as people were whipped around by the Whippet.

Eddie bought them each a long chain of paper tickets and told them to go have a good time. That first year, it was so hot and humid everyone was still dressed like it was summer time. As they left the fair and headed back to the parking lot, over the loudspeakers the song *Brown-Eyed Girl* began to play. Eddie tossed the stuffed alligator he'd won into Bea's arms and grabbed Janet by the hand. He pulled her out of the dark toward the light of the white stone fountain whose water was still running. They began dancing around the edge of the fountain which drew a small crowd that paused and watched as if it were the last bit of entertainment before they all climbed into their station wagons and returned to regular life of tuna fish sandwiches, shirts from the dry cleaners and school buses. At the end, Janet jumped into the water and Eddie followed her. People cheered.

On the drive home, Eddie and Janet were laughing, together.

"Did you see old Bill Burnett's face?" Eddie rocked his head forward and back with his shoulders tight, like he wanted to bounce up and down. "He wanted to give us a fine right there." This was the Eddie that Janet liked. The one who liked breaking rules. Being bad.

"I wish he had," said Janet, her hair damp, her arm draped so that her fingers touched Eddie's shoulder. "I would've tossed it in the fountain."

"Like a wish."

"Like a wish that would send him straight to hell," Janet laughed.

But the Fireman's Fair was only once a year.

Most nights, if they were eating at home and not having guests for dinner, Eddie liked to have the radio on low so he could listen to the game even though they were all at the kitchen table eating dinner. Mona carried the conversation with stories of her day. Back from a trip to the fabric and wallpaper store with Mrs. Meredith, she recounted each decision and choice in detail.

Janet watched Eddie's attention drift, far from the table.

"Almost as good as watching paint dry," she called across to Eddie over the top of her wine glass, trying to win him back.

Mona's excitement collapsed slowly like the frenzy of soda foam that has risen quickly almost to the rim of your glass, only to descend into bubbles burrowing under cubes of ice.

Bea wished she knew the words Mona would most want to hear.

"That sounds really pretty," she offered.

"Oh shut up," said Mona. "Who cares what you think? All your drawings are in black and white. You're probably color blind."

"You may not speak to your sister like that and you know perfectly well we do not use the words "shut up" in this house," said Eddie. "You may go to your room now."

"She hasn't finished her dinner," objected Janet.

"I don't care," Mona stormed out, her chair nearly toppling over. She shouted over the railing as she pounded up the stairs. "I hate all of you." Her voice was filled with tears.

Bea was left with the grown-ups and yet, invisible.

"You need to do something," said Eddie, feeding cut hot dog under the table to Miss Flossy who was staying with them while Louise visited Mackinac Island with her bridge club.

"She's a little girl. Little girls have fits."

"And you're a grown woman. Women teach their daughters how to behave."

Tennis was always the escape. Until the Spring when Ricky went to Canada.

March 1969. Bea was tapped to play in the state invitationals. She was only a junior but everyone kept telling her she would be voted captain of the team when she got back and the season began.

"What tremendous news," said Mr. Stewart. "Your parents must be so proud."

Mrs. Stewart smiled at her and offered her the platter of English muffins. Bea declined. She'd already eaten three. Outside the window it still looked like winter. She didn't normally come over on a Saturday morning for brunch if she hadn't been playing with Mr. Stewart first, but she'd wanted to tell him and this seemed the best time to come round. Jenna had already asked to be excused but her dishes still sat on the table in front of where she had been sitting. Bo sat between his parents. He ate strips of bacon, with his fingers, one at a time, trying to get the whole piece in without breaking it.

"That's quite enough, Robert," his mother said. "Use your fork and knife."

She turned to look as she heard Ricky come down the back stairs. Her entire countenance filled with light.

"Ricky! Good morning, my angel. Did you sleep well?"

"I should hope so," said Mr. Stewart. "It's nearly noon."

Ricky bent down, wrapped his arms around his mother's shoulders from behind and buried his face into her neck. He stood up and pushed his hair out of his eyes. He smiled at Bea who willed herself to look casual but she could feel the flush spreading across her neck and cheeks.

"Sit sweetheart," Mrs. Stewart got up and Ricky slid his long limbs into her seat. "How do you want your eggs?"

"Portrait eggs, thanks Mom."

"At Dougie's house they call it toad in the hole," said Bo.

"Oh, that's not so nice, is it," said Mrs. Stewart.

"Toad in the hole. Toad in the hole," said Bo.

"Robert," said Mrs. Stewart not scolding exactly, as she knew he was trying to tease her. It was more that her voice was bored, as if she found him tiresome.

"Bea's playing in the state invitationals next weekend," Mr. Stewart said to Ricky.

"Swell." Ricky lifted his glass of orange juice to her before taking a swig.

"I said her parents must be really proud of her," said Mr. Stewart.

Ricky nodded, sitting back in his chair so his mother could slide the portrait eggs onto his plate. He cut into the toast and forked a chunk of toast and egg into his mouth.

"So good, Mom."

She beamed and set a small bowl of cut fruit next to his plate before sitting down in Jenna's chair.

"Ricky is a wonderful tennis player," she said to Bea.

"Was," said Mr. Stewart.

"Well, Pops," smiled Ricky, he seemed to be ready for a volley. "I'm still a good player whether or not I have an insignia on my blazer."

"There's a difference between champions and dilettantes," returned Mr. Stewart.

"Oh, vocabulary lessons," said Ricky calmly eating his toast and eggs. "What's the difference between a sycophant and a boot-licker—oh wait, you win. Those are synonyms."

Mr. Stewart's face and throat went dark red, his hands slammed the table as he stood up to lunge his torso across the table at Ricky. Bo looked frightened. Mrs. Stewart began trembling.

"Oh dear, oh dear. Boys. Boys. Please. Boys." Her voice a whisper.

Only Ricky looked utterly unperturbed. He looked up at his father who had frozen into the posture as there was nowhere for him to go and his violent movement had not caused any response from Ricky, who continued eating.

"Can you pass me the salt and pepper?" He asked Bea, gesturing to the white ceramic ducks that sat in front of her.

Mr. Stewart walked over to Ricky and pulled on his arm.

"Let's go."

"Where're we going, Pops?" said Ricky.

"Don't make a scene in front of your mother. Time for a conversation. Let's go."

"Is it my mother or your protege you are concerned about, Pops?"

Mr. Stewart wrenched Ricky by the shoulder, which must have hurt because Ricky jumped to his feet. Bea had never realized how much taller than Mr. Stewart he was.

"Boys. Boys. Please. Please don't," Mrs. Stewart seemed as if she might burst into tears any minute. Ricky put his napkin on the table but not before shaking off Mr. Stewart's hand. Then he walked out of the kitchen down the hallway toward the living room with Mr. Stewart walking behind him.

Mrs. Stewart began gathering up the dishes. Normally, Bea would have stepped in to help, but she was hoping she had become invisible and that nobody knew she was still there. Bo did. He looked over at her and shrugged before lifting up the last strip of bacon that crumbled before he could get the whole piece into his mouth.

"Don't worry. This is nothing compared to what they usually do."

That wasn't the last time she saw Ricky. She was there when he drove out of town the next morning. He had come to get her. Just like in the fairy tales. He lobbed a tennis ball at her window. She was already awake and threw back the covers to see what the sound was. Maybe a bird had crashed into the glass and needed help, but when she lifted the sash and looked down, there was Ricky in a coat with a long plaid scarf looped around his neck that covered the ends of his hair. His head bare even though it was so cold her breath made white mist. He didn't speak. He made a sign for her to come down. There was a knapsack on his back and a duffle bag on the ground next to him.

Her heart was pounding in her throat. Were they eloping? Were they going to run away together? What would she bring? She pulled on clothes as fast as she could, stuffing extra socks into a shoulder bag with her sketchbook. She had eleven dollars she had saved from babysitting at the Tamamotos that she tucked into her front pocket.

She closed the kitchen door as quietly as she could and did her best to hurry, though every crunch of her boots on the frozen grass sounded louder than the last. The driveway was empty. Had she dreamed it? Then, Ricky stepped out from where he'd been standing behind a fir tree.

"What's happening?" Bea whispered, her breath crystalizing and making everything even more magical. She and Ricky were in her driveway. In the dark. He had come for her.

"I'm going to Canada. We're meeting up behind Watson. I don't want my mom to find me in the kitchen. So can you help me? Can you bring me some food? And, can you grab a bottle of liquor? Something that won't get you in trouble that your parents won't miss? Can you hurry? We want to get on the road before it gets light."

Bea gathered up peanut butter, some bananas, half a loaf of bread—anything she thought Janet wouldn't notice too much missing. A jar of almonds. A box of raisins. She went into the dining room where the liquor cabinet was and opened the door in panic. She had no idea what any of it was. Which one did he want? Which one would get her in trouble? The pressure of time made her just grab the bottle at the back. It looked the oldest and seemed like nobody would miss it.

They walked to the Watson elementary school along the aqueduct so nobody would see them on the road. As they walked, Ricky explained he wasn't going to college and be a puppet all his life like his father. But if he didn't go to college, he'd get drafted, so he and Tommy were driving up to Canada. Tommy's aunt lived up there. They were going to stay with her.

"I want to come, too," said Bea. "Can I come with you?"

Ricky stopped and put down his end of the duffle they were toting between them. He took her face in his hands.

"Oh pretty lady, if only you could. But you're not eighteen and that would be kidnapping." She thought he might kiss her, but he didn't.

"I'll be eighteen soon."

"When?"

"Next October."

"Okay, well then next October I'll come get you." He stroked her hair. "We'll have things all settled by then and we'll need your help with the gardens."

The woods ended right at the edge of the school parking lot and Tommy's blue Mustang was already there with a circle of people around it. Lori was there, her tan coat had fluffy fake fur on the cuffs and around the hood. Patty was wearing a ski jacket and cowboy boots.

"You're late," Tommy said, grabbing the duffel and jamming it into the trunk that seemed like it could not possibly fit one more thing.

"Food and Glenfiddich!" Ricky held up the sack of food Bea had given him as if it were a prize or a bag of gold.

"Good. Let's go," said Tommy and he held the seat forward so the girls could climb into the back.

"You're all going?" said Bea. He hadn't said that Lori and Patty were going, too.

"Next October," Ricky's hands were on her shoulders. Then, a funny look came into his eyes. Tommy called to him again. Ricky looked down at Bea.

"Don't let them make you into one of their puppets. You are too good for that. Don't let this tennis thing make you into one of those Swellsville mannequins."

"No. No—I won't. I'm—I'm quitting tennis anyway." Bea had never thought about quitting tennis until that minute, but she could feel how big a moment this was; she knew that Ricky had quit tennis and she wanted him to come back for her. He had pledged he would come back for her in October, she wanted to make a pledge to him.

She knew she had said the right thing because his whole face lit up with the biggest smile. Then, he kissed her. On the lips.

She watched as he climbed into the front seat of the car. The windows were all rolled up but she could see Lori and Ricky waving to her. She waved back and watched as they drove away. He had kissed her. On the lips. In front of everybody.

All morning she floated in a bubble. Over and over she kept counting out how many months exactly to make sure she had it right. Seven months to October. Twenty-eight weeks. Two hundred and fourteen days. She started to make a special sketchbook to keep track of the days, but then her mom called that she had to come join them. Bea didn't mind at all. She knew Louise was downstairs so she changed into an outfit she knew her mom would like. Now that Bea knew that Ricky loved her, that it was only a matter of months before she would be out of this house and with him in Canada, a wellspring of wanting to make things right with Janet sprang up within her. She walked into the living room and smiled at everybody in it. Her mother lifted her eyebrows in approval. *Well, well.*

Louise sat in the wing chair with Miss Flossy on her lap. She was recounting only the most boring details of her recent trip. Bea could see that Mona was struggling not to fidget so she sat next to Mona and whispered in her ear how pretty she looked and that she had a new story to tell her, later. Mona seemed to relax, somewhat. Bea felt the sofa cushions behind her back, soft support. This must be what it felt like to be Nana, always calm and happy in the midst of all the sharp energies. Bea watched as Louise sent arrows across the room at Janet who deflected them with words, shrugs and another glass of sherry.

Louise stood up to leave. Everyone holding in a sigh of relief that she would be gone momentarily. She put Miss Flossy on the ground and looked over at Bea.

"I trust you will be practicing extra hard this week. You don't want to make them sorry they invited you now, do you?" It wasn't a question, so Bea didn't answer it.

"Mother," said Eddie. "Nobody's gonna be sorry. Bea's gonna be terrific, aren't you, Bea?"

"I'm not going," said Bea. The sensation of being wrapped in molten gold dropped away as the words landed. Ice in a glass. "I'm not playing any more tennis."

"You most certainly are," huffed Louise. Her mouth pushed up toward her nose.

Janet stood up and began escorting Louise toward the door.

"Thank you, Mother Stewart. Eddie and I will talk with Bea."

"You don't talk to a child. You tell them what's what."

"Thank you again," said Janet, holding the door open so that Miss Flossy could run out. "So glad your trip was a success."

"Miss Flossy, come here," Louise commanded the dog who only returned as far as the front steps. "Eddie. You will have to get this situation sorted. That child cannot be allowed to quit."

Eddie gave his mother a kiss on the cheek then stood next to Janet and put an arm around his wife's waist.

"We'll talk to Bea, but if she doesn't want to play, she doesn't have to play."

Bea's golden feeling returned. She had never loved Eddie before that moment. With Eddie by her side, Janet was a sea of calm in the face of Louise's fury.

"Indulgence! What kind of parent allows their child to grow up without discipline? These are the moments that form the character." She shifted her gaze from Eddie to unload on Janet. "Mark my words. Your permissive ways will ruin that girl. Don't come running to me when you see what you've done. If you allow her to be a quitter, she won't even have the wherewithal to run a proper household."

"My daughters are not being raised to run households," said Janet.

"Well, I never." And with that, she was gone. Janet shut the door.

Bea let her knees go from where she had been holding them tight against her chest. "I am so sorry," said Bea.

Janet pulled her cigarettes out from the side table drawer where she put them whenever Louise visited and lit one quickly. She looked around the room at the cheese tray she had put out for Louise that had gone untouched.

"I guess I'll go get dinner started." She sounded exhausted.

"I think it's a night for Howard Johnson's," said Eddie.

Mona jumped from the sofa. "Really!?"

"Girls," said Janet, her energy immediately bright. "Let's get washed up."

Janet followed Mona up the stairs.

Bea was incredulous. Shouldn't she be punished? Instead they were getting the biggest treat? She walked over to Eddie who was freshening his drink at the cart. His hands were shaking and she could see that his whole body was trembling. She felt extra guilty about the bottle of liquor she took for Ricky. *I'll tell him what I did*, she thought. She still had her eleven dollars. She would buy him another bottle.

He turned, surprised she was standing so close. Standing next to Eddie, Bea realized she was tall. He was only an inch, maybe two, taller than her. He put down his glass and let her come all the way in. His arm wrapped lightly around her shoulder. She wrapped her arm around his waist. His cologne was so nice. In his ear, for only him to hear, Bea said, "Thank you."

She would tell him about the bottle of liquor later.

At HoJos, Eddie was loose and charming which made Janet sparkle. Mona let Eddie be the one with all the stories. She was bursting with happiness to have all three of them in a good mood at the same time. When the waitress arrived, Mona proclaimed, "I love Howard Johnson's so much!" which caused all the adults to laugh.

After the waitress left with their order, Eddie launched into the story of how lucky HoJo was. The mayor of Boston had banned the production of a play called *Strange Interlude* so the people putting on the play moved it to Quincy instead. It was a really long play that lasted hours and hours so they had to pause in the middle and let everybody have dinner. As it happened, the first Howard Johnson's restaurant was near the theater in Quincy so that's where people went, and since most of them were from Boston, they all spread the word about this scrummy restaurant in Quincy.

"Scrummy!" repeated Janet. She liked fun words.

"Why did the mean man want to stop the people from having their play?" asked Mona.

"Sex, darling," Janet answered.

"Janet!" Eddie was a bit scandalized, but Bea could tell it was also what he loved about her. "Keep your voice down. The Hammond's are right over there."

"Why would he be allowed to keep them from putting on a play?" asked Bea. "It's just a play. How can there be a law about that?"

"Oh darling," Janet's heavy sigh released a big exhale of smoke. It was her heavy grown-up sigh: *the world is just too much to explain and you'll just have to learn and see.*

The waitress began setting down their drinks. In front of Mona was an enormous glass whose curvy silhouette was streaked on the inside with drips of chocolate syrup. It was filled to overflowing, chocolate soda foaming at the top and crowned with a scoop of chocolate ice cream so large it looked like it could topple at any minute.

Mona burst into tears.

Eddie looked to Janet for explanation.

"Is that not what you wanted?" The waitress was confused.

Mona shook her head violently, unable to speak for the sobbing.

"She said chocolate ice cream soda," the waitress said to Eddie in her defense.

"No!" said Mona. "I meant milkshake. A chocolate milkshake."

"Okay sweetie. We can fix that," said Janet, reaching out to stroke Mona's head.

"I'll drink it," Bea offered, but Mona had passed the point of no return in her upset. Eddie smiled at the waitress and waved her off. "We're fine," he said.

To Janet, he leaned in and said, "you need to get that child calmed down."

Janet put her napkin on the table and slid out of her chair. She took Mona by the shoulders and guided her to the ladies room. Eddie finished his scotch. Bea pretended she had the beads in her fingers and started the words in her head without them. When Janet and Mona came back, the chocolate ice cream soda was gone and so was the happy energy of the night. Mona was subdued. She apologized to Eddie for the disruption, then sat with her chin to her chest for the rest of the night. She didn't eat her frankfurter. Janet put it in a doggie bag.

The weekend after the state invitationals, Bea pushed back the green door and splashed across the court into the Stewart's backyard. The rain was cold. She held the hood of her jacket with both hands as she made a jagged dash to the Stewart's back door trying to avoid the worst of the puddles. Mrs. Stewart was inside sitting at the table sorting packets of seeds. Bea rapped on the glass.

The door yanked open. It was Bo.

"Go away," he said.

"Robert," Mrs. Stewart turned to see who was at the door. "Oh," was all she said before turning back to her seeds. Bea stood dumbly in the doorway. Rain pounded on the roof. Gutters gushed out into the lawn that was so sodden it couldn't absorb any more water.

"My dad is so mad at you," said Bo.

Mr. Stewart? Mad at her? Bea's stomach lurched. And Mrs. Stewart? Did they all hate her now? Was it because she had given Ricky food? Liquor? How could they know that? Did they think it was her fault he left? Was she supposed to come and tell them?

Without turning to look at her, Mrs. Stewart spoke directly to Bea. She laid out seed packets with thoughtful placement as if she were playing a game of solitaire.

"Mr. Stewart was very disappointed to learn you stopped playing tennis."

"Just at school," Bea's voice was thin, her hands icy. "I still like to play."

"Very disappointing," repeated Mrs. Stewart. "He drove all the way out to see you play in the invitationals. Wanted to surprise you, I imagine. Probably best to stay away for a while, dear. Things are not quite what they were."

"Dad kicked Ricky out of the house," said Bo, a certain pleasure in his eyes that he got to share news he thought would shatter Bea.

"Robert," said Mrs. Stewart, her voice mild as ever. "Please shut the door. It's coming down like Niagra out there."

Bo shut the door, but not before sticking his tongue out at Bea. She stepped back, still facing the closed kitchen door. Out from under the shelter of the portico, the rain pummeled her bare head.

• • •

The night before Easter, supper was simple, baked beans and grilled cheese sandwiches. Janet and Bea had been cooking all afternoon for tomorrow's Sunday dinner with Louise, some of her friends and Charlie, of course. Eddie had the radio on low.

"What happened to Mrs. Stewart?" Mona asked as she nibbled at her sandwich, not eating the crust.

"Something happened to Mrs. Stewart?" Bea looked at Janet.

"It's okay, honey." Janet was nonchalant as she scooped baked beans from the tureen in the center of the table onto her plate. "She's getting treatment for being an alcoholic."

Eddie, who had been in another world before this moment, reared to life.

"What did you just say?"

Janet seemed to be done with trying to get his attention or, maybe this was a different way of getting his attention.

"I answered my daughter's question."

"That is not a topic of conversation for young girls."

"What—are you forbidding me? Verboten to show her that the object of her worship, she of the perfect hedge and red red tomatoes, has clay feet?"

Eddie's chair scraped as he stood. "May I speak to you in the other room?"

It wasn't a question.

Janet followed him and the argument exploded before he had even shut the door behind them. Bea looked at Mona.

"What did you see?"

"I didn't see anything. I heard Mommy on the phone."

The argument got louder but they didn't seem to be talking about Mrs. Stewart anymore. Someone threw something that crashed.

Bea began eating her potato salad. Mona inched closer to Bea. Bea rubbed Mona's back with one hand. "It's okay. Don't be scared."

"Why did he get so mad? What's an alka lick?"

"Alcoholic. It's when you drink too much."

"But isn't that what they all do?"

Mona must have misunderstood. Janet could not be telling the truth. Mrs. Stewart was never at any of Eddie and Janet's parties or at the country club where everyone drank cocktails on the veranda that looked out over the golf course. Bea had seen people drinking too much, getting tight as Eddie called it. She saw adults being ugly, getting sloppy, acting stupid, but never Mrs. Stewart.

That Spring, Saturday mornings were crushing. Bea would count how many days until October. It felt unbearable. She would remind herself of the sister with six brothers who got turned into swans and to save them, the sister had to never speak a word and knit each brother a shirt from nettles and she was almost burned alive at the stake, but the brothers came back. She broke the spell by not giving in.

It was a relief to drive out to Louise's house in Siasconset as they had the past three summers. Away from the empty tennis court, Bea could pretend everything was the same as it ever was. Eddie would dance with Mona in the living room in the way he and Janet danced. Louise would sit in her chair with a bowl of butterscotch candies next to her and work on her needlepoint pillowtop. Eddie tried to teach Bea how to dance but she could never get it right the way Mona could, so she preferred to sit on the window seat where she could watch the sea on one side and the dancing on the other. Janet buried herself into books.

Louise never mentioned tennis and Bea knew she never would.

People came to visit them while they were at Louise's house. Some rented houses nearby, some filled the back guestrooms. There was always someone who came in with bulging brown paper bags that held lobsters, their strong claws shackled by thick rubber bands. Bea would never eat them. She had seen Louise put them into the giant cooking pot filled with boiling water. Before she dropped each one in, Bea saw it wriggling, its antennae fluttering, helpless. They were alive.

Around the table people wore paper bibs around their necks, cracked the claws, dug out the white flesh, dipped it into melted butter, mouths greasy, fingers slick. *You don't like lobster,* they would say in amazement. *Definitely not from around here*, they would laugh.

At night they played charades, board games and cribbage. Days were spent biking, playing on the beach, building sandcastles and, whenever she could, Bea would join whoever it was that wanted to bike down to the municipal courts and play tennis.

The one person who never came for the weekend was Charlie. Bea hadn't even thought about it until she walked in on Eddie and Louise having it out in the living room. It made sense that Eddie would want his best friend to come out for the weekend. She didn't understand why Louise was adamant that he was not welcome.

Bea had turned back from the group biking out to the lighthouse and raced in from the side porch. Her steps must have been light or their shouting was too strong because they both whirled in shock when she ran into the living room. They stopped fighting but not before she had heard Eddie screaming at his mother, almost in tears.

"I have done everything. I have done everything you asked. And you won't—"

He stopped and they both looked at Bea standing there stunned. Louise didn't miss a beat.

"Oh Beatrice darling, you're not going to the lighthouse with everyone?"

"Yes, I—wanted the binoculars. I'm sorry. Excuse me. I—"

"Oh of course darling—Eddie and I are just working out some summer plans, aren't we darling?"

Eddie had turned his back to both of them but Bea could see the tops of his ears were scarlet.

She ran up the stairs, grabbed the binoculars and shouted out a goodbye as she left through the kitchen door, making sure to slam the door loudly so they knew she was gone.

❖ ❖ ❖

Bea had never been to Vermont before the day she got off the bus that had dropped her in front of the Middlebury Inn. Eddie had volunteered to drive her. He and Charlie would make a road trip of it, but Janet shook her head.

"She can take the bus," said Janet.

It wasn't a long walk to the campus but it was uphill and her suitcases were heavy so she was pouring sweat by the time she stood in line to get her orientation packet. Nobody else in line was carrying luggage. There were more adults than kids in line as each new student had at least two parents with them, some had grandparents, too. Bea had never felt so misplaced in her life.

When she finally found the room assigned to her, she dropped the bags and collapsed face down onto the mattress. There were no sheets. She was supposed to have brought her own. Why did Janet not tell her? But she didn't care. The muscles in her arms ached. She was drenched in sweat. The room was stifling. She sat up and shoved the window sash up to get some air. A cluster of white birches grew directly across from her window. Trees. There had to be trees. That's what she had told the college counselor.

The fall of her senior year, everyone was talking about college except Bea. Ricky had not come back. Bea refused to go anywhere but school. She refused to go downstairs and join in the dinner parties Eddie and Janet had. There was nothing either of them could say, no threat that could make her do anything. She didn't care.

"You're grounded."

"Fine."

"You're cleaning the kitchen every night for a month."

"Fine."

"You're not coming with us to Howard Johnson's."

"Fine."

The fights between Janet and Eddie were getting worse. In the morning the whole house would be in a deep freeze of nobody talking. Except Mona. Mona would do everything she could to get a response from someone, anyone, but the best she got was a *that's nice, baby*, from Janet or an explosion from Bea to *stop bugging me*. School became Bea's favorite place; she could just shuffle her body from classroom to classroom and sit at her desk, a stone in the river.

She was required to meet with the college counselor who asked what kind of school she was looking for. Bea shrugged. He reminded her of the way Mr. Stewart had been once upon a time, so optimistic and encouraging.

"Okay, so—can you tell me the one thing that matters most to you?"

Bea took a breath and decided to try and make an effort. He was a nice guy.

"Trees," she said.

The counselor didn't laugh. He pushed a few brochures across the desk toward her. One had a photograph of a boy and girl walking down a white path through green grass with great red and yellow maples all around them.

"Where's this?"

"That's Middlebury. It's in Vermont."

"Where's Vermont?"

He smiled at her. Surely now she was kidding.

"Between here and Canada."

"Okay," said Bea. "I'll go there."

sex, lies, and the divine feminine

This must be what it feels like to be a baby or, the King of England. People waiting on me hand and foot, carrying off my bedpan, changing my clothes, massaging my feet, bringing me food and, sometimes, outside my window is that sweet Brazilian man doing gardening things.

Bea is in the ugly chair knitting. It looks like she is doing nothing, but I know she's here, staying close, taking care of me. I once heard Janet tell Auntie Annie that everyone needs to take care of themselves. Such bullshit. Janet was never on the frontline by herself. She always had a man. Even Bea has people in her life. Nice people.

Well, Ellen isn't exactly nice. She doesn't care if I like her or not, but that's what I like about her. I wonder where she grew up.

"So you are the one who talked my sister into buying this—this place. Why didn't you find her a real house?"

"Muggins," Ellen moves her peg down the cribbage board. Damn, I got distracted.

"You're taking advantage of a dying woman."

"The Buddha says we begin to die the moment we are born."

"Pair of Jacks for two, one for his nobs," I say.

Ellen pegs for me.

"I'm guessing the Buddha didn't die of pancreatic cancer when he was only thirty-four," I say. "So maybe you don't want to quote him to me."

"I lost count how many houses I showed her," she says. "She didn't want them. This is what she wanted."

"Is that true?" I look over at Bea.

"She walked in and said, 'I want a small house with a big yard'."

"And she ended up with—"

Ellen interrupts me. "A mouse-filled sugar shack with 82 acres."

I look over at Bea again. Still no reaction. How does it feel to listen to someone else tell your story? Is she not even listening?

Did she always live in her own world or did she fade away when we moved to Wellesley? It was like she never forgave Janet, but I don't get it. How could she not see how much better everything was than what we had in California? The homes in Wellesley were like giant dollhouses. I got in trouble for touching all the things. Mrs. Meredith had the prettiest, though not the biggest, house. She never told me I was being rude.

I pretended to want to be friends with her daughter, Cookie, but really I only went to their house so I could be with Mrs. Meredith. Cookie was dull like her father, cake batter before you put it in the oven. Her real name was Constance but only the teachers called her that. Mrs. Meredith was always changing things around in the house even when it looked perfect, but then, I did the same thing with my dollhouse.

Sometimes I was there on a Saturday and she would ask if we wanted to come with her. Cookie would say no—all she ever wanted to do was watch cartoons. I would say, *yes please!* And Mrs. Meredith would tell me what lovely manners I had and make Cookie come with us. She would pull up to the bottom of Eddie's driveway and make me run in to get permission from Janet. I would run up the drive and hide in the bushes, count to ten, then barrel down to her big station wagon and say, *she said yes I can go!*

I sat up front with Mrs. Meredith. Cookie would make all kinds of screams from the backseat. "I hate going on errands," Cookie howled.

"Cookie," said Mrs. Meredith in that voice mothers use that never works. She would make threats about things she would do but never did. Mostly she promised Cookie that we would go to Bailey's for ice cream if she behaved. I didn't care where we went. Shopping with Mrs. Meredith was always fun. She would bring us to the hardware store and let us roam around while she talked with the man who worked there. In the back there were rolls and rolls of wallpaper, boxes of shiny white bathroom tiles that clicked when you touched them together and all kinds of door knockers.

Cookie pinched my arm.

"I don't like you," she told me.

"Girls," Mrs. Meredith called for us.

One day I went over. Mrs. Meredith stood behind the glass of the front door.

"I'm sorry, Mona," she said. "Cookie isn't here right now."

That was a lie. I knew her stupid, mean face was sprawled on the family room floor watching cartoons and flipping Pez into her mouth.

"Okay," I say. I want to tell Mrs. Meredith I'd like to go with her on errands even if Cookie doesn't want to, but I don't. I just go home.

. . .

"That was a tough night," Bea puts a cool cloth on my forehead then lightly presses it against each cheek. A cool cloth to the back of my neck.

She has no idea. I've stopped calling it a headache. The pain in my skull doesn't ever go away now; it just quiets and flares. I must have done something pretty heinous in a past life. How else to explain this hell.

"Bryan's gonna be here this morning," she says.

I know she wants me to be glad, or happy, or make some sign that there is anything that can make me feel better, but there's not so I just close my eyes.

"Can I read something to you?" I don't answer. She begins telling me about the books that she would read to me when I was little. Lulu, her hero. She goes over to the green bureau and tugs on one of the drawers. She brings over a small stack of ratty old comic books, barely hanging together. I can't smell them, but they look like they smell of mold or sad old things.

"This one." She holds one up with Lulu dressed in a deerskin dress and wearing a papoose on her back. "This was the first one I ever got."

She tells me about Pippi Longstocking. There was a copy in the school library but she couldn't keep it. She wanted one of her very own and one day she found one in a box on the driveway of someone's garage sale.

I'm not really listening. I can't. It takes too much effort. I had a favorite book, too. Nothing famous like Lulu or Pippi. I don't know where it came from. I don't even know what the name of it was, but I loved it. Secretly. Kept it hidden under my bed. If Janet or Eddie's mother got hold of it they would have taken it away. You're too old for that, they would have said. It was a picture book, probably written for a little girl of four or five but we lived in Wellesley when I had it, so I had to be at least seven or eight, maybe nine. It must've gotten left behind when we moved to Montreal.

In the story, the little girl goes out to play, jumping in leaves, and comes in with cheeks pink. Her mother has lunch on the table. The page I remember most clearly has a picture of the little girl sitting down at a table with a blue and white checked tablecloth. On her plate is a piece of meat, bright green peas and mashed potatoes. After lunch, the little girl takes a nap. Then, the mommy and the little girl walk to the train station to pick up Daddy from work. The little girl walks home from the train station in between Mommy and Daddy, all three holding hands. No one else is in the story. No other children, friends or siblings. It was so comforting. I wanted to be that little girl with the pink cheeks and the healthy lunch.

"Bea said you had a rough time of it last night," Bryan is holding my hand between his palms. There's nothing he can do. He knows it. He doesn't say things like *how are we feeling?*

"Has there ever been a Saint Bryan?" I ask.

"I might be the first."

"The Patron Saint of Modesty."

"And strong calves."

"Is that why you're always in cargo shorts? To show off your sainted calves?"

Nursey comes in. I heard her car in the drive. Bryan's shift is over.

"How are we feeling?" she asks.

I want to curse her out so badly, but I don't. I don't say ugly things in front of Bryan. He lays my hand down on the bed, so lightly. He smells of ginger and coconut and there is so much light in his eyes I can never hold his gaze for long.

Nursey fusses about the room. She doesn't want to touch me.

"Get Bea," I tell her.

When Bea comes in I tell her no more talk about books.

"What was the last movie you saw?" she asks.

"*Sex, Lies, and Videotape.*"

"Seriously? That was like, how many years ago?"

"You saw it?"

"Yeah, sure," says Bea. "But I liked that actress better in *Groundhog Day*."

"God. No." My throat clogs and she has to get me some water.

"You didn't like it?"

"Hated it. How could you possibly like that?"

"Wait," says Bea. "That only just came out. So *Sex, Lies, and Videotape* wasn't the last movie you saw."

"The last one I liked."

"What did you like about it?"

"It was different. It was about love."

"What movie did you see? It wasn't about love. It was about two sisters."

"No—"

"Yes."

"I don't remember it that way. Why did you like *Groundhog Day*? I thought I would lose my mind if that alarm clock went off one more goddamned time."

For someone who never talks, Bea has a lot to say about the most boring movie ever. She likes how the guy starts out as a dick but is transformed by love.

"That's not love," I say. "He just wants to have sex with her."

"At first," Bea agrees. "But then, over the course of the movie, because that is the only thing motivating him—to get her to fall in love with him—he does love her."

"Bull. Shit." How can we never agree on anything?

"The movie is like a thousand lifetimes rolled into one," says Bea, ignoring me. "He tries to kill himself, but he can't because he just keeps coming back. Over and over. So then he decides, I'll just get all the money but then, he finds that is a total dead end. So then, he starts helping people and practicing things like piano and ice sculpture just because he has the time and there's nothing else to do and he becomes this wonderful person. It doesn't happen all at once. Iterations. And then, one day, when he does all the things he does without ever expecting a different outcome, boom. He's crossed a threshold. She loves him. And together they wake up into a new day."

Bea is flushed and excited.

"You should write a dissertation."

"Don't be so cynical."

"Don't tell me what to be."

She walks over to the window and pokes at the seedlings.

"I don't want to write a dissertation," she says from across the room. "I want someone to write the movie a different way. Instead of a man who needs to grow his soul, I want someone to write it about a woman who needs to learn to fall in love with herself."

"Oh, that's gonna sell tickets."

"See? Even you don't value the divine feminine."

"What's that? Narcissus? Falling in love with herself?"

"Forget it."

She's walking to the door. I've pissed her off.

"Don't go," I say.

"I need to do something outside—" She is such a shitty liar.

I can't let her go. I will listen to anything.

"Please. I'm sorry. Explain it better. I'm super foggy."

"It's just really disrespectful."

"I said I'm sorry."

"No, I mean—that's what I am talking about. We've lost all respect for the divine feminine. Do you think it is women-owned companies poisoning the planet? Women are starting all the wars, selling guns?"

"They don't have the time," I say. "They're too busy tearing each other apart."

I gesture for her to adjust my bed. She comes over and helps to move things around.

"Better?"

I say yes although it doesn't make any difference at all. She sits in the chair. The light hitting the wall behind her makes everything golden, for a moment, and then the room grows darker.

"Hey Bea, is it weird neither of us are married? No kids?"

Bea stretches her arms and then cracks her knuckles.

"Stop. I hate that."

She stands up.

"You've seen a marriage that you want?" she asks as she walks out the door making some blah blah about chores before it's too dark.

Have I seen a marriage that I would want? Who were the married people we knew? There was Mrs. Stewart next door that was an alcoholic; she looked like a hobbit and her husband was way too fucking cheerful. Something was very wrong there. Creepy Mrs. Grayson and her husband that always wore the Christmas sweaters she picked out for him. The March family with that little boy who'd been in that accident, that had to be why they were so messed up. That young couple who moved into the old Eberlee place. I babysat for them a couple of times. I don't know how old they were but Janet always called them 'that young couple.' The wife wore her blonde hair in a tight ponytail. Her house was immaculate, but cold. Not pretty like Mrs. Meredith's. It felt desperate, pushing, trying too hard. What was her name? She was always trying to get into the newspaper or magazines where they had society stuff. I don't remember the husband. Maybe they were happy? Janet and Eddie, dear god.

Is Bea right? Have I never seen a good relationship? What about some of those families in Montreal where Janet worked, up past Murray Hill in Westmount?

Oh, damn. Damn. *Putain*. Of course Westmount's gonna make me think of Sami. That's where he lived. Sami, my first boyfriend.

I remember everything about what I was wearing the day we met because I went straight home and looked in the mirror so I could see what he saw. Loose cotton skirt the color of dandelions that grazed the top of my knees. It had deep pockets for my key and a few coins in case I wanted a coffee or some gum, white v-neck t-shirt with a very good bra underneath. Janet said French women always had the best lingerie shops and by French, she meant Montreal. I had on white tennis shoes because that's what I always wore when I wanted to get out of the house, away from Janet and Antoine. I had the camera Eddie had given me the Christmas before, our last Christmas in Wellesley. That's all I did. Walk around. Take photographs, but mostly walking and noticing what kind of shoes women wore.

It was pretty warm that day so I stopped to sit across the street from a small cafe with a few tables on the sidewalk. A boy walked out of the cafe with his *copains*. He was the tallest of the three. Dark hair, white jeans. One of his arms was mounded around a big plastic motorcycle helmet. They did that short goodbye handshake that French boys do and the two walked off while the really cute one went over to an orange motorcycle that was parked in a spot as if it were a car.

He straddled the bike and then looked over at me, letting the helmet sit in his lap. I didn't look away.

On y va? He smiled and gestured to the seat to show there was room enough for me to ride behind him.

I shook my head and stood up. I began walking down the center of the park's gravel path. I couldn't walk too fast or the camera would swing on its strap and begin thumping on my chest. I heard a quiet purring motor come up behind me. It was him. I stepped aside to let him pass but he trundled along beside me, the motor impatient in its slow speed. He gunned it just a bit and then, getting no response from me, sped off down the pedestrian way. He's going to get in trouble for that, I thought. But when I came to the edge of the garden, about to begin the walk home, there he was. He sat on the bike with both boots on the ground, leaning back on the orange bike as if it were a stool at a bar. I really couldn't remember ever meeting anyone so handsome. His hair so black the curves of his curls seemed almost blue. His teeth when he smiled, like a movie star.

I walked over, not quite all the way.

"An orange motorcycle," I said.

"Yeah—it's a Beemer, R90S." As if that should mean something to me. And then, misinterpreting my puzzled look for disdain, "Yeah, it's a lot but I earned it. My dad got it for me because I got into the college he wanted."

"Which one?"

"You won't have heard of it—MIT ."

"Massachusetts Institute of Technology. Our neighbor is a professor there. I mean, my used to be neighbor. We don't live there anymore. In Massachusetts, I mean."

He looked at me with a suddenness that made me have to look away. Somehow just knowing about a smart college made him think I was smart.

He tried again to get me to go for a ride with him but I pointed at my skirt and shook my head. I didn't want to tell him the real reason was that the very idea of riding on a motorcycle without knowing where it was going made me want to throw up.

"Meet me here tomorrow," he said, pulling the helmet down onto his head and clipping the chin strap. "And wear jeans."

He started up the engine and again, I was so surprised by how it wasn't loud and snappy, but more humming. He flicked his fingers in a wave and then sped off.

The next day was Sunday. Janet and Antoine were gathering up things, a blanket, a bowl of blueberries and strawberries with a sheet of foil crimped overtop, bottles of white wine and sunhats.

"We'll be back late," Janet said, fluttering her feet in the air so the polish on her toes would dry faster.

"Can I come?"

Antoine walked into the room and said, "what?" in answer to Janet's face that looked filled with surprise.

"She wants to come," said Janet.

Formidable, said Antoine.

So for the whole day, I wore a pair of my mother's dark sunglasses and a scarf over my head like some of the other women Janet's age who were all gathered, grass poking through where the carpet of blankets didn't touch. After everyone had finished eating dinner and the baskets were out of the way, I lay back and watched the sky get dark. It was so easy to see the stars here, far away from the lights of the city. The grass was a little bit wet but I didn't care at all. I felt such tremendous relief knowing he could never find me here and now I could go back to the city knowing I would never see him again. The concert was still going when Janet said she'd had enough and we walked back to Antoine's vw van.

"I'm so glad you wanted to come," Janet said, wrapping her arm through mine and we crossed the field like that, as if we were the kind of mother and daughter that walked arm in arm.

A few days later I stepped out of the camera shop, my photos a thick stack in the glassine envelope. I walked down the street slowly, moving past feet as I flipped through the images, careful to keep the strip of negatives from falling out. And then a pair of black boots stopped me. I looked up.

"Did you know there are three places you can get pictures developed around here?"

"The one on St. Viateur isn't good—I've used them before," I said.

He put out a hand for me to show him the photos. I hand them over. He looks through them.

"It's too bad you don't shoot in color. That's what's so great about summer—all the colors come back."

I shrugged. I wasn't going to tell him that color prints cost way more money.

He pointed across the street. "Ice Cream?"

Was there anything I loved more than ice cream? Plus, he was buying.

He ordered a cone of pistachio. I ordered a small cup of strawberry with the cone sitting on top.

Sami was Algerian. Well, his parents were. They were in Paris for three weeks. He was shocked, maybe a bit turned off that I knew nothing about the French colonisation of Algeria or the war that killed so many. Why were we even talking about this? *Putain*. I didn't tell him that I had read *L'Etranger* and liked it. I just sat there, embarrassed. All of the wars were so confusing. I heard about Khmer Rouge and Vietnam, these foreign places where horrible things were happening but I didn't know why. I asked Janet, but she was no help.

"Oh honey, men and war. I don't know where it starts and I have no idea how it will ever end. I wish I knew what to tell you, I really do. Mostly, I would say try to stay out of it."

No help at all.

Eventually, he talked me into riding on the back of his motorcycle. He had a helmet for me and everything. It was amazing. Amazing. I'd never seen the city like this before. I told him he should name his bike.

"Only girls do things like that," he said.

Every day he'd be waiting for me outside Antoine's apartment right around lunch time but he never wanted lunch because he had only just woken up. He took me to restaurants and cafes that would make him eggs or crepes.

"She'll have waffles," he would say to the waiter.

"I'm sorry, *monsieur*. We are on lunch menu now."

"Oh come on," Sami would say. "Look at this girl. Tell me she isn't deserving of an exception this one time. This girl right here, she is the one in a million."

The waffles would arrive with a pat of butter melting in the middle, whipped cream on top and a pitcher of maple syrup. I would let him eat most of them, but the bites I had were pure heaven.

Sami always got what he wanted which meant if he liked me so much, I must be special. I started to relax and let myself like him and then, really like him. Like love him, like him. This is what grown-ups do. This is what real boyfriends and girlfriends do. He had so much energy, always wanting to do something new, see something he hadn't seen before.

Museums and movie theaters were air conditioned so we spent most afternoons there. In the movie theaters, we would make out in the back row. In museums we would walk around and choose the paintings we would put in our house. He was partial to Franz Marc, de Kooning and Chagall. My favorites were Klimt and O'Keeffe. We both loved Rothko. I drew the line at a sculpture of a wooden grizzly bear that he wanted to put in our bedroom.

"Absolutely not" I said.

"But he's cute," Sami wheedled. "Look at those teeth."

"You can put it in your study."

"See?" he said, wrapping me in a big hug and kissing me. "Look at how good we are at compromise."

"You probably didn't even want it in the bedroom," I said, letting him hug me without hugging him back.

He took my hand and lead me into the next room. "You understand me completely."

One afternoon he pulled the bike up in front of a shop.

"This is my cousin's place," he said. Inside there were piles of rugs and more hanging on the walls. Above our heads, the ceiling was filled with hammered tin light fixtures, all sizes, some have colored glass. There was a big silver one that looked like it had a genie who lived inside.

Sami motioned to his cousin to take it down for me.

"Don't!" I said, horrified. "It's too expensive."

I shouldn't have told him I liked it.

The cousin grinned. His jelly belly flashed out from under his shirt as he reached up to bring the lamp down.

The ride home was like being in a movie. I could see people looking at us. People in the bus next to us looked down when we were at a stop light. Pretty girl on motorcycle with handsome boy carrying beautiful Moroccan lamp. Did I look wild, young and free? I had the lamp gripped under one arm and clung to Sami with the other.

When I got back to Antoine's building, I went down to the basement where we had storage space. I wrapped the hanging lamp in a winter blanket and hid it behind some of Janet's boxes. There's no way I could show it to her, yet. But soon, I could. It wasn't exactly an engagement ring, but it was big and silver and special. And he had bought it for me. Janet would like him because he was rich and lived in Westmount and went to Brebeuf. I began imagining where I would set up the introductions. At a restaurant. Sunday brunch so it won't be too expensive. I was going to tell Janet once I had invited Sami, but I never got the chance. That was the week his parents came home.

He had brought me there to meet them. His mother left the room. His father asked for me to excuse them and pulled Sami into the library. I stood there, not knowing what to do. I could hear Sami and his dad arguing. They were shouting in French. Maybe his dad didn't think I spoke French?

She has no family, his father said. That was the last thing I heard.

Sami came out, trying to pretend everything was okay. I wouldn't let him give me a ride home. I didn't have my bus pass with me, so I walked the whole way home. It was so hot. I felt disgusting. Like garbage. I went into my room and didn't come out until the day Antoine made me ride with him to deliver paintings to MT GALLANT.

It was only years later when Janet insisted I come up to Montreal to help her move out of Antoine's that I found the lamp. I had actually forgotten all about it.

"Where did this come from?" Janet asked in amazement.

"Some client of Marie-Thérèse was getting rid of it."

"It's beautiful," she said, a bit envious. "You keeping it?"

I wasn't planning to, but as soon as I realized she would take it if I didn't I said yes. My apartment was too small but someday I'd have a foyer where I could hang it.

It didn't take us long to finish digging through all her stuff. Janet was leaving most of it behind.

"I don't want to drag old stuff into my new life," she said.

"What about all this?" I tapped my foot on the boxes that held all her manicure supplies.

"Good riddance," she said.

Even though Antoine supported us pretty much and had the apartment for free, Janet needed cash flow. She began giving in-house manicures to the women of Westmount. It was a word-of-mouth success. She made cash under the table plus her offers to the same clients to spring clean their closets got her hand-me-downs that she sold at consignment shops. Not before she squirreled away the best bits, of course, careful to keep track of which pieces belonged to who, so no one ever saw one of their former blouses or skirts or handbags on her.

My gut churns at the memory of the shoes I let her give me.

"Look," she dragged the word out as she held the shoes up for me to admire. "Aren't they beautiful? Too small for me, *tant pis,* but you try them."

My foot slipped in easily. Even though they were a bit worn in, you could tell the shoes had been very expensive—soft leather, the color of dark apricots and the most perfect heel. I knew that once I had polished and buffed them they would be sensational.

Janet tried to take them back. "They're too old for you," she said, but I loved them. They made me feel rich. I wore them so often that I forgot where they came from until that day one of Marie-Thérèse's clients got a look on her face as I walked across the room. She was waiting for Marie-Thérèse to join her on the sofa. She looked like so many of the women I saw here every day—

brows groomed, hair styled as if she had just come from a salon. The woman stared at my feet.

"Where did you get those shoes?" she asked.

I stopped. At first, I thought she was simply admiring them. I smiled.

"Oh, a lucky find," I said.

"Around here?" Her question was more pointed. She wasn't admiring them. She recognized them. She knew I was lying.

"No—" my voice wavered. "A little shop down in Boston." Marie-Thérèse was walking toward us. I tried to get away but my feet wouldn't move.

"Boston," the woman repeated. She leaned back into the sofa and smiled up at Marie-Thérèse who was placing samples down onto the coffee table. With one hand, the woman adjusted the pink cashmere shawl that was draped across her shoulders, with the other she accepted the demitasse of coffee that Marie-Thérèse held out to her, rings and bracelets glittering.

"I had a pair just like those that I got in Barcelona. Handmade."

I smiled and nodded, still unable to move away from her gaze that ripped the clothes off my body. My lying, garbage-digging self completely exposed to the woman whose shoes I was wearing. Marie-Thérèse waved me off which released the curse on my feet and I escaped to the backroom where I stayed until the woman was gone.

That night I carried the shoes in a plastic bag as I walked down the alley behind Antoine's apartment. I scooped up dog poop and dumped it on top of the shoes. At the end of the alley was a trash can. I tied the bag tight with a double knot and tossed it in.

Holy shit. How did I never realize this before? Did that woman know Sami's mother? Did Sami's mother know who Janet was and that I was her daughter? Is that possible? Of course it's possible, you idiot. How is it only now you are making that connection? Oh, that's right. Because you are the stupidest, most blind moron that the world has ever known. How did you ever trick anyone into believing you were smart? You are such a fucking imbecile. *Nul. Nul. Nul.*

Bea smoothes the covers and tries to calm me down.

"It's okay, it's okay," she says.

I shake her off. There's nothing she can do. She thinks it's because of the bedsores. And they're bad. It's all one long knifepoint of misery, but I sink into that pain. The physical pain is a relief, so much easier than the memories that keep surfacing.

unconventional for the win

Mona is on a blanket in the grass. She tips over as she tries to sit up. Bea squats from behind and lifts Mona by the shoulders. She pulls her back a few inches toward the big maple and tucks pillows between Mona's back and the tree.

"There you go, " Bea says. "That's better."

"It'd be better if you brought me that chaise lounge."

Bea gets up and begins heading down the hill, the dogs running alongside.

Mona wants to call out she was only kidding, but she doesn't have the breath.

There are no sounds here except some birds, and that chippy noise—is that a chipmunk or a squirrel? She closes her eyes and lets the breeze roll across her face.

Mosquitoes.

She spritzes more of the concoction Giusita has given her, trying to make sweeping arcs as she would put on perfume, shoulder to shoulder, behind her head, up and down the blanket. Wrists. Behind the ears.

She settles back and gazes over the green and gold hills. The soft purple mountains in the distance. From up here, Bea's house, plus the one she built for Giusita and Diogo, plus the garden sheds and outbuildings, looks like a compound of Greene and Greene bungalows with paths and gardens weaving in-between.

She watches as Bea and Diogo carry the chaise lounge up the hill.

They set it down on the flattest area. Diogo lifts Mona up and places her onto the chaise, then wraps the blanket over her legs. He wedges a couple of big stones under the front wheels.

"We don't want you rolling down the hill, now do we?"

"I don't know," says Mona. "It could be fun."

"If you want to get yourself killed." Bea tucks the blanket up over Mona's lap.

"Might be a good way to go," says Mona.

"Only if the neck snaps in a clean break," says Bea. "Otherwise you could be in agony and who knows how long it would take to get an EMT crew up here. Might be a slow, horrible, protracted death with a lot of pain."

"Sounds fast and easy to me," say Mona.

Diogo looks horrified. He cannot join in. The dogs follow him a bit as he walks off, but then they turn and come back to where Bea and Mona are sitting.

"I think we offended your handyman," says Mona.

"He is not my handyman."

They watch as Giusita opens the gate and lets the pigs out for the day.

"You just let them roam free?"

"Yep."

"They won't run away? Or get hurt?"

"Nope."

"Why do you even have them if you're not going to eat them?"

Bea looks up at Mona from where she sits in the grass next to the chaise lounge.

"Spend some time with pigs," says Bea. "And then ask me that."

Mona reaches down and rips up a handful of grass to throw at Bea's head but it mostly scatters across the blanket.

"Yeah, I'll get right on that. How about this summer? Good for you if I spend the summer here getting to know your pigs? Or a couple months next fall? Or Christmas?"

Mona starts to cry. "How about I come and visit the pigs at Christmas?"

As she sobs, Bea reaches up and rubs Mona's ankle, her shin.

"Stop it," she says, kicking Bea's hand away. "I'm not one of your dogs. *Putain*."

They watch as two cars come up the hill with dust in their wake. Little Bear and Luka leap to their feet and race down the hill barking for all they are worth.

The cars pull to a stop. Ellen gets out of her vw. The dogs greet Ellen and then circle the jeep carrying the strangers.

Two men, each with a briefcase, step down from the jeep. One reaches out to pet the dogs.

"What kind of lawyer drives a jeep?" says Mona.

"If it were the middle of February you wouldn't be asking that question."

Bea stands up.

"I want to stay here forever," Mona says.

"Well, that can be arranged, but right now we need to go down and meet these guys."

"Why can't they come up here?"

• • •

Thank god there are people in this world who are good at dealing with the nitty gritty details of life, thinks Bea as she combs burrs out from where they are buried in the thick fur of Little Bear's chest. She and the dogs sit a distance away from where Mona is holding court.

If the nurses were watching from the kitchen window, it must have looked like a strange procession. Bea and Ellen carrying two chairs and a stool up to the giant maple tree with the lawyers walking behind.

Ellen settles on the stool to Mona's right. The lawyers sit in chairs on her left. Not a typical day at the office, one of them says. He is trying to make light of why they were there. Mona does not smile. They bring out the paperwork and begin the process.

Little Bear squirms as the comb gets stuck behind a tangle of burrs. Bea murmurs into her ear and strokes her head as she gently works the knot until the sticky ball of fur and burrs is in her hand. She tosses it into the grass.

All better, all better, she whispers to Little Bear. She puts the comb back in her pocket and begins giving the dog long strokes up and down its spine. Luka comes over to get some love too, which causes Little Bear to get up and walk away.

Bea tries not to listen to the conversation. She focuses her attention on Ellen and watches her as if she were seeing her for the first time. What would she ever have done without Ellen? Ellen, who never met a contract she couldn't decipher. Ellen, who talked Bea through getting the pilot light back on when it went out during a snowstorm. Ellen who got Bea in with the best vet in the area even though he wasn't taking on new clients. Ellen, who in a matter of days, has won over the trust and affection of her never satisfied little sister.

"Mona named you as her executor," says Ellen.

They stand in the drive next to the vw. The jeep is gone. Bea scrolls lines into the dirt with the toe of her boot.

"Just a heads up, she has quite a bit of debt to clear."

Bea stops scrolling. "Are you serious? I thought she was rich."

Ellen rattles off a slew of details from the meeting but the only one Bea hears is that the apartment is a rental and will need to be vacated by the end of August when the lease is up. The lawyers are sending a letter to the property manager.

"Here," says Ellen, handing a slip of paper to Bea with the name of a trucking company that will help her. "And you thought your moving days were over."

The attic of Eddie's house had to be 100 degrees, baking under the August sun, but that was not why Bea's heart was pounding; she was scared of what her mother would do if she saw what Bea had found hidden in one of the suitcases.

"For god's sake," Janet called up. "What are you doing up there?"

"Everything is super dirty," Bea's voice was choked, clogged with dust and a storm of emotion. "I found them. I'm just cleaning them off."

It was a lie. She had done nothing but open the manila envelope of photographs that she held in her hands. Sweat gathered at the nape of her neck and dripped down her spine.

Bea had no memory of Ray photographing her. She had gone up to the attic to find suitcases that she could take to college. Under the fabric covered cardboard bottom of one of the big ones they never used, she found the manila envelope. Did Janet even remember she had put it there when they left L.A.?

The envelope was flat with two narrow strips of yellowed masking tape, the decayed adhesive disintegrating, barely holding on. Inside were three large black and white photographs, the kind professional photographers make.

The first one was of Bea as a toddler in a dress of ruffles that ended mid-chubby thigh. She peered up at the camera, confused. Her hair was a messy mop of curls. In the distance behind her was Janet, whose hair was coiffed into a chignon, her long legs bare and tucked neatly at the ankles. Janet's head was in one hand, her elbow propped on the sofa arm, as she watched Bea. Her mother looked old because of the black and white photo and the old-fashioned clothes, but when Bea peered closer, she saw that her mother was actually very young. She didn't seem that much older than Bea was now.

The next photo was of Bea standing on a stool behind her mother, pretending to play hairdresser to Janet who sat at a vanity. The little girl was very serious, a fistful of her mother's hair lifted high. The mother was laughing into a cigarette. The oval mirror reflected them and the ornate carvings on the silver backed brush that sat on the vanity table. Bea recognized that brush. Her stomach heaved and pitched to one side. That brush was now on the dresser in Janet and Eddie's room. Bea could walk downstairs and put her hand on it if she wanted to.

The last photo. Bea from the back, older now, maybe four years old, barrettes in her hair, a white blouse with tiny puffs at the shoulders, a swiss dot pinafore, two straps crisscrossing over her back. Bea seemed to be asking a question, looking up to Janet who sat at the edge of a bench in a garden or park somewhere. Janet's fingers cupped each of Bea's shoulders as if she might answer the little girl but her gaze was directed into the lens of the camera. Ever inscrutable, she was giving her full attention, her mysterious smile to the man behind the camera, daring him to guess her thoughts.

A kind of stabbing went through Bea's chest. She felt a loss for something she didn't even know existed. Were there other photographs of Bea's childhood that Janet left behind? Had there been photos of her with Setsuko that she never saw?

Her mother called out again for her to hurry up.

Bea stuffed the envelope back into its hiding place but the zipper caught on the frayed fabric and wouldn't close. Panic. She shut the suitcase then clambered down the rickety ladder that folded back up into the ceiling. Janet was waiting, hands on hips.

"God, I'd forgotten that old thing." Janet reached to take the handle out of Bea's hands, but Bea shifted to hold it behind her. Their eyes connected. Her mother flinched.

"Clean it off," she said, one hand on the banister as she went down the stairs. Mona had been watching from the threshold of her bedroom.

"You can't bring that to college. People will think you're weird. Mom!"

Mona galloped down the stairs after her mother. A shopping opportunity had arisen. "She needs a new suitcase. She can't use your old one. The other girls will tease her."

· · ·

Mona led the way as they entered the luggage store.

"You really should have a set," Mona advised Bea. The salesman beamed at the precocious eleven-year-old who was clearly in charge.

"She's not getting a set," said Janet.

Mona pressed from a number of directions. Finally, with input from the salesman, Janet caved and a four-piece set of light blue hardcase luggage, replete with a small train case that Mona had explored in detail—lifting out the tray and putting her hands into the pockets that lined the case—was brought up to the register.

As they left the store, Mona again led the way back to the car. She carried the train case in one hand and the smaller suitcase in the other. Bea brought up the rear with the two large cases, empty and banging against her bare legs.

Janet fiddled with the rearview mirror and lit a cigarette. Mona sat in the backseat with the train case on her lap. She beamed with pride as she talked about the locks, the inner pockets, how it had straps to hold things in place, the zippered pocket you can unsnap, how pretty the blue is.

"It has a mirror in the top!" After each announcement, she waited for Bea's response. A thank you or some kind of recognition for this marvelous gift she had just made happen.

Bea rolled her window all the way down. The heat was unbearable. She felt sick for how much it all cost, barely able to keep from bursting into tears when she thought about the photographs in the brown paper package with the yellowed bits of masking tape now hidden under her mattress.

"Can we go now?" Bea said, her words directed out the open window.

"Don't use that tone with me, missy," snapped Janet. "How dare you be so ungrateful. I should never have let him talk me into all that."

Janet jabbed the bar on the steering wheel into reverse and backed out of the parking space.

"I didn't ask for any of this," Bea replied.

The wheels squealed as Janet shifted the car into drive and pulled out of the lot.

"You really are something," Janet growled in her sharpest, ugly voice that she mostly used with Eddie. "You know that?"

Bea felt Mona behind her. She turned to look at her little sister.

"You can keep that one," she said, pointing to the train kit. "I don't want it."

• • •

Two weeks before she graduated from college, Bea traded the blue suitcases for a knapsack and duffle bag. She was headed to San Francisco right after commencement and needed to pack light as Alex, the guy who had posted the ride share that she answered, had made it clear there wouldn't be much room for her stuff.

Bea took the job because she didn't want to disappoint Professor Tamamoto, who had told her to apply for it, and because she thought returning to California was a good idea. But the moment she and Alex arrived, she knew San Francisco was a mistake.

The engine strained and the muffler coughed hairballs as they inched up the impossibly steep hill. The city did not feel at all like she thought it would. She tried to tell herself that it was ten days on the road that had eaten her excitement and energy, but she knew what the problem was. She didn't belong here.

Weeks, then months passed, but the feeling did not change. It felt like there was a dark energy underneath San Francisco even though it looked so colorful on the surface with longhaired girls in tie-dyed tee shirts who danced barefoot in the grass, Indian cotton skirts swirling at their calves. If she went over to Berkeley, or later when she moved down to Cupertino, the feeling wasn't there so she knew it was part of living on that rocky hill, but she never told anyone. Well, except Alex, the one who was her boyfriend until he wasn't.

"You said the same thing about being at your grandparents in Pennsylvania," he had answered. He stood barefoot in the kitchen wearing beat-up board shorts, no shirt. He had stopped cutting his hair once they arrived and it was now nearly touching his naked shoulders. He grabbed a beer from the tiny refrigerator that sat on the countertop of their impossibly small kitchen.

No, she thought. Pennsylvania didn't have this dark sorrow energy. It was just that summers there were muggy and oppressive. Not the same. But she knew better than to try and explain how things felt to another person. They would tell her to stop being so sensitive or weird, mostly stop being so weird.

High school hadn't been too bad as long as she was playing tennis. Once she quit, nobody knew what to make of her. College was better once she transferred into the nerd dorm where she didn't stand out at all since everybody in there was some kind of castoff. Plus, she soon became the reigning queen of Pong, which actually gave her whatever kind of status you could have with people who ate Fluffernutter on white bread for dinner and whose idea of a big night out meant going downstairs to the basement lounge to compete to see who knew more world capitals or debate Kant's beliefs about space and time.

College was easy as long as she stuck to the math and science classes. Totally straightforward: practice, memorize and study. Her focus paid off. She got an internship at MIT the summer after her freshman year which was perfect timing since it meant she could avoid being dragged into Janet's latest crime scene.

· · ·

Bea was in the dorm's basement lounge with a couple of people from her linear algebra class, prepping for finals when somebody yelled down that she had a phone call.

It was Mona, sobbing. Bea could hardly understand her. Janet had left Eddie. She'd met an artist named Antoine and decided to move to Montreal to be with him. Mona was hysterical. Among the many things she was saying was that she couldn't bring all her things with her, she listed out clothes and toys that had been left behind. Two suitcases, Janet had limited her to two suitcases.

"Okay, that's quite enough," Bea listened as Janet took the phone away and Mona ran screaming into another room. A door slammed.

"Darling," Janet purred into the phone as if they were off on holiday and not leaving a trail of wreckage in her wake.

"She's being her sweet dramatic self. You know she doesn't like change at first. She'll settle in. Can you imagine how lucky we would be to get to go to school in Montreal? I would have given my right thumb at her age. And let's not even talk about how fabulous it's going to be for her French. And you, my darling bunny, this is perfect timing. You are only a hop skip and a jump from Montreal. As soon as you finish your exams and whatnot, grab a bus and come up here. You will love it. There's a summer jazz festival and lots of places you can be a waitress if that's what you want to do."

When Bea didn't answer, her way of saying she would not be getting a bus to Montreal, Janet played her winning card.

"You know I wouldn't ask, but it's for your sister. Mona really needs you, darling. I think it will help so much for her to have you here with us."

Bea hung up the phone knowing full well the person it would help most.

The fact that Janet had to pretend not to be pissed off that Bea preferred to be in Wellesley with her former neighbors, the Tamamotos, was just an added bonus.

Janet had never met the Tamamotos. They lived a few streets away from Eddie's house and were never at any of the parties. The summer after Ricky left, the days were unbearable for Bea and she'd go for a long walk only to find herself standing outside the Tamamoto house.

She had babysat for Professor and Mrs. Tamamoto a number of times, but that summer after Ricky left, she knocked at the door, hoping Mrs. Tamamoto would want to see her. Nobody invited the Tamamotos to their cookouts. It didn't seem to Bea that Mrs. Tamamoto had made friends with any of the other women in the neighborhood. Maybe she was lonely, too.

At first, Bea always brought a gift—a tomato plant she had bought at the garden club sale, a plate of brownies that she made, a small posy of cuttings she took from along the aqueduct—but soon she didn't have to bring anything anymore. Mrs. Tamamoto always seemed genuinely pleased to see her.

She had two little kids and her husband, a professor at MIT, worked long hours. Their house, a cape painted dark gray with a lighter gray trim on the windows, had a bright yellow door and was the smallest on the street. A trio of massive juniper bushes provided a hedge of privacy.

Bea had loved it from the moment she first stepped inside. It reminded her of Setsuko's house, how there were slippers by the door where you were to leave your shoes, how they didn't have things like wallpaper, flowered slipcovers pulled tight over fat sofas or chandeliers in the foyer. Everything was simpler, quieter, even Mrs. Tamamoto. Part of the quiet between them was that Mrs. Tamamoto's English was not strong but mostly, Bea knew, she was like her, happier not to talk if you didn't have to.

When Bea stood in the doorway to a tiny room—not much bigger than a closet, really, where Mrs. Tamamoto had a table and chair for her watercolors—and asked if she was an artist, Mrs. Tamamoto blushed hard and buried her head down as she shook it, no. Emphatic. No. Bea looked again. There was a smock, paints, paper, pens, a row of brushes wrapped in cloth, two small ceramic bowls for ink and water. Her small paintings had thin black lines to give shape to a flower or landscape and then Mrs. Tamamoto would fill it out with watercolor paint.

Bea was confused. Why wouldn't she call herself an artist?

Mrs. Tamamoto offered food in small bowls or on curved rectangular plates. Plump half moons of tangerine arranged in a fan, apples sliced so you could see the star in the middle. Sometimes Bea would bring Mrs. Tamamoto something she had found in the woods—Queen Anne's lace, moss, stones. Mrs. Tamamoto put the flowers in a green ceramic vase, misted the moss and set the rocks, in groups, on the windowsill.

When the children were napping or busy scribbling in coloring books, Mrs. Tamamoto taught Bea how to hold the bamboo brush with its soft, teardrop-shaped bristles, how to stroke black ink on to white paper. Slow. Careful. Precise. Dip, stroke.

She pointed at the torn back pocket of Bea's Levis. Bea had been exploring the woods past old man Mueller's farm and jumped down from a fence without realizing the pocket had gotten caught. She didn't want to throw her jeans out because they were finally broken in the way she liked them. Mrs. Tamamoto brought her sewing pouch to the table. As they sat, Bea watched Mrs. Tamamoto unroll the pouch to reveal small sections that held needles, pins and a thimble. She held out three kinds of thread for Bea to choose. Bea chose the red one.

The children clapped their hands to their mouths and squealed with laughter when Bea came back into the room wearing a pair of Mrs. Tamamoto's long, linen culottes. They thought it was hilarious to see Bea in their mother's clothes. Bea handed the Levis to Mrs. Tamamoto, but she handed them back.

"No, you do," she said.

She showed Bea how to hold her wrist, how to use the thimble, how to make a series of stitches beyond the original rip so it looked less like a scar and more, just, pretty.

Before she left for college, Mrs. Tamamoto gave her a cloth bundle. Under the wrap was a small painting of trees blooming, masses of pink blossoms tumbling and there, so tiny underneath, a girl crossing a bridge.

When she first got to Vermont, Bea sent postcards to Mrs. Tamamoto. Postcards with lots of leaves and trees and, whenever she could find a good one, a bridge.

· · ·

It was because of Professor Tamamoto that she got the summer internship at MIT, so Bea stayed with them for those weeks in a small room down in the basement of their house. It was such a change from dormitory life. She loved coming up the stairs into the spare, quiet house each morning. Green plants in dark ceramic urns. Lamps with carved wood bases and fragile white paper shades. The kitchen had sliding glass doors that opened into the back garden. The only awkward thing about that summer was being back in the old neighborhood, but she did all she could to avoid Eddie's house as well as the Stewart's.

Once, she saw Mrs. Stewart outside the grocery store. She wanted to rush up and tell her all that had happened since they last rubbed mushrooms clean and set bulbs into perfectly measured holes, to tell her how she had created a whole series of books about *Carrot Girl*. She wanted to know how Ricky was. Was he still in Canada? But Jenna was with her so she just watched as the mother and daughter loaded their bags into the station wagon and drove away.

Mornings, she would ride into Cambridge with Professor Tamamoto. Together they would walk to Building 4 where they would each buy a bagel from the coffee cart. Then he would give her a funny bow-wave-nod as he headed to his office. At the end of the day, she usually finished before he did, she would sit on the steps of Building 10 to wait for him there. She loved the routine, the consistency and Professor Tamamoto's courtesy. How he always waited for the song to finish before turning the radio off. How he never failed to offer her a napkin for her bagel. She wondered sometimes if this is what it was like to have a father. Someone who wants to help you, who likes to spend time with you, who makes you feel like you can do anything.

The Tamamotos didn't go to the seashore or do traditional holiday things, but every Sunday they would go for long walks at the Arnold Arboretum or drive up to New Hampshire and climb Mt. Monadnock, and she was always included.

Sometimes, she realized she was holding her breath. What was the word for this? She paused, gazing around the living room, Mrs. Tamamoto's dark eyebrows lifted as if to say, is there a question? Bea smiled and shook her head no, exhaling, looking back to the stitching in her lap. The word was warm across her chest, privileged.

When she got back to Middlebury, feeling filled up with the peace and gentleness that was part of her daily life with the Tamamotos she found a single postcard sitting at an angle behind the little metal door to her mailbox. The photo was of a street mime wearing a black bowler, a black and white striped t-shirt and black pants. In one hand he held a red umbrella.

On the back, Mona had scrawled, *I hate you forever.*

A few weeks later Bea was on a bus heading to Montreal for Canadian Thanksgiving.

Antoine's apartment had three bedrooms and a back deck where he painted scenes from the neighborhood. Antoine was much younger than Eddie. He may have been younger than Janet.

The four of them crowded around a table in a busy cafe. Janet and Antoine drank espresso and finished each other's sentences. They had a physical intimacy as if they'd been together for years. Mona was sullen, her only response to any question was a shrug. Bea watched how easily Janet fit her body against this man, his arm resting across her shoulder. She realized her mother was a trapeze artist, the impeccable timing of letting one bar go as the next one swings into reach.

Auntie Annie was joining them for this first Canadian Thanksgiving which meant Bea had to sleep on the floor of Mona's room. Her sister had still not said a single word to Bea, but, as always, once Auntie Annie arrived, things got much better.

"What's going on?" Auntie Annie asked.

"She's shunning me," said Bea.

"Well, glad to see someone's got some religion around here," laughed Auntie Annie. When Mona looked confused, Auntie Annie patted the seat next to her.

"Come here, poppet. Quakers shun. It's their way of punishment. Good choice, darling. So much better than those dreadful Catholics with their guilt and shame."

"Or, you know, torture, inquisition and burning at the stake," said Janet, handing Auntie Annie a glass of red wine.

Auntie Annie took Mona shopping and treated her like a princess.

"Look," Mona raced into the room. She held out her ten fingertips all painted pink.

Janet hung Auntie Annie's coat on one of the hooks by the door. No front hall closet here. They settled on the sofa. Mona put on a fashion show with the clothes that Auntie Annie had bought her.

"You should have come with us, Bea," said Auntie Annie. "I would have spoiled you, too."

Antoine brought in a bottle of Beaujolais and a tray with olives and cut baguette. He settled in next to Janet. They talked about jazz, Pollack, Motherwell. Antoine asked Auntie Annie all kinds of questions about her life in New York. Janet looked so much younger. Her hair was long and she wore it loose, no hairspray. Bea didn't know what she'd done with all the clothes she used to wear in Wellesley, but here she wore brown corduroy bell bottoms with her shirt tied in a knot at the waist.

When Antoine took Auntie Annie and Mona for a walk through the neighborhood, Bea followed her mother into the kitchen. It was the first time they had been alone all weekend.

"So," Janet turned with a bright smile to say, *see, didn't everything work out just as I told you it would?*

Bea couldn't deny Janet seemed happy and Antoine seemed nice, but there was something so wrong about what she had done. Shouldn't she be punished for ripping Mona out of the life she had made her believe she could have? It was confusing. Bea walked back into the living room without saying anything. Her mother followed.

"Look, I have done everything for you girls. I have always put you first. I left L.A. and got buried alive in Tupperware just so you kids could have a storybook childhood. I did that for you. Now I have a chance to find myself again and it is perfect timing for Mona. Do you know they call her Monique here? How fabulous is that? She has a fresh slate. She can be anyone she wants. You should see the high school, it's positively cosmopolitan. It's going to be like going to college in Paris for god's sake."

"This is not Paris, Mom."

"What was she going to learn in that graham cracker box of a high school? Would you want her to grow up and be like one of those women? Think about what happened to Sylvia Plath."

"Who's Sylvia Plath?"

"Oh for god's sake. I think you just want to be mad at me so you can be mad at me. Well have at it."

Janet blew smoke out the open window and looked down to the street.

"Have you ever seen anything so darling as that mailbox on the corner?"

"What about Eddie? You made us believe we were a family."

"There they are. I see them," Janet got up and opened the door. She came back to the window and stubbed out her cigarette with a sigh.

"Oh bunny, I told him ages ago that I was ready for change. I tried to get him out of there, to make a move with me."

"That's crazy. Eddie would never leave Wellesley. He's not going to come live in some strange city and leave his job and the golf and the country club and Louise and Charlie. He grew up there. It's his home."

"Exactly," said Janet.

How does she always win? Bea reached across to the hors d'oeuvres Janet had set out and began snapping a breadstick into pieces.

"Stop that," said Janet. "You're making a mess."

They listened as Antoine, Mona and Auntie Annie thumped up the stairs.

Janet beamed as they come into the room, red-cheeked. "How was the walk?"

Bea hadn't thought much about how she would get out to San Francisco and then, walking through the student center she noticed the bright blue index card on the bulletin board. She liked the handwriting; it was strong, clean, confident.

Alex wasn't part of her nerd dorm but he wasn't a frat guy either.

He had majored in English and wanted to be the next John Steinbeck. They had spent four years together on the same campus but had never met until she answered his posting. He was looking for someone to split gas and driving. It didn't mention he had a crappy VW bug that would break down every third day, but she didn't mind, too much. He was cute and liked to talk about the books he was going to write. He introduced her to Bob Marley and Gordon Lightfoot. When it was her turn to choose, she always picked the *Moondance* cassette by Van Morrison until Alex told her he was going to throw it out the window if she played it one more time.

Alex didn't have a job lined up. He was a free spirit and wanted to see what the universe would bring. It was Bea's salary that landed them the first and last month's rent and security deposit on their apartment, but the company Professor Tamamoto had been so excited about for her turned out to be a bust. Somehow they hadn't looked too closely at her paperwork because they all seemed to be surprised and dismayed that she was female. Instead of working with the electrical engineers as she had been led to expect, she was delegated to catalogue documentation.

"I think you'll be happier with this assignment," said the human resources man as he left her in the windowless room they called the library. It was on the same floor that housed the company cantina which meant she was often asked to make another pot of coffee.

One Saturday morning, Bea passed a bakery whose front window was filled with plants, many of them needing help. She walked in, slipped off her knapsack and began gently removing the dead leaves and talking to the plants.

"Want a job?" a voice called out from across the room.

Bea turned to see Parvati, a woman with bleached blond hair and tattooed arms who was loading freshly baked sourdough batards into baskets.

"Yes," answered Bea.

Parvati had been kidding. Bea wasn't.

Because Parvati didn't ask her to stop, Bea proceeded to prune each plant carefully, whispering encouragement to it as she wiped the dust off each leaf with a wet paper napkin. She gathered up the debris, carried it back to the kitchen and tossed it into a trashcan. She asked where she could find a watering can. There wasn't one, but with a bucket of water and a coffee cup, she gave each plant a good drink.

When she was finished, Parvati came over and handed Bea a mug of coffee that had been sprinkled with sugar, cocoa powder and cinnamon.

"What I need is four a.m. help," said Parvati. "You an early riser?"

Bea never went back to the company. She wrote them a letter and dropped it into the blue metal box that stood at the end of Parvati's street. No more dark, boring, windowless room shelving stacks of paper. Behind the bakery was a courtyard with the most lovely plum tree whose blossoms seemed to last forever and dropped to the ground like fat carnations. The birds loved the courtyard almost as much as Bea, probably because of all the breadcrumbs, but maybe, like her, they were in love with the tree.

Suddenly her life in San Francisco became an entirely different experience. Slipping out of bed so she wouldn't wake Alex, she would stretch her arms up to the sky, wiggling fingertips hello as she walked through dark, empty streets. She had a key to get in but the lights would be on and the kitchen fired up as the two bakers had been prepping loaves and pastries since midnight. Around five a.m. they would unwrap their aprons and hang them on the hook by the door, leaving Bea to continue until Parvati showed up around nine.

Parvati came into this world as Polly Gunderson from Edina, Minnesota. Bea learned this because from the moment Parvati walked into the bakery each morning, a steady stream of chatter ran from her mouth. Every once in a while Parvati said something that was useful, but not often.

She had a tattoo of a peacock on one arm, a trust fund, divorced parents and a moon in Capricorn. At first, it seemed like Parvati was unlike anyone Bea had met at college. But after a little while, Bea came to see that underneath the hair, the bohemian clothes and the name change, Parvati was just like the suburban girls she had grown up with. She might talk a lot about free love and independence, but Parvati defined the world with labels like everybody else. When a child ran after a woman crying because the mother had absentmindedly left the bakery without her, Parvati sniffed.

"Probably an Aquarian. Not a great inclination toward motherhood. Now Cancers. Or, a Taurus with a Libra moon, give me that, right? What's your sign?"

"Oh," replied Bea. "I don't know anything about tarot."

"Astrology, not tarot. You should read up. Makes life easier."

Doubtful, thought Bea. Parvati seemed to be in a constant state of struggle—with boyfriends, with girlfriends, with running the bakery, with getting up in the morning, with falling asleep at night. Every day was a new drama.

One morning, Bea arrived to find Parvati sitting at the counter looking more like a sad seventeenth-century French courtesan than the cool party girl she thought she was. Thin rivulets of mascara scrolled down her cheeks. This was Bea's sacred hour, cherished for its quiet, and here was Parvati crying and filling the space with her empty words. She hobbled about in thigh-high black patent leather boots, insisting on trying to help because she didn't want to go home.

"Wash your hands first," snapped LaDonna, the nicer of the two bakers. LaDonna rolled her eyes at Bea as Parvati went to the sink. It wasn't often that LaDonna spoke to her and Bea wanted desperately to say the right thing. Ever since Bea had remarked in passing that for the longest time she had misunderstood and thought their boss had renamed herself 'Poverty,' LaDonna had been warmer to her.

"I think she's a little drunk," said Bea.

"That's the least of her problems," said LaDonna, slashing quick cuts into a loaf of bread.

For anyone who didn't work at the bakery and see behind the scenes, Parvati must have seemed like the girl who had created this beautiful place where all the cool kids wanted to hang out. And, the flipside of her irresponsible attitude toward business was that she was easy going and generous to a fault. People were always leaving with a little something extra tucked into their waxed bag of baked goods. She called everyone Sugar in her broad midwestern accent. But a sack of broken cookies as a bonus to her pay wasn't enough for Bea so she picked up a job as a bar-back six nights a week at the Tin Lizard, thanks to one of Parvati's regulars. The job was to keep the coolers full and the glasses washed, basically help the bartender do his job. But pretty quickly Bea was pulled into tending bar. Earl, one of the bartenders who had been there the longest, taught her about the rack.

"It's different depending where you serve," he explained in a Texan drawl. "But in this town you want these five: vodka, rum, gin, tequila, bourbon."

Earl taught her how to make a Gimlet, a Manhattan and the perfect Martini. For that, Earl said, "you just wave the vermouth at it."

He was a good teacher and she learned quickly. Best of all were the tips. At the end of the night they would split a fat pile of money as the waitresses also had to give them a portion of their tips. Bea understood why the waitresses resented her. They had to wear outfits and do their hair and make-up. They had to wind their way through crowds carrying a heavy tray. They had to bend down to put the drinks on the table while the men looked down their shirts and the women ignored them. And, they had to give the bartenders a cut of their tips.

Bea wore jeans and a black t-shirt. No make-up required. There was a slab of wood, eighteen inches deep between her and the customer. Customers were seated and she was standing. Everything was different. Especially the money. She could not believe how much money people left for her. All she did was nod and listen, looking directly into their eyes as they talked.

You couldn't say alcohol made people talk. Some people sat all night without ever saying anything, but there were only so many combinations of people and alcohol and it wasn't long before she had a shorthand of what to expect.

By and large, gin drinkers were mean. Vodka were the true alcoholics. Rum meant flirting, cuddles and an eventual swift exodus for the nearest bed or bathroom stall. Tequila had a few different flavors; it drew the dancers, the fighters and the artists. Bourbon was for posers. And beer drinkers were the least interesting to Bea. As a rule of thumb, beer drinkers were stupid and thought they were hilarious.

Earl worked Wednesday, Thursday, Friday. Those were the good nights. He was professional and fair. He never let her carry the cases up from the basement, not because she couldn't do it, but because he said it was important to protect her back. She assumed he meant for when she had babies someday. She didn't tell Earl that she was never having babies because carrying the cases really did make her back ache. Earl also mopped the floor and cleaned the tables while she washed and stacked the glasses which meant they got out sooner.

"You, are a Knight of the Templar," she told him as they parted ways at the corner of a street that was heaving with people in a spectacular range of attire, platform shoes, hats, boas and bare chests. Bea thought she and Earl, in their plain clothes, looked like a pair of orderlies standing by to make sure no one got hurt.

"And you," said Earl, taking her hand and bringing it to his lips for a kiss. "Are my Maid Marion."

She smiled all the way back to the apartment. Still smiling as she brushed her teeth and spit into the sink. Did he really not know the difference between King Arthur and Robin Hood? Or was he giving her the highest compliment in not calling her Guinevere but the independent shepherdess who was on equal footing with her beloved?

Monday, Tuesday and Saturday nights she had to work with Mickey, who spent his days looking for modeling gigs. He was tall and looked like Michael Landon, at least that's what the women would coo to him as they leaned over the bar to get a better look at the top shelf liquors and give Mickey a chance to see their boobs.

Mickey always wanted to have 'one last cigarette' with his scotch to relax before cleaning up which meant he would sit at the bar watching Bea as she made trips down and back to the basement, bringing up cases of beer to fill the coolers. He would talk about the bands he saw the night before, the disco he was headed to once they finished. She never asked him to mop the floors because she only had to do it again.

The good thing about working with Mickey was that he would focus on the women and Bea would focus on the men. And, he could make her laugh. He loved to tell silly jokes and goof around. The tiresome thing about working with Mickey, besides the fact that he was lazy and messy, was that he was always trying to get into her pants.

It seemed inconceivable to him that she wasn't interested. By day she had to deal with Parvati's planet pluto ramblings, three nights a week she had to put up with Mickey's hands on her ass, on her shoulders, in her hair. When she finally lost it, smacked his hand away and told him to *cut the shit* while two waitresses who were standing waiting for their orders to be filled looked on, he got an ugly look on his face.

"What's your problem?" and then a lightbulb went off.

"Oh I get it, I thought Alex was your boyfriend, but I get it, Alex is a girl."

Mornings she would be at the bakery by four a.m. and usually not get out until ten-thirty or eleven. Nights she was at the Tin Lizard from six p.m. to midnight.

That's where the real money was, but she never told Alex. She had made a false pocket in the bottom of her knapsack where she stuffed the wad of dollars at the end of the night until she could get to the bank to deposit them.

Sometimes Alex was home when she got back, sometimes he didn't get in until she was brushing her teeth getting ready to head to the bakery.

After the first year, routine and predictability made things feel less strange. She never felt at home, but she had begun to want to.

. . .

"I heard what you did," said LaDonna.

Bea slowed the motions of hanging her jacket on the hook. Her heart was racing. Why was she always scared of getting in trouble? She couldn't think of anything she'd done wrong. What was LaDonna talking about?

When Bea didn't reply, LaDonna gave her another clue as if this was a game of twenty questions.

"My cousin Teesha is a waitress at the Tin Lizard."

"I know Teesha."

"Um hmm," LaDonna hummed as she ran the rolling pin out and back. "She said some guy told you that you should be wearing a bra and you told him to stop looking at your titties if it bothered him so much."

Bea relaxed. Oh, she wasn't in trouble. LaDonna liked what she'd done.

"I said boobs."

"I would have liked to see that." LaDonna whacked the rolling pin onto the dough. She was smiling. She looked up at Bea.

"You're alright," she said.

"I didn't know Teesha was your cousin." Bea would never have imagined the waitress who wore her hair big, her earrings bigger and her lips red would be related to LaDonna who oiled and scraped her hair back into a tight ponytail and never wore a scrap of make-up.

"She told me to invite you to the bar-b-que we're having tomorrow."

Bea was excited that LaDonna wanted to be friends but wait, *was* that an invitation? She wasn't sure.

"I work tomorrow night," Bea said.

"So come by in the afternoon. It's an all day, all night thing. For me. I finished."

LaDonna worked these crazy hours so she could get a degree as a vet tech.

"You finished. That's great."

"Come by around two. Here," LaDonna scribbled the address onto a piece of paper.

. . .

LaDonna lived with her mom and sisters in a house that was connected to a house where her grandmother lived. The bar-b-q was in their shared yard and when Bea arrived people were sitting in lawn chairs watching a couple of guys grilling meat. She didn't see LaDonna or Teesha right away. Her face flushed with embarrassment at the awkwardness. The pan of peach cobbler she'd made felt like lead weight in her hands.

"Hey girl," Teesha called, the heels of her strappy sandals clicking as she walked across the patio. "Get in here."

Teesha showed her where to put the cobbler, got her a drink and a chair. It took Bea some time to realize no one was going to make her talk. Nobody asked her where she was from, what she did for work or where she lived. It wasn't that they were rude, she got compliments on the cobbler and LaDonna came by and said she was glad Bea came. It was just easy. LaDonna's grandmother and her friends played cards under a beach umbrella. Kids were hula hooping. Music played. A woman with muddy sneakers pulled a chair over and sat next to Bea. She wore a tee shirt with the sleeves cut off and held a chihuahua in one arm.

"You like dogs?"

"Sure," said Bea.

The woman put the chihuahua into Bea's lap and the dog promptly peed on Bea's leg. That's how she met Randi.

Randi had an animal shelter outside the city. Mostly dogs, she told Bea, but some cats and every once in a while a rabbit or a guinea pig.

"You should come by," she said. "I can always use help."

It was strange to go into the bakery and have LaDonna not be there. It had taken all year for them to finally connect and now she was gone. Bea had thought they were going to be friends but after the bar-b-que she never saw her again.

Sunday mornings she would drive to Randi's shelter and spend hours there. Sometimes she helped with cleaning cages but mostly she cuddled the kitties and took the dogs out for walks. Around noon she would leave and it always hurt. She hated putting them back into cages. She wished she could take them all home with her. What helped was when she would arrive on a Sunday morning and see the adoptions that had happened over the week. Of course, the ones that never got adopted were the ones she gave the most attention to. She understood them the best.

Once in a while, she would drive to Glen Canyon. There was a loop she liked to walk that had a secret dugout by a creek where she would settle in with a bag of pretzels, a can of ginger ale and her sketchbook.

Carrot Girl was how she worked out all the people stuff she didn't understand. When her wrist got tired. She would put the pen away and lie back. Sometimes she would think about Ricky Stewart. She would imagine him walking into the Tin Lizard or maybe the bakery. He would tell her that he came back from Canada to find she was gone and how he'd been looking for her ever since. They would get married on a hill above the sea and live in a house with a back stairway filled with family photographs on the walls. There would be a garden with vegetables and flowers and they would name their dogs Stella, Georgia and Rosemary. She didn't know why their dogs were always female, but they always were.

Alex was usually around when she got home on Sunday afternoon and they'd get pizza, or egg rolls and lo mein, and climb onto the couch to watch *The Six Million Dollar Man* or the ABC movie or *Columbo*, whatever Alex wanted. Bea didn't care. What she liked was how Alex would stretch out and put his head in her lap or, sometimes, how they would both stretch out and she would fall asleep like that, the TV droning on, his arms wrapped around her.

One day, making a deposit at the bank, she was shocked to see how the money had piled up. She didn't know anything about having money like this. She began paying attention to the guys talking at the bar. Real Estate. It made sense. It had more appeal for her than bonds or stocks or things that felt like throwing her money into outer space.

Buying an apartment seemed like the most daring thing she had ever thought about. For weeks she turned the idea over and over, worried that she was making a terrible mistake. Her mother had never bought anything, not a home, not a car. She always rented or lived with a man. Somehow thinking about this spurred Bea forward. Buying a place of her own seemed like something Janet would never do.

When it was all said and done, though, there was nothing particularly hard or scary about the process. Randi gave her the name of a realtor who quickly understood what Bea was looking for. It was sort of like going into a second-hand store where the chair is marked thirty dollars and you offer twenty-two. The sale went through easily.

As she showered and got dressed for work, the keys for her 900 square foot apartment on top of the bureau, Bea stopped to look at herself in the mirror. Why did she think she couldn't do this?

She had seen four places before she found the apartment that, luckily enough, was only a few blocks from the bakery. She knew it immediately because of the light, because it had a big old porcelain sink like the one in Nana's kitchen, and because it was on the top floor; she would not have to listen to anyone above her.

It was her very own private hideaway.

The apartment became her obsession. She began spending afternoons scouring for furniture and fixtures, sanding the walls and painting with a stereo playing Linda Ronstadt's *Retrospective* album on repeat. She would sing along as she knew every word by heart. She didn't tell Alex she had bought the apartment. She simply told him she was moving out.

"You're leaving?" He was in the middle of eating a peanut butter sandwich. "How'm I gonna pay for this place on my own?"

You'll find another girl, is what Bea thought.

"You'll figure it out," is what she said.

"Where are you going?"

"I'm moving to L.A." She didn't want him showing up on her doorstep like a sad-eyed puppy because she knew she would take him in. She could leave him like this because it was Sunday morning, the sun was coming in the window making everything look bright and, because she had stocked the kitchen with bread, peanut butter, bananas and beer. She knew he wouldn't really start to worry for a couple of days and by then she would be waking up in her pretty bedroom with the yellow bedspread and the Georgia O'Keeffe print on the wall.

But her new life didn't last long. Nine weeks after she had settled into her hideaway apartment, she got a postcard. The Tamamoto family had moved to Elmwood. Professor Tamamoto was now teaching at Berkeley. She was beyond happy to see them again, but when he learned what had happened with the job he had lined up for her, and that she was working as a bartender, Professor Tamamoto got angry. He tried to talk Bea into applying to another company, but she buried her face into Meri's neck who was sitting on her lap as if she were still five years old and shook her head no.

"The same thing will happen," Bea told him. "You know it's true."

Not long after that, Professor Tamamoto called Bea to say, "I have given your name to someone. Couple of guys have started a small enterprise, if they call, please consider it."

Small enterprise. Bea had to smile at Professor Tamomoto's choice of words.

The company was in Cupertino, housed in a building that looked like a Quonset hut someone had ordered from the Sears catalogue. Everywhere was just a scramble of stuff. Guys walking around as if it were a Saturday and they were building something for a soapbox derby. Not a suit jacket or a necktie in sight, but she didn't mind.

Professor Tamamoto was right. This was a good place for her. The company, anyway. Outside flattened her spirits. It seemed like there might have been some farms here once, but now it was a bit desolate. The building sat on the side of a moderately busy road with a gas station on one side and a Bob's, Home of the Big Boy Hamburger restaurant on the other.

Maybe she took the job because Cupertino didn't have the dark sorrow energy coming up from the ground. Maybe she wanted to please Professor Tamamoto and not disappoint him by being a bartender. Maybe it was because the guy who hired her said that he liked weird people.

"You're quirky and eccentric," he said, as she sat there thinking he must be mistaken. Wasn't Parvati what quirky and eccentric looked like?

"That's what we are looking for. I want people that have sharp creative minds. Independent thinkers who challenge the status quo."

Janet would have rolled her eyes at his wish list and Bea would have agreed since all she ever did was work on testing and verification, hardly setting the world on fire, but it used her mind in a whole different way from the bar and the bakery. And, she liked that she got the job because nobody seemed to care particularly that she was female.

That first impression, that it was just a bunch of guys goofing around, was way off the mark. The pace was grueling in a way working two jobs had never been. Sometimes Bea fell into bed having only eaten moments before, often wearing the same clothes she would head back to the office in, the next morning.

Saturdays she got up a bit later, time to indulge in a coffee that she didn't make herself, but still heading into the office that looked just the same as it did on a Tuesday or Wednesday, heads bent over glorified typewriters, the smell of unwashed hair and bodies part of the stale odor that carpeted the space. Maybe this is what they meant by purgatory, a gray place you go and stay until you aren't there anymore.

She had rented a room with kitchen privileges in a woman's house near DeAnza College and rented out her apartment in San Francisco to Parvati's cousin Jilly who had moved in from Chicago and needed a place to stay for a little while. That felt like a good solution because she didn't think this job would last long. Everything about it felt so temporary but she ended up living at Mrs. Cooper's place for nearly eight years.

Again, her bank account swelled. The money she got renting out her apartment covered both her mortgage and what Mrs. Cooper charged her. There wasn't anything to spend money on except her annual trips back east at Christmas time when she'd be asked over and over, *how can you live like that? That's no life. Get out of that dead end job. Why don't you move to Montreal?* Or later, when Mona relocated to New York City, *come to New York* was on repeat. They never came to visit her. Janet probably couldn't afford it or maybe she was afraid of returning to California. She never went backwards. Her movement was always on to the next thing. Mona would have seen it as a waste of time, which was how she referred to any activity away from the quest to reach the heights of Coco Chanel or Sister Parish or whoever was her current role model.

Sometimes their lack of interest in her life felt hurtful, but then she thought about it and realized, she wasn't particularly interested in their lives either.

Part of what she liked about the job in Cupertino were the people. They wore flannel shirts in June and never seemed to think it strange that she would have found objects—stones, bones, feathers and branches on the shelves above her desk.

A few of them were readers, mostly science fiction buffs, but they all bonded over Vonnegut. At the end of the day, on days when no big bosses were around to ask why things weren't done already, Bea would walk down to the far end of the cubicle row where there was a small empty area that became their defacto lounge. She never went all the way in because she didn't want to get trapped in there in case the conversation veered off into *Lord of the Rings*. She would sit on the edge of one table and listen as they talked about what they were reading. When she said she didn't know who Tom Robbins was, a copy of *Still Life With Woodpecker* was tossed at her which she devoured in a matter of days.

It was as if the drab cubicle world wasn't the real world and this little band she was part of understood that. The empty cubicle lounge slowly accumulated plastic action figures, dice and a shelf with cast-off books and magazines for everyone to share. It became one of her favorite places to be. Without anyone calling a meeting or sending out a memo, they all found themselves there regularly. Each of them had the place they always sat. Without even trying, she found she was part of a club. What would Lulu have thought about that, she wondered.

She still went up to the animal shelter every Sunday. The drive wasn't terrible. Early Sunday morning it usually didn't even take a full hour to get there. And when she did get stuck in traffic, she liked being able to look out the window and let her mind fly. She missed her pretty, hideaway apartment but she felt free in a way she had never experienced before. Plus, there was Joe, her boss.

It was funny to think of him as her boss because he wasn't at all bossy. Even when software wasn't working, deadlines were missed and people were charging up and down between the cubicles blowing up like the world was ending, Joe would just laugh. He took nothing seriously and everybody respected him. Even the very top guy whose company it was deferred to Joe. The most common phrase when people were uncertain about the best path forward was, *let's go ask Joe.*

He was gentle, kind and ridiculously smart. Crazy smart. She decided this must be what men who grow up in California are like.

For some reason, Joe took Bea under his wing. He looped her in when her oblivion to background politics might have taken her down, gave her a raise when she didn't ask for it, put her in charge of teams that were all men, taught her how to conduct meetings and how to get people who were arguing to find consensus. It felt to her that Joe was a kind of spiritual mentor, but she would never have said that to him. He was way too much of an engineer for any of that Parvati talk, but she knew how lucky she was. She knew he was the best life teacher she ever had.

There was nothing romantic about her admiration for Joe. It was more like how she felt about Gregory Peck in *To Kill a Mockingbird*. He was that kind of guy. Older than most of the guys she worked with, but not old enough to be her father. Joe and his wife, who he clearly adored because he mentioned her often, had twin girls, but Bea never met his wife because she never came to any of the company picnics, Christmas parties or project launch celebrations. Bea heard a secretary say Joe's wife never came because she was sick and then watched the secretary point to her head and spiral one finger.

Oh, thought Bea. *She's probably like me.*

One afternoon things had run late and they were sitting in his office waiting for some trials to finish. She learned his real name wasn't Joseph, but Josiah.

"Oh," Bea said.

"A-yup," he stretched back in his chair. "Born and raised in Vermont."

She was so surprised. She told him that she had gone to school there.

"A Midd kid," he laughed. "That I didn't see coming."

There were surprises everywhere in that unconventional little enterprise.

One day in early December, Joe brought her into his office and closed the door. He never closed the door when it was just the two of them.

"There's going to be a big payout," he told her. The company had been sold and because she was vested, she was going to receive a lot of money.

"Do not tell anyone you have this money," he counseled her. "People behave very differently when they know you have a lot of money."

Later, there was a meeting with about ten of them in the conference room. Bea knew there were going to be several groups of ten shuffled through here because there had to be at least thirty or forty on the payout list and the conference room only sat twelve.

Joe was in her group. At one end of the room were three men wearing suits, ties and dress shoes. They came around the table and shook everyone's hand. They stood at the front of the room and explained that they were financial advisors.

"Financial planners," said the one who had to stand the whole time or prop himself on the edge of the table as there wasn't a chair for him. "We want to help you plan for your future."

Really, thought Bea. *You weren't able to plan that you would need a chair today.*

The men pointed to charts and dropped a glossy binder down in front of each of them that had photos of smiling young families on green lawns, guys laughing on the golf course, an older couple on a sailboat and more charts and graphs.

When they finished, they stood by the table at the front and people formed a line to sign up with them to help them manage their money prudently and wisely.

Bea left the binder on the table and walked back to her office.

A while later the three men were in her space.

"We noticed you left a little early," said the one who had done the most talking. "Were there any questions we can answer for you?"

The planner without a chair had dropped a bit of cream cheese onto the lapel of his jacket and done a bad job cleaning it off. He made a move to put the binder she had left behind onto her desk.

"No," she said. He stopped and looked surprised.

"Here?" he gestured to leave it on the shelf where she had a bird's nest, rocks and dried flowers she'd brought in over the years from the lot.

"No."

She shooed them out into the corridor and shut the door. The smell of their cologne and aftershave lingered.

The next morning Joe tapped on her door.

"You will need to deal with this," he said. "It can get complicated. If you don't want these guys, you need to find someone who can give you advice and take care of the legal side of things."

"Okay. Thank you."

She looked back at the work on her desk.

"Beatrice," Joe said. "Just curious. This is a great firm. Very well respected. Everyone in the company uses them, including me. What didn't you like about them?"

Bea thought for a moment and then smiled at Joe.

"Everything."

He laughed and rapped his knuckles on her door, before walking down the corridor.

That Christmas she packed two boxes of Sees chocolates and a first edition of *House of Mirth*, Janet's favorite book. She bought a second suitcase simply to hold the antique Chinese wedding basket she had found for Mona. The basket felt precious because it was made of thin strips of wood painstakingly pressed tightly together with a single, perfectly shaped piece of wood looped at the top for a handle. The lid came off so you could look inside and see the precision of the work even more clearly. It was the color that had caught Bea's eye. The red lacquer paint must have been glossy once upon a time, but now it had grown dull with age and softened into a rich shade of maple. She made sure the slip with its provenance was taped to the bottom, otherwise, she knew, Mona wouldn't know its value.

On the flight, she began to worry that she had made a big mistake. Mona hated old things. She should have bought her some perfume or a scarf, but she didn't know what kind she would like and Mona's opinions were so exacting it paralyzed Bea. She had seen the wedding basket in the window of the shop. It was so pretty and, she thought, rather romantic.

Turns, out, she had wasted her time worrying.

When she got off the plane, Janet was there to meet her with a man she introduced as Marcus, her fiance.

"Just Marc," he smiled and shook her hand before picking up Bea's bag and walking ahead of the mother and daughter.

Mona was spending Christmas in London. Antoine had moved to Vancouver. Janet was leaving Montreal to live with Marcus in Rhode Island.

Bea had been prepared for the shock of snow and cold. She was not, she realized with a sort of embarrassment that she had never comprehended this before, ever prepared for Janet. Was that even possible?

They spent the week in Old Port. Marc had booked rooms at Le Saint Sulpice.

Most of the time it was the three of them walking around the city, browsing bookstores, wandering into galleries, getting wonderful meals in cafes and restaurants. She didn't have any time alone with her mother until the morning Marcus announced he was going off to do some cross-country skiing and would be back for dinner. Bea could not remember the last time they had been together like that, just the two of them.

Janet seemed to be circling Bea. As if there was something she wanted to say but wasn't sure how she was going to tell her. This made Bea nervous and so the entire day was spent in awkwardness until they landed in a coffee shop late in the afternoon. Snow was swirling outside the window and the street lights were on. Janet cupped her cappuccino in two hands and licked at the foam like a cat.

"Mom. Stop. That's gross."

Janet exaggerated the movement. She lifted a huge curl of foam with her tongue.

Bea couldn't help it. She started to laugh.

"You are so gross."

Ow. *Putain*. Janet said suddenly. The cup landed onto the dish with a crash.

"I just burnt my tongue."

Then they were both howling with laughter.

When the waitress brought the check, Bea grabbed it.

"I've got this," she said.

"Beatrice," her mother had grown serious. *Here it comes*, thought Bea. *That thing she wants to tell me*. She felt herself bracing. Her neck growing tight. She crossed her arms over her chest.

"I'm in love." It was almost a whisper. Her mother's cheeks were pink. She looked scared and excited.

Bea waited for the other shoe to drop, but that was it. That was what she had been trying all day to tell her. She gazed expectantly at Bea.

Bea put down the money for the coffees, making sure to leave a thirty percent tip. Slowly she put each arm into her coat and buttoned it from the bottom to the top. She picked up her shoulder bag and looked over at her mother who was sitting with her hands in her lap like a little girl.

"Congratulations," she said and walked out the door without looking back.

Christmas day they sat in the hotel lobby in front of the fireplace while staff brought them coffee, fresh squeezed orange juice and croissants. Bea gave the chocolates to Marcus and presented the red wooden pail to them both.

"A wedding basket," her mother said, amazed. She held it up for her fiance to see, turning it so that he could see it from all sides. "How did you know?"

"I'm psychic," said Bea as she sank back into the soft pillows of the hotel sofa to stare at the mantel that was strewn with garlands of artificial balsam and fairy lights.

"Isn't this magical?" crooned Janet. She wore a white turtleneck, white trousers and shiny gold boots. Her only jewelry was the ruby ring on her wedding finger. Marcus tried to make conversation with Bea but Janet shook her head at him and squeezed his arm.

"She's not a talker," she explained.

wherein Bea learns about the third chakra

On the flight back to California, after Christmas in Montreal with Janet and Marcus, Bea stared out the window. *Good thing she hadn't moved to Montreal*, but the thought brought no comfort. The strange ache that Janet always stirred in her got stronger. Under the cover of a blanket so no one could see, she fished the beads from her pocket and began repeating the words until she fell asleep.

When the plane touched down in San Francisco, she had finished an orange juice and two coffees and knew exactly what she would do about the money question.

Earl. She would find Earl. He was the most fair, hard-working person she had ever met. Joe was great, but his judgement was clouded by having a family dependent on him and spending so much time with corporate types. Of course, she could just open a phone book and look under financial services, but she was certain Earl would be able to help her do better than that. He would have some good ideas about how to invest the money from the company sale.

The airport was crowded and stressed in that way particular to the holiday season. As she headed for baggage claim, passing one of the sports bars that had three televisions running, a hand reached out and grabbed her shoulder. She jumped back. It was more than the normal bumping into strangers that happened as you pushed your way through the terminal.

She looked at the man who had grabbed her. It was Bo Stewart. In a navy three-piece suit. *He's all grown up,* she realized with a shock. Somehow, she had never thought about that, but here he was telling her to come in so he could buy her a drink.

He had been sitting at the bar, but they found a table by the window where she could see the runway path with white lights and carts shuttling luggage. It was too cold by the window to take off her coat, but Bo had been there awhile and a few drinks had warmed him up. He hung his blazer off the back of the chair so that he was just in his shirt and vest, the tie neat.

An investment banker like his dad, Bo was married with two children. They lived in Needham. "Can't quite afford Swellsville, yet," he joked. "But soon."

He'd only been in town a few days and was headed home on the red-eye. Just landed something big. He seemed annoyed that Bea didn't ask anything about the big deal.

"How's your mom?" Bea asked.

"You mean after Jenna?" said Bo.

Bea looked at him blankly.

"Oh you didn't know? That's right, your mom ditched town before then."

Bea didn't give him the satisfaction of seeing how much his dig cut. She waited.

"Jenna died. Yeah. When I was in college. My sophomore year. So—1973. Yeah."

"Ten years ago."

Bo smirked. "You always were good at math."

Bea felt like she had been cornered by a rattlesnake. An angry rattlesnake in a Brooks Brothers suit with an expensive red tie. She knew better than to move or speak.

"Fucking horses, right? God. Don't you just love how fucking insane it all is?"

Bea watched this man in his very expensive suit and very expensive haircut and very expensive shoes speak gutter language. Mrs. Stewart hated vulgarity. But Bea understood. Whoever can use the more foul, more vulgar, most violent expression wields the power in this world. She realized he hadn't spoken in a while.

"A riding accident?" she offered.

"No. No. You'd think that, right? With all her jumping and ribbons and steeplechasing, but no. Happened in a stall. Nobody knows for sure but she must've been behind it, when the horse got spooked. Nobody knows. One of the staff found her. Head stove in. Had to be a closed casket."

Bea imagined Jenna as a newborn baby, like Mona. That sweet bald head so heavy. How you have to hold it under the neck. So little. So fragile. Mrs. Stewart. Mr. Stewart. How do you live after you've seen your baby with her head bashed in?

Bo shook his glass of ice cubes at the waitress. The waitress put down a fresh drink and took the finished one away. She gave Bea's ginger ale a cursory glance; she knew who her customer was.

Bea remembered the last time she saw Jenna and Mrs. Stewart. In the grocery store parking lot when she was living with the Tamamotos. The summer she did the internship. She let them drive away without going over and saying hello.

"It feels good to sit with you," said Bo. "I mean, you never know. People change but you just have a nice way of sitting with someone."

Bea got that unsettled feeling. Was he going to hit on her?

"So, your mom—" she said.

"Oh yeah. Well, that was the final blow, ha. They split up."

"No," the word gushed from Bea's chest. Her mind was spinning. It was too much to process. She put her hands to her eyes.

"Yeah. Funny isn't it? I was always complaining about being the forgotten middle kid and here I am orphan of a broken marriage. Crazy, right?"

"Orphan?" Bea looked at him in confusion. "They're dead?"

"No—not orphan—don't get all fucking word shit on me—I meant only child. That's what I meant. From ignored middle to only child."

He was definitely trying to get Bea to feel sorry for him. It was making her stomach heavy and icky. She wanted to leave, but she had to know.

"Ricky is, dead?"

"Might as well be," said Bo. "He showed up at the funeral. Hit my father up for a couple hundred bucks cash—can you fucking believe that fucking asshole. Course he was stoned out of his gourd the whole time. My poor mother—" Bo choked back a wave of tears but got more angry instead. "That fucking bastard. Always about him, right?"

"How did he get out of Canada without getting caught?"

"Oh whoever knows with that dickwad. He finds his way. He always finds his way. Last I heard he was in some shit backwater town in Vermont working as a landscaper. Ha. Fancy word for growing weed. Mom went back to Maine. My grandparents' place. She really is a landscaper, grows varieties of rugosa and blueberries. Weezie and I take the kids up to see her in the summer. She won't come back down."

Weezie, his wife Louisa Webster. Bea remembered the small blonde girl with strong legs; she was a good tennis player.

"How about your dad?" asked Bea.

"Oh, he's fine." Bo dragged out the word fine like someone from the South.

"Remarried. She's your age, just about. They have a couple of kids, same ages as mine. How's that for a head trip? And, get this, they live at the old homestead. Disgusting. My mom bought that house."

Bo leaned back in his chair. "He's probably teaching them to play tennis."

She wanted to ask him so many more questions, but could feel things were not headed in a good direction. She needed to get away from him. She stood up.

"Where're you going?" Bo growled. "Siddown. My flight's not for another hour."

"I've got to go," said Bea. "I'm sorry. Good to see you."

Only one of those was true.

"Good to see you? What the fuck. Oh, fuck you. You always thought you were so much better than us. Sitting there watching from above Miss High and Mighty, so perfect, huh. No drugs. No boyfriends because you were pining after the one all the girls wanted. You were no different than any of them, you know. You know that, right? You are just the same as the rest of those stupid bitches coming around the house in heat for him. Stinky hippie bitches."

Bea was frozen.

Bo shifted his tone. Tried to be charming. Gestured to her chair with his glass. "Siddown. Just stay for one more drink. Be a sport."

She was not going to sit but she wanted to say something.

"Bo—I,"

He waved her off. "See ya!" His effort at coaxing gone in a flash.

He got up, gathered his coat off the chair and finished his drink in one go. Bea stepped back to give him room. There was something in his body that felt dangerous to her.

"I'm gonna go sit at the bar with some real people," he said.

He walked off without looking back, bumping into a couple of empty chairs on his way.

The cab dropped her at a hotel that wasn't too far a walk from the Tin Lizard. She wanted a place to stow her bags, but also to have a day or two if making investments was going to take time.

She took a long shower to shake off what had just happened at the airport. Seeing Bo Stewart had been a shock. Physically. Emotionally. She forced herself to not think about that now. She still hadn't worked through Christmas with Janet and wanted to call Mona to see how she was dealing with the news of Marcus. Had Mona known what happened to Jenna Stewart? Bea wanted badly to talk to her sister about these things that nobody else in the world would understand, but when she sat and imagined getting Mona on the phone, she knew it would probably make everything worse. Mona was on holiday. Don't spoil that. *Later, not now*, she repeated to herself.

The next morning she could hardly get out of bed. It was late afternoon before she finally got outside to discover that San Francisco felt the same as ever, but the Tin Lizard was no more. It was now called Enoteca. The bar had always been more upscale than its neighbors, but now it had been remodeled to look like a place you'd see in Europe. Bea walked through the room of empty chairs to the bar that was being wiped down and stocked up.

"We don't open until five-thirty," said the woman as she scooped olives out of a jar and spooned them into the garnish tray. It was Teesha.

"Hey Teesha," said Bea.

"Oh my god. Wow. I didn't recognize you. Hi. How's it going?"

Behind her was a guy, also in black pants and a white shirt, loading beers into the coolers.

"You're bartending now," said Bea.

"Yeah, so much better. How about you? You work around here?"

"Cupertino."

Teesha's face seemed a bit surprised, definitely unimpressed, but then she covered it quickly as she rubbed a white towel over the bar.

"Really? You get good tips there?"

"Sometimes," Bea said. "Listen, I was hoping to catch up with Earl. Do you know how I might find him?"

Teesha straightened up and rested her hands on the cloth.

"He's gone."

Bea waited for her to explain what she meant.

"He got really sick and went back to where he was from. Texas, I think."

"Well, do you know what town, or what his last name was—did he leave—"

"I think he died. He had that thing. You know."

Bea shook her head. She was trying to stop the buzzing in her ears. Earl, sick? He never got sick. He was so strong and vibrant. What thing was Teesha talking about?

"Gay cancer," the guy behind her said. "You can at least fucking say it."

Teesha shook him off. "Did anyone invite you into this conversation? Don't tell me what I can say. I will say whatever the hell I want." She turned back to Bea.

"I don't know anything more, but his boyfriend still tends bar down at the Met. His name is Bruce and he would know more. I'm sorry. You guys were friends?"

On the drive down to Cupertino, she remembered Earl coming up behind her and whispering in her ear.

"No bill for the guy at the end. On the house."

A vet, Earl explained later. Bea had noticed he stood apart from the rest with his collared shirts and wounded eyes, but she hadn't made the connection. When they were closing up, she looked up from where she was bent over the little metal sink, scrubbing rocks glasses two at a time to watch Earl waltzing the mop across the floor.

"Did you go?" she asked him. He was the right age.

Earl shook his head. Both his brothers did. Both were killed.

All gone. That's the thought that kept tumbling over and over in Bea's mind as she drove. Earl's mother. Three babies. All gone. And then she had the most tremendous sense of relief wash over her. And then, guilt. She pulled the car to a stop in Mrs. Cooper's drive and willed herself not to think such a selfish thing, but there was nothing to be done. It had come in and she could not turn it away. Ricky Stewart was safe. He had dodged and gone to Canada. He was alive. And that's when she began to cry. Her forehead pressing into the hard plastic of the steering wheel. Not in grief for one of the most beautiful men she had ever met who had been so good to her, who treated everyone with such kindness. Not in sorrow for his mother whom she'd never met but imagined was prostrate in some cornfield somewhere, her chest blown right through, a charred, burnt hole with smoke trailing out of it as if she had been felled by a meteorite. No, the watershed was relief that somewhere safe and good, Ricky Stewart was still waking up, still part of this cloven world.

· · ·

When she returned to work, she realized the pattern. Every year, January would roll around and she would think this would be it, time to move on and get a real life, find out where she belonged, but then the project she was on had another few months to go and while she was working to wrap that one up, a new one would begin that lasted at least fourteen months and on and on. There was always just one more thing to finish.

Days got longer with less time to hang out. There seemed to be more pressure to get things done faster. More people got hired and the empty cubicle area had long since been converted into six new workspaces. The little book club was no more.

Outside, strip malls seemed to be multiplying like a chemistry experiment gone wrong. What kept her connected and breathing was the lot behind the old bus station. It wasn't big, maybe twice the size of Parvati's bakery. There were no trees, but in March the little white flowers called milkmaids would blossom. Then there would come shooting stars. A fiery name for such a delicate bloom, but the name made sense. The dark base like an engine that has rocketed the flower out of the earth into the sky with bright yellow flames banded by the thinnest orb of white that extended into those graceful petals of violet, exquisite. She didn't know what the small clump of red flowers were that cropped up in one far corner, but it made her think of a cross between echinacea and butterfly bush. The butterflies did seem to love it. And then came the poppies. When the poppies began to bloom, usually the beginning of May, she tried to get out there at least once in the middle of the day and she would always go there before heading home to sit, watching until it got dark. It must have been the birds that seeded this place, she decided. And the lack of trees made for quite the meadow.

After that last Christmas in Montreal, three things happened in one week.

First, was Henry.

Henry came into the shelter on Easter Sunday. The family had decided their little girl would rather have a bunny. Bea spent every spare moment trying to think how she could bring him home. She had told Randi he was hers. She would be back for him, but how.

On Tuesday, a reminder of her ten year college reunion arrived in the mail.

Thursday, she grabbed her sandwich and ginger ale out of the fridge in the break room and headed to the lot to have her lunch. She'd been thinking maybe what she needed to do was buy a house close to work so she could visit Henry every few hours during the day when she turned the corner and saw what had happened.

The soda dropped to the ground. And then the sandwich.

Someone had mowed the lot. Savaged it. Every growing thing had been ripped out and a sign hammered into the ground that announced the name of the fast food restaurant that would be built there that summer.

She turned her back on the scene and crouched down, crying as she brought to mind each of the beautiful plants that had lived there. All the bugs, animals, birds and insects that had loved it as she had. Where would they live now? Their home was gone.

She cried until she couldn't cry anymore. She walked back to the office building, down the corridor to her office, stood at her desk as she typed out four sentences, clicked print, went down the hall to the printer, pulled the sheet of paper off, signed it and knocked on Joe's open door.

She handed him her two weeks notice.

It took him a few minutes to even know what to say. He was not laughing. He'd never looked so serious.

"Why?" he seemed almost hurt. Shocked, but even more so, confused.

"It's just time for me to go," was all she said.

"Do you have another job?"

"I don't want another job."

During those last weeks, she sold her apartment in San Francisco which, that guy at the bar was right, was ten times better than a savings account. She bought a brand-new Toyota pick-up truck with a matching cab. And best of all, when she left the shelter, Henry was with her.

. . .

That drive across country with Henry was, without a doubt, the best time of her life. She had never spent 24/7 with a dog before and the companionship and understanding was better than anything she had ever known. Thanks to Henry, they stopped often. She would choose places she thought he might like, pretty campgrounds, lakes, places they could go for a hike. It was a completely different way of driving than how she and Alex had done it ten years earlier.

They slept together in the cab on a mattress she had set up there, her few boxes of things set neatly to the side. Brushing him, keeping him clean, watching him run, how tentative he was around water, how grateful he seemed to be. He would put his head on her belly. He would lick her wrist. And she would stroke his ears and say, *no, no. I am the lucky one.*

They got to Burlington a few days before the reunion, time enough for Bea to get a haircut, find a dress and some shoes to go with it. She deliberately didn't stay in Middlebury in case she ran into someone she knew. In the end, she didn't attend the reunion. She almost did, but then sat on the edge of the bed, lipstick feeling ugly on her lips, the new shoes already uncomfortable and the dress, well, she never felt good when she was supposed to be dressed up. She imagined walking up to the groups of people gathered about. She tried to think of someone she would be happy to see, someone who had lived on her floor, one of her professors. But all she could imagine was walking around with a smile pasted on her face feeling lost and alone. She imagined running into Sally who she learned from the alumni newsletter was married with two children and living in Marblehead. And she imagined the pain of being different, of being judged for wanting something they didn't understand, of not wanting what they wanted.

She took off the shoes and the dress. Put her shorts and t-shirt back on. Then she and Henry went for a long walk along Lake Champlain. The next day, she went into Ellen Grady Realty and said, "I'm looking to buy a house."

• • •

It was Ellen who sorted her financial situation.

"You just need a good accountant," Ellen had said as she cracked a pistachio on her back teeth, tossed the shells into the bowl and ate the nut.

She arched her eyebrows at Bea. "It's not rocket science."

With Ellen's help, Bea found a small firm in Burlington who kept it simple. Once they had gotten Bea's accounts sorted they knew exactly how to set up the anonymous donation she wanted sent to Randi along with a fund named the EARL foundation, that would kick off an annual sum to pay volunteers at the shelter.

"That's a lot of money," her accountant said. "Do you want to designate it so that it is a college fund for high schoolers helping out?"

Hell no, thought Bea. *They get to do what they want with the money.*

But she just smiled and said, "no, thanks."

For months after she bought the sugarbush, Bea would swing through Ellen's office and leave gifts on her desk, a bottle of Jim

Beam, a pecan pie in November, a small, foil-wrapped poinsettia with blossoms the color of cantaloupe in December.

It took five months, three weeks and a day before the construction was far enough along for her and Henry to move in. In the early weeks, when the foundation was getting poured and the septic system put in, Bea and Henry camped up by the job site. By the end of September the nights were just too cold. Ellen found them an apartment she could rent on a monthly basis which is where they lived until March.

Nearly a year to the day that she had come upon the desecrated lot, Bea stood on the porch of her little house, a cup of fresh coffee in her hand, and gazed out at acres of muddy grass peppered with patches of snow. She looked down at Henry who was always by her side.

"What do you think, big guy? We did good, huh."

People couldn't see her place from the road, so Bea assumed no one in town, aside from Ellen, had any idea what she had actually built. However, it didn't take her long to understand how things worked in a small town. Every carpenter, electrician, mason, plumber and painter who had been on the job were like field reporters keeping everyone informed right down to how much she had spent to put in a mudroom with an enclosed tub to bathe her dog.

Though she didn't appreciate the lack of privacy, she supposed there were trade-offs anywhere you lived and there was one aspect of life that very much agreed with her: the perfectly acceptable one-syllable reply.

"You the lady who bought the old sugarbush off of Gage Hill Road?"

"Yep."

"Some of the best syrup I ever tasted came off that hill. When I was a kid, we'd go sledding up there. You gonna be sugaring?"

"Nope."

When the house was done, it was nothing like those columned brick Georgian affairs in Wellesley or the sprawling shingled cottages of Nantucket that could sleep fourteen people with everyone in their own bed. It looked exactly like the home she had always dreamed of. Simple, low to the ground, with a feeling of spaciousness inside thanks to the twelve-foot ceilings. The house faced south with a kitchen on the east side, two bedrooms on the west and a studio on the north.

Bea had done drawings of what she wanted and the builders had delivered in spades. They didn't mind using the reclaimed wood and architectural elements that she and Henry would dig out of old salvage yards. Her years of learning with Joe how to work with guys made it easy to create good teamwork.

She wrote the checks. She was the boss.

If a guy gave her attitude or showed up late, she cut him loose. When things got done the way she asked, everyone drove off with six packs of beer and a fat envelope of bonus cash. Word got around that good money was to be made and she soon had a team that pushed hard to make sure they were working inside before the heavy snows came.

As she shaped and created her small house, she imagined Setsuko coming for a visit. Should she try and locate her childhood friend? Who knows if they would even still like each other after all these years? But it didn't matter. As she made decisions and found pieces, she always brought Setsuko and Mrs. Tamamoto to mind. She liked imagining them walking in the front door and feeling at home.

Trolling through the public library in Burlington, Bea found a book on Swedish country living that inspired her to paint all the floors white and the mullions of the kitchen windows a pale, cornflower blue. It also gave her the idea to paint the bathroom floor a deep red and stencil it with thin outlines of overlapping, oversized white blossoms.

Winter was Ellen's slow season, so she would often ride shotgun in Bea's pickup with Henry snuggled between them. Ellen knew every back road between Bristol and Peacham and introduced Bea to the best places to score secondhand furniture, rugs, lamps, vintage knobs and drawer pulls, garden tools and textiles.

Ellen was not impressed with the green bureau that Bea found in the back of a garage in Waitsfield.

"Overpriced," Ellen mouthed to her and shook her head, no.

Bea didn't care. Even if she hadn't already saved loads of money in so many places she still would have paid whatever they were asking for this bureau. It was the exact same weathered green that had been on the big wooden door into the Stewart's backyard. She had to have it.

As she watched the bureau get loaded into the back of the truck, she had the thought, *maybe this is a sign. Maybe Ricky will find me, soon.* The whole drive back she was lost in the most wonderful reverie, imagining him seeing the sugarbush for the first time, meeting Henry, he would have a dog, too. Her name would be Scout and she and Henry would be best friends. Bea and Ricky would sit on the porch drinking coffee in the morning watching the rays of sun illuminate the mist. He would tell her about how after Canada he had gone to India to learn Sanskrit the way he always wanted to and then how he ended up in Kenya helping fight elephant poachers. She would tell him about her time in California.

"Such a wasteland," she would say, shaking her head in embarrassment that she had spent so many years there, especially in comparison to all the exotic travel and important work he had done. He would smile in that way he always did, not letting her talk down about herself.

They would make plans for the gardens.

"If I didn't know better, I'd think there was a genie in that bureau," said Ellen as she climbed out of the cab when Bea pulled up in front of her house.

"You look like you just won the lottery."

Bea smiled and nodded.

"Yep," she said.

❖ ❖ ❖

Bea gazes across the room at Mona's face. Mona always had a round face, a sweet round face, but that's probably what caused her to be so relentless in her dieting. Her face is still round despite everything, or maybe the drugs keep it puffed, Bea doesn't know. Only the lamp in the corner is on as Bryan is trying to help her find a way to fall asleep. Bea watches from the shadows as Mona struggles to get comfortable and all she can see is Mona as a baby, little girl, teenager, woman of the world. Now she is dying, with rumpled hair and that dear sweet body that she hated so much. The shoulders with their pretty bones, her jawbones and temple, her lips and eyes, all so lovely and never enough.

Is it irony that Mona dieted her entire adult life and now her choice is a voluntary refusal of food and drink as a means of bringing about the end? Bryan told Bea that it can take a person between five and ten days to die this way as they gradually slip into a coma, followed by death. She watches as he holds her sister's hand and listens as he tells Mona about the solar system mobile his daughter built for science class. How would she have survived these days without Bryan? He was the most wonderful man she had ever met in her entire life.

Mona is finally asleep. Bryan looks over at Bea and gestures to the kitchen. It's an invitation to sit and talk, maybe have a slice of pie together as they usually do, but she shakes her head, no. He nods, understanding. But he doesn't understand. And Bea isn't going to tell him that in this moment it's all she can do to keep from kissing him. Once he leaves the room, she releases her hands from under her thighs where she had been sitting on them. The guilt is intense. She gazes at Mona's pale, perfect forehead. She doesn't want Mona to die not only because she is too young to die, but because when she does, that will mean the end of Bryan.

But then, Jenna Stewart was fifteen when a horse kicked her in the face.

❖ ❖ ❖

One day in March, or maybe it was April, so hard to tell when the late winter weeks stick together in one long rut of mud and heavy rain, Bea picked up two books at the church rummage sale.

The years of living up on the hill had found their rhythm and she didn't need much most days except during the endless dregs of winter.

"These are the times that test a woman's soul," she said to the dogs that morning as they all pressed themselves against the back wall of the porch while the rain pounded the earth and splashed up at them from the stone steps. Bea carried her coffee back inside to where it was warm and dry. She watched out the window as the dogs leapt off the porch and began their morning inspection of the yard same as any other day. Weather just didn't matter in their world. They plowed their bodies through deep snow as if they were body surfing waves in Bali. In the worst of the hot summer days, they dug cool dens under the lean-tos Bea had set out onto the hill for them and watched the world go by. Always happy to walk, just as happy to lay down for a nap, happy to eat, or forget about food when they were absorbed in chasing squirrels. There was only one channel on their television set: happy.

Bea was not a dog. Life on the hill was more than she had ever dreamed of in so many ways and she didn't want to seem ungrateful when she knew just how lucky she was, but there were also times when she questioned everything and wondered if having some people up here with her might make things easier.

They would have to live in their own place, she decided as she slowly picked the truck down the road into town, wipers a metronome of fury. Henry's damp body pressed against her. She reached her right hand down to stroke his head, it came back wet and covered in hair. She rubbed it off on the beach towel he was wrapped in. He thumped his tail, not able to distinguish her rubbing her hand clean on his back from giving him some love.

The idea of building another small house woke up some energy inside her. She had loved the process of building her house and learned so many things that she would do differently, better if she did it a second time. It could be fun; those excursions with Ellen had been like treasure hunting. Who would come and live there, though. That was the question.

She pulled the truck under the shelter of the gas station since it was closed and nobody would care if she parked there for a little bit. This way Henry would feel safer while she ran inside.

She had seen the sign about the book sale days earlier and made a note on the calendar. Not even pouring rain was going to keep her away. Her desperation for diversion surprised her. Wasn't she the one Janet always said entertained herself? Wasn't she the one who thought living remotely was the answer to her need to be away from people? And this sad sack of a church basement with crappy paperbacks in abundance, piles upon piles of murder mysteries, crime dramas, police dramas, serial killers, is this is what the people in her town were reading for pleasure? For entertainment? Dismemberment, murdered girls, the weary detective, the cynical, wise-cracking police force with their token female. How many times can this same story be told? How many times would they want to hear it?

Many, many times Bea understood as she dug through the shelves in the hopes of finding something that wasn't mass produced, something without violence.

Over by the stairs, a card table had been set up with a money box. Underneath were a couple of boxes with old hardcover books in them. She found two that seemed interesting.

One was called *Down the Garden Path*, by Beverley Nichols, the other a book about being an artist by Robert Henri. She liked it for his name though she spelled Henry's name differently and because she opened to a page that said about artwork, "the better or more personal you are the less likely they are of acceptance." This struck hard.

She had to sit on the steps for a minute to let the storm of feeling pass through. Waves of memory slammed into her. She had totally forgotten that day, and yet, here it was, buried alive somewhere in her cells, called to the surface in full force with every stinging detail clear.

San Francisco. A gray afternoon, probably this time of year, March, maybe April. She had brought a few of her *Carrot Girl* books to that guy in the comic store.

At Parvati's bakery, a table of twenty-somethings were talking about a place that published zines and graphic novels. She wasn't sure what a graphic novel was, or a zine, but it gave her the idea that they might be open to her illustrated *Carrot Girl* stories. It wasn't a comfortable idea and she continued to question why she was doing it as she walked down the street to the shop that was littered with trash, a street so narrow it really should have been called an alley.

The moment she pushed the door open she knew this was not a good place and should leave, but she overrode her intuition by telling herself she needed to be brave. That she was being a scaredy cat. She wanted to be open to possibility as Parvati was incessantly poking at her to do. How will you ever be anything in this world if you don't even try, Parvati would say to her again and again.

Bea didn't know if she wanted to be something, but she wasn't sure that she wasn't supposed to want to. And, she did love *Carrot Girl*.

Her adventures had grown in all sorts of ways she never expected and they could make her laugh out loud. She imagined another girl like her somewhere, a little girl in a room alone who liked the world of stories, who needed them as she had. What would she have done without Lulu? Without Pippi? That is what pushed her on.

The shop stank of reefer, patchouli and B.O. The shelves were crowded with comic books, plastic action figures, the occasional G.I Joe and crates of comedy LPs. Even the albums in their plastic sheaths had a sheen of grime. A skinny guy wearing a gray sweatshirt sat at one side of the counter twisting a Rubik's cube. He seemed to be there to keep the other guy company. The guy behind the counter wore his hair pulled back into a ponytail that lay across one shoulder like a limp husk of corn. Sunglasses were perched on his head.

"Yeah?" he asked her.

Bea used as few words as possible to explain she had some original comic books and was wondering if they published them here.

"Sometimes," he said, and then paused. "You?"

Bea understood what he meant—that she was not edgy enough, not groovy enough, not goth, no pink streaks in her hair, no tattoos or multiple piercings up the curve of her ear. She didn't look like a comic book writer was supposed to look.

Behind him sat a pizza box with the lid flipped open, a couple slices getting cold. Pepperoni, that was part of the smell, too.

"Lemme see." He made a stab at wiping his fingers. She didn't want him touching her paper. Still, she undid the portfolio and slipped out the most recent one that she had finished. Since it was her latest, chances were it was her best.

He flipped through. The skinny guy came and stood behind him also looking though he couldn't have read from that far away. She hadn't realized how exposed she would feel. Why was that other guy looking? When pizza face guy got to the end, he flipped it back and forth as if to say, that's it? He pushed it back to her.

Bea hurried to tuck it back with the others and tied up the portfolio without even checking if he had left grease prints on it.

"I have more," she said, feeling a need to defend. Hating herself for having shown this dick her work. He sucked on a straw that stuck out from the lid on a giant waxed paper cup. He put two fingers to his lips, then rolled out a burp from the side of his mouth, "Sorry," he said.

"Your drawings aren't bad, but you need some drama, you know? Like, she's a superhero, right? So give her more to fight about and you gotta sex it up. Maybe a bikini top and the tassels are the tops of carrots."

His face lit up at this idea and he nodded at Bea as his imagination gained momentum.

"And she doesn't get into enough trouble. Maybe she gets gang-raped and then goes on a revenge spree, you know? Spraying everyone with pesticide."

He sucked on the soda, nodding and smiling. "Also, maybe think about getting rid of the vegetable thing and go for something like I don't know, a mermaid, that could be cool, right?" The skinny guy nodded, jumping in.

"Yeah, cool. Her trident could be a laser gun."

Bea's chest was so tight she could hardly breathe. A storm of insult, humiliation and fury sat behind her eyes in two fists of hot tears. She couldn't speak. She didn't even have words for this. She needed air. She rushed to the door and heard him call out.

"Hey, a thank you might be nice. Just gave you a shit load of ideas for free, you know."

Standing in the church rummage sale, reading those words brought it all back. Her stomach heaved with nausea at the memory. How could she have been such an idiot? Why would she share *Carrot Girl* with them? How could so much shame be so alive inside of her? That was years ago. Why was she even feeling shame? What was wrong with her? Why was she always such a baby? When would she ever be okay in this world? Why couldn't she be more like Mona or Janet? They didn't let anything stop them.

The basement was hot and stuffy, she pulled off her jacket and tried to find her beads. They were on her bureau. She had left them at home.

"Are you okay, dear?" A woman was leaning over her, touching her on the shoulder. Bea nodded and buried her face into her knees.

"I'll bring you some tea." She heard the steps over to the table with the paper tablecloth where lemon cookies sat on a plate and two big silver canisters with black lids and little red lights sat with handwritten signs in front, coffee, tea. Were they the only two people in this place?

"Here you are, dear. I put some honey in it for you." The woman was holding a small white styrofoam cup to her. Bea took it and smiled her thanks.

She sat up. The woman went back to her chair and picked up the crochet she was working on. Bea felt the gift of privacy she had just been given. The tea was too hot to sip, so she put it next to her and opened the book to the page with the words she had read. She read them again, and again.

The better the art, the more personal, the less likely it will be accepted.

Yes, Bea nodded, the tea finally cool enough to drink. Or understood and appreciated, she added.

The books were a quarter each. She bought both and then tucked a twenty dollar bill into the donation box that sat on the tea table behind the lemon cookies.

She fought the truck up the hill as far as she could before parking it. Any further in she might get it stuck. She walked the last half mile, her wellies a gift in weather like this. Henry was drenched by the time they got to the house. Of course, he loved nothing more than when she rubbed him dry. They all did, so she gave them all towel rubs and then handed out three soup bones to gnaw on to burn off some of their energy. There was no big walk for them until the weather cleared. She was not going out into the rain again.

She left her wet clothes in the mudroom and pulled on socks, leggings, a clean t-shirt and her favorite sweater. It was cashmere, a tender sage green that Mona had given to her for Christmas. It could not be more perfect. Mona was a shopping savant.

Bea stoked the wood stove and settled onto the sofa to examine her books.

She liked what Henri was saying but quickly got exhausted replacing every him with her. Finally, she just stopped. She could not get past his insistence on brotherhood, brotherhood, brotherhood, page after page. Written in 1923, sure, she understood on some level, but this guy was an art teacher talking about staying open, not getting stuck, the importance of a change of perspective. This guy. Can't see Mary Cassatt? Can't see Elisabeth Vigee-Lebrun? Are there no females in any of his classes, ever?

She opened the grate, threw the book in and wrenched the door shut. The flames dove onto it and ate it with relish. She decided not to start the other book. Better to put on some music and get out her sketchbook instead.

What would *Carrot Girl* be doing on a rainy day when her heart hurt?

That night, after taking the dogs out for nearly two hours, they were all shellacked. The dogs crashed by the wood stove. Bea carried her dinner into the living room and settled onto the couch. She dug the garden book out from under her butt. This one she had grabbed because in the very first paragraph the author talked about how she bought the house on a whim, having been there once and having a profound memory of the garden. This impulsive move connected with Bea who felt she had done the same thing in buying the sugarbush; some undefinable force that compelled her when she couldn't possibly explain it to anyone else.

But the author wasn't a woman. Beverley. A guy. Must be a British thing, she decided. The book had its moments but the section she read and re-read, then tore out and pasted into her journal was from the chapter titled 'The Professor'. He wasn't a made up character. This Professor existed which meant she wasn't alone. There were other people like her.

She filled one page of her sketchbook with the passage that read,

"Just because Nature may produce a thousand seeds in order to grow one plant, have we any right to assume that all the other seeds are wasted? We don't know—we haven't the least idea—what those other seeds are doing; whether they are falling to the ground and fertilizing it for the one chosen seed…" He straightened himself and glared at me. "The one thing of which we are certain in an uncertain universe, is that the energy is never lost. It is transformed, but it never disappears."

From another chapter she copied out the words, *to me, all the woods are enchanted. I cannot imagine being lonely in them.*

She got up and went to the closet where she stored her art supplies and settled at the kitchen table. She wrote the words out across the bottom of a large piece of watercolor paper and then filled the page with a drawing of the sugarbush. She took the drawing into the studio and began painting on it for days. When it was dry, she went on the hunt for a frame which she found at a yard sale for two dollars.

After she hung the picture on the wall above the green dresser, she crawled onto the bed and Henry leaped up to settle in next to her. She gazed at her painting. The crown of each tree merged into the next to create a halo of yellow-green over the still dark winter wood of the sugarbush, it was a promise of spring.

"If I saw that in a store," she whispered to Henry whose head was on her chest, "I would buy it." Luka and Little Bear whined for the same special treatment so she let them all up on the bed which was too small for all of them together and didn't last more than a few minutes, but those minutes were perfection as she was surrounded with love and snuggles while outside heavy rain resumed pounding on the windows.

Bea has been sitting at the top of the hill for hours. She watches the long grass show how the breeze ripples in and out of the field, invisible without the grass giving it away. The grass moves like seaweed bobbing in the wake of a passing motorboat.

She intended to help, but Ginny and Paulette are getting Mona bathed and dressed. Giusita is in the kitchen spreading pesto on bread toasts.

"Go," she waves Bea off. "I'm all set."

And she was. The back patio has an old but freshly ironed tablecloth set with plates and a pitcher of daffodils. Three chairs have been set at the table with room enough for Mona's wheelchair to be rolled into place.

Bea hears the car before she sees it. Lucky the roads are dry. That black sedan has almost no clearance and would never make it through a puddle let alone a muddy road. Three people get out. Their city decibel voices reach Bea easily. She listens as they squeal in greeting Mona who has been wheeled out onto the patio. She has insisted all interior doors be shut during the visit so if anyone uses the bathroom, they will not see the rest of the place.

She's embarrassed of me, thinks Bea, which adds to her already low mood. She stretches out against Henry's grave on her belly with one arm across the mound she had planted with creeping geraniums. She hopes they will create a purple blanket for him each summer and get thicker year by year.

It seems weird that she can be consumed with such piercing loneliness when the sound of voices, laughing and talking as if nobody is dying, is only a few hundred feet away. Her cheek presses into the dirt and she traces her fingers through the letters of his name that are carved in stone.

She has never missed anyone the way that she misses Henry. That makes her weird, too. She is so tired of feeling weird and wrong and embarrassing. She rolls over onto her back and watches the sky. Air soft, breeze playful. Grass smells so sweet and hums with crickets and bees. Overhead, branches bob with tight yellow green balls. The balls are made up of hundreds of tiny yellow green buds that will soon spread open into leaves.

When she wakes up, her neck is stiff and she has to scramble to pick up the loose pages that have blown out of her sketchbook and across the meadow. The black sedan is still there, but she is thirsty. She walks toward the drive, trying to avoid the group, but someone calls out.

"Is that your sister?"

"Are you Bea?"

"Come join us!"

The woman in charge looks to be about her age. Clary, they call her. Feels like someone Bea has met before. Typical preppie, not even three p.m. and she is in the bag. The other two seem harmless enough. Bea stands, letting them rake her with their gazes.

"You're Monique's sister?"

"You don't look anything alike."

"Different dads," says Clary.

Bea looks at Mona wanting an explanation, but Mona is half-asleep with a dopey smile on her face. It's the first time Bea has seen her look happy since she arrived.

"This place is amazing," says the woman in sunglasses.

"So beautiful," the guy next to her agrees. They both smile up at Bea expecting her to respond. She looks out across the fields and it does look exceptionally pretty today. Diogo has mowed the meadow around the house and up one hill which helps define the space and show off the maples.

"Oh yes," says Giusita, gliding out to begin gathering up the plates and platters that had been covered in grilled veggies, bread and olives. "Very shabby chic meets Kyoto machiya."

"Exactly!" shouts Clary and you can see she wishes she had been the one to come up with that observation.

Mona nods like a queen. Bea isn't sure what Giusita just said but she can see that her words have elevated everyone's perception of where they are sitting. No longer a dumpy junk shop at the side of the road. *Now all we need to do is keep anyone from seeing the hospital bed looming with its oxygen tank and morphine drip which would bring the curtains crashing down on set*, thought Bea.

Bea picks up some of the spent glasses and follows Giusita into the kitchen. The nurses get to their feet.

"It's time for them to go," says Ginny. The nurses head out to end the party.

Bea sits on the small red chair in the corner furthest from the door and watches as Giusita scrapes and stacks the plates.

"This is super nice of you," says Bea.

Giusita shakes off the compliment. "Please, this is nothing."

"It's everything. I would never have been able to make it look like this and she is so happy. Did you see how happy she is?"

"These are all your things, Beatrice. Give yourself some credit, would you."

Giusita pours a splash of red wine into a hobnail juice glass and hands it to Bea.

Bea shakes her off.

"I don't drink alcohol."

"It's wine. Drink it."

"It'll make me sick."

"No, just today. You'll see."

Bea swallows it all in two gulps then hands it back to Giusita. It feels like she was giving her medicine. It feels like she is the grown-up in the room when Bea is easily ten or twelve years older than her.

The wine does make her feel better. She leans back against the wall and notices how everything has softened. How does Giusita know all these things?

Over the sound of dishes being washed, Bea hears the goodbyes, the car doors slamming, the gravel spitting as the engine floats off.

"That's some crazy friends she's got," Giusita says for Bea's ears only.

Are they crazy? Bea thought that's what cool people look like, but it seems Giusita isn't impressed. Diogo comes in and grabs a beer from the fridge. He snaps it open and smiles over at Bea.

"How are you doing? That was a big day."

From down the hall they can hear Mona chatting to the nurses as they get her changed and back into bed.

"Aren't my friends the best? Aren't they the coolest? They came all the way up here to see me. To see me."

"You shouldn't have had anything to drink," Paulette scolds Mona.

"What, am I gonna DIE?" Mona laughs. The bedroom door closes.

"You guys did all the work," Bea says. "I ran and hid in the field."

Diogo takes the plate of food he has assembled and sits next to Bea at the table. He bites into his sandwich. His hands are washed. He shaved this morning.

Giusita checks to see that the bedroom door is closed and that she won't be overheard. She brings a bowl of peas over to the table and begins shelling them. Bea tries not to stare at Diogo, but he doesn't seem to notice. Diogo reminds her of Joe; he has the same quiet confidence and gentle manner. And he adores Giusita. Not like Janet's guys who were like needy little puppies, there's no passive aggressive manipulations or insincere bullshit. They seem like partners. Their skills complement so beautifully when you put them together, it's like they are one person. And yet, two totally different countries, two different languages. Venezuela and Brazil. Though she knows better than to believe in perfect people. Giusita and Diogo are the most perfect people she has ever known. His dedication to the land. Her knowledge of herbs and plants. It's like they are land artists or artists of life. Giusita has her hair held back with a head scarf that doesn't look like a sad hippie but regal, like an African princess.

"Her friends are not really friends, you know? I see better now the third chakra issues," says Giusita. Sometimes her accent throws Bea off. She isn't sure she understands what Giusita is saying.

Bea shakes her head. "I don't know what that is."

"The third chakra? Or chakras in general?"

"Yeah, I don't know what you are talking about. Is this like astrology?"

Diogo nods yes. Giusita pushes at his shoulder.

"Stop," she says.

"It's all voodoo woo woo witchy woman stuff," he says.

"You love it," says Giusita.

He smiles. "I love you."

Bea is embarrassed to be blushing. She doesn't know what to do. She is kind of pinned in and can't get up without making Diogo get up.

"You're making Beatrice uncomfortable," says Giusita.

"Am I?" He melts her with his smile.

She shakes her head but her cheeks give her away. Damn wine.

"Yes, you are. Go be your manly man self and clean the tractor or something. Dig some holes. Tote some peat moss."

"Yes boss," he says gathering up his plate and crushing his empty beer can before tossing it into the recycling. He turns back to them. "For the record, I am one with the woo woo."

"*Mentiroso*," says Giusita. She waves her hand toward the door.

He sits to pull on his boots then goes out the side door. Bea watches as he drops down off the porch onto the grass and walks away without looking back.

"Sorry, " says Giusita. "He can be so annoying."

"He's fine."

This cloud of embarrassment that fills her chest is not about them. She has had it many times. It is that awful sense of confusion she gets when younger people seem to have so much more figured out then she does. How do they do it? How do some people just seem to have so much smartness? Giusita knows about herbs and plants and how to use them for healing. She knows how to hang laundry with the least amount of clothespins and yet they never fall to the ground, she knows who Count Basie is and David Byrne, Rickie Lee Jones and Joan Armatrading. Bea once watched as Giusita got too hot and took off her tank top, rolled it up with ice cubes in the middle then tied it so the ice cubes rested against the back of her neck and held it in place by looping the ends through the armholes, pulling it tight like a French scarf.

It feels like she knows everything. And she has the best guy ever.

Why didn't Bea know about chakras when she was twenty-seven?

Giusita brings an empty bowl to the table and dumps half the peas into it for Bea to help her. They sit shelling.

"Chakras are energy centers in the body. There are seven basic ones. The third is located at your solar plexus, and why I said I understood better how your sister's cancer was pancreatic versus breast or some other organ."

Bea listens closely. Giusita explains how the third chakra is all about self-esteem, self-confidence, the ego, will, drive, power. She also talks about the energy in the pancreas. When it is weak, says

Giusita, people have trouble receiving love.

"Don't I have the same third chakra as Mona?"

"Oh no, no. Your third chakra is radiant."

"How do you know?"

"Look at what you've created. You follow your own drummer. I think you are confusing shy with being confident. You might be shy, but you know very clearly what you like and what you don't like and you don't do what other people think you should."

"So," Bea asks. "This place, living on a farm is a third chakra?"

"No, this is all first chakra. Number one. The ground floor, security, hearth and home. Roof over your head. Grounded. The color of the first chakra is red and you live in a sugarbush."

"But I am leaving."

"Which means you are done," says Giusita. "You are grounded and ready for the next chakra."

"Which one?"

"I'm not sure, but if I had to guess I would say your fifth."

"What does the fifth one mean?" Bea asks.

"Self-expression. Finding your voice."

The bedroom door opens and the two nurses come in to collect their bags and coats.

"She's sleeping. Probably going to have a tough night because of all the food and alcohol."

Ginny glares her blame at Giusita, who beams a smile up at her as she sweeps the last of the empty peapods into the compost bin.

"We're leaving now," says Paulette. "Bryan will be here by 5:30. Can you sign please?"

Bea signed their paperwork and the two women walked out to their cars.

Giusita snorts. "How ridiculous that they each drive a car when they live almost next door to each other."

"Well, they hate each other," says Bea.

"Like I said, ridiculous."

. . .

Bea settles into the chair across from Mona's bed. She watches her sister sleep. She was so happy when her friends were here. That bright, shining energy. She was like Janet when she turns on the wattage. Now, she looks like a little girl. A very sick little girl with dark rings under her eyes. Her hair flattened. Her skin the yellow of spent tulips. Her hands, so small.

Did Mona always have friends? Bea tries to remember. It seems like she did. Did she ever have friends like Setsuko and Mrs. Tamamoto? But could she call Mrs. Tamamoto a friend? Was Mrs. Stewart her friend? Did grown-ups count as real friends?

That first year they were in Montreal, Mona had breathed into the phone so that Janet couldn't overhear.

"You have to come for the real Thanksgiving day, please say you'll come."

But Bea didn't go to Montreal. Her roommate Sally had invited her to come to her house in Marblehead for Thanksgiving. Or rather, Sally's mother did.

The house was enormous with a lawn that reached to the sea. The family seemed oddly familiar to her as if they had been transplanted from Wellesley, but no one had ever been as blunt as Sally's grandfather, a smug old fart in glasses with a belly the size of a small keg girded in place by a belt stitched with red anchors. The belly poking through the suspenders that matched his bow tie, like a toddler's round head between stair railings.

"And where's your home, dear?" He asked upon being introduced to Bea. His eyes milky blue behind the bifocals, his country club smile, a pretense at hospitality as if this were just a friendly question and not a giant sniff up her butt.

"Wellesley," she said. Not entirely a lie, but exactly how to return the serve.

"Oh, very nice, very nice," he said, tottering back to his chair giving the glass in his hand a shake so that what remained of the melted ice cubes rattled like a little bell. Sally's mother came over and took the drink from his hand and left the room. She returned with a freshly filled glass, the ice cubes fat and visible above the rim, that she placed onto a coaster on the end table next to where he sat holding court from a large wing chair. He lifted the glass and swigged deeply without so much as a thank you or acknowledgement that his unspoken request had been satisfied.

"He's old school," Sally said, half apologizing, half secretly proud that his arrogance dated back to ancestors who knew Emerson and Alcott. They were finally back in the room on the third floor of the house where they had been assigned and were changing into pajamas before climbing into bunk beds as if they were ten years old and not college students. Bea chose to be on top even though it meant she kept banging her head into the ceiling.

"No problem," replied Bea. "G'night." But it was a problem. Back on campus, she could not fit in with Sally's plans which included joining a sorority, spending hours on hair, make-up and talking about boys, and very little interest in classes except to complain about how much homework they were being assigned.

"It's the weekend for god's sake," Sally huffed, dropping her books onto the bed as if they were rocks from a prison yard. "Do they expect us not to have a life?"

Bea moved out at the end of that first semester, citing her preference for waking up early as the reason, but they both knew why and Sally was visibly relieved at the pretense.

"Oh yes, I can see how that would work better for you. I'll miss you though," and they fake hugged. Bea packed up her blue suitcases and lugged them across campus to her room in the dorm where nobody was invited to frat parties.

Avoiding frat parties had not been the reason she changed dorms, but after witnessing the panty raids that happened that winter—at all the girl's dorms, that is—her co-ed weirdo dorm held no interest for the marauding bands of drunk boys in rugby shirts shouting and chanting, sometimes breaking into song, locking arms to do the Monkees walk while singing *here we come, walking down the street.*

How was it possible to make a silly song she knew as a kid sound menacing? But they were just having fun. The dean had waved off the objections and told the girls it was a tradition, to not take it too seriously, to be good sports. Some of the girls liked the attention, clearly. Bea watched as a group of girls opened their window and called down to the boys, dangling their lingerie before squealing and slamming the window shut when the boys roared in response and raced into their dorm.

She didn't know if Sally thought it was fun or not, but once, late in the spring a few weeks before the semester ended, she crossed paths with her early in the morning after a frat party.

Outside of the few times when Bea saw Sally in the dining hall and Sally pretended not to see her, they had not seen each other in months. Bea had just come up from the river where she liked to walk before breakfast and Sally was barefooting down the stone steps of the Delta Epsilon house, her high-heeled shoes in one hand. The typical debris of a morning after was in full evidence: beer cans scattered across the lawn, empty kegs tipped on their side, beer bottles and cigarette butts overflowing from pails filled with sand that held the doors propped open.

Sally was wearing a dress that must've been what she had gone out in the night before, but it was barely on her. One sleeve was ripped at the shoulder and the ties of her belt, unfastened, flapped against her hips. Bea had never seen Sally with her hair in such a tangle or with mascara smeared down to her cheekbones. Bea felt a pressure in her chest. Something was very wrong.

"Hey Sally," said Bea.

Sally seemed unsteady on her feet. She looked at Bea, but she didn't seem to recognize her old roommate. She looked stunned. Like she had just been in a car accident.

She clearly wasn't okay, but Bea didn't know what else to say so she reached out with a hand to touch her on the shoulder and asked, "are you okay?"

Sally reared back.

"Don't touch me!" she choked. "Don't touch me." She pulled her shoes into her chest and hobbled quickly away from Bea, weaving across the wide empty expanse of the quad, back toward her dorm.

· · ·

"Something is touching my foot." Mona is awake and in an awful mood. It is Little Bear; she is licking Mona's foot that is sticking out from the edge of the sheet. The dog stops licking and looks up at Bea in confusion. Bea likes being woken up with a kiss on the toes. Bea rubs Little Bear's head and tells her to go lay down.

"I'm so thirsty. I'm so thirsty." All Mona's bright energy from the afternoon is gone. Bea helps her sit up and sip from the cup of water. She lays a chilled washcloth across her forehead.

"Oh my god, my head, my head. Everything hurts."

"How about some Excedrin? Yes?"

"Anything. Oh my god, anything. Why did you let me do that? I'm so sick. I'm so sick. Why did you let me do that?"

Mona rolls to one side. An explosion of farts is followed by the stench of diarrhea. Wetness spreads under the sheets. Mona's eyes are pressed shut but tears are running down her cheeks, dripping down her nose. Her sobs are interrupted by sharp hiccups.

Bea goes to the door and calls to Bryan for help.

"Oh, somebody had too good of a time," he says trying to make light of the mess they were cleaning up.

"Shut up, shut up." Mona isn't sobbing exactly. It's more like convulsions of pain as her body expels everything in it through every orifice possible.

"Okay, okay," says Bryan, and even Bea is soothed by his voice. So low, so comforting. In the midst of getting her clean while the bed is full of vomit and piss and the most rank smelling watery poo, Bryan is talking sweet talk. His motions are swift, efficient, practiced. He has done this many, many times before. How is he so cheerful, so kind? Bea had never thought about a man as a nurse. She just assumed all nurses were female, but he is so much more caring than either Ginny or Paulette. And better in so many ways because he is strong enough to do things alone, like lifting Mona up so Bea can scoot all the sheets out from under her.

Bea walks the pile of sheets out to the porch, holding her breath until they are in the giant plastic trash can they use for this purpose only. She stops at the bathroom to wash her arms and hands. She goes to her room and changes her clothes. When she comes back in, Bryan has Mona on the drip. She is in clean pajamas. Clean sheets folded snugly under her lower belly. He has smoothed her hair back from her forehead and washed her face.

"You had a nice time with your friends," Bryan says as he opens the windows and lights one of Giusita's scented candles.

"No," says Mona. "They are horrible people and I hate them."

Bea sits in the upholstered chair.

"What are you talking about?" says Bea. "You were having a great time"

Mona looks at Bea with exasperation. It was the face of corporate Mona.

"*T'es bete?*" she says coldly.

"I heard you. You said—"

"Clary Endicott—"

"She's the one you always talked about. Your best friend."

Bea sees Bryan leaving the room. He makes a sign to say *I'll be in the kitchen if you need me.*

"I thought she was my friend, but she just used me. That's what she does. She uses people. And then, when I became her boss—"

"You were her boss? How could you be her boss. You're so young. She's my age."

"Whose side are you on?"

"What happened?"

"It was a timing thing, a re-org." Mona recounts the details like she was giving a deposition.

"The year I finished my MBA, we got a new leadership team who wanted to change the reporting structures. Sales and Marketing got combined under my boss and I was put in charge of the division that oversaw the creative team. Clary was still the Art Director because she was good, but no one was going to promote her because she had burned a lot of bridges. Now she reported to me. Which I knew would be a disaster, but she stood in my office and said it was no problem at all. That she was happy for me. But it was all a lie. She wouldn't spend time with me anymore because I was her boss and she said it would look bad, which was such horseshit since she crawled into anyone's office that had a warm beer. She started telling people that I was an ambitious bitch that would step on anyone and that I had used her."

Bea picks up the knitting she had left in the chair from the night before. It is a blanket, mindless, but it helps her focus as Mona tells the story of how Clary went on a smear campaign against her. How she turned the whole office against Mona by saying she had slept her way to the top. How she made sure Mona was never included when people got together for drinks or dinner. How she did these little shit moves during meetings that mocked Mona and there was nothing Mona could do to stop her.

"I would go up to the seventh floor and hide in the bathroom stalls to cry. My stomach was clenched in terror all the time, worried about what people were saying about me. I couldn't eat. It was horrible. I can't believe I let her come see me. She wanted to see me sick. Wanted to see me like this. She wins. I lose."

"She was jealous," says Bea.

"Jealous?" Mona spits the word back at Bea. "Jealous of what?"

"You."

Mona looks at her like she is making no sense. Bea doesn't understand how they aren't understanding each other. It is so clear. How can Mona not see this?

"You're young, beautiful—your smile lights up a room. She's got a face like Andy Rooney's bastard son. You are creative and smart. You're the full package. You even did an MBA while working full time. Do you think Miss Cocktail Hour could even fill out an application for graduate school without slurring her words?"

"*Alors*," Mona sinks back into the pillow, pleased. "*Comme tu es mechante. On ne savait pas. C'est formidable.*"

"You have no idea how powerful you are. People will do anything you ask them. You get middle-aged European men to sign million dollar contracts without so much as a glimpse of your thigh."

"Oh, they may have gotten a glimpse."

"But they didn't touch it."

Mona smiles. "No."

Bea lets the last of the emotion roll off her and settles back to the chair to catch her breath. She didn't like the sensation of this fierce energy that raged through her. Only Mona ever brought it out in her.

Mona looks across the bed at Bea. "Is that how you see me?"

"Of course. That's how everyone sees you. Don't you remember that thing Janet said?"

"About me?"

"Yeah, how if Rome was ever gonna be built in a day, you'd be the one to do it."

"She never said that."

"You think I made it up?"

"You make a lot of things up."

Bea puts her knitting onto her lap and holds up one hand.

"Hand to God."

"I don't believe in God."

"Well, hand to Gucci, then. Janet said it. I thought you were there."

"I never heard her say anything like that."

Pause.

"You think Clary was jealous? Of me?"

"How could she not be?"

"What do you mean? She is a legend. Everybody wants to be her."

"Oh, honey," says Bea. "You are in marketing. You know this better than me. She's a storefront. That hair all Andy Warhol and her crazy clothes and fat lipstick, that's a costume. You know that, right? It's just a costume. You were her best friend and she sabotaged you. That's a very messed up person who does that."

They sit. They listen to the radio in the kitchen. Linda Ronstadt.

"You loved her," says Mona.

Bea remembers long hours on the living room floor with her head by the speakers, getting up only to start the record again. *Rock Me on the Wate*r and *I Fall to Pieces* over and over. Eddie would come in and kick the soles of her feet and tell her to stop playing such sad music. Put on something happy, he would say. Linda didn't make her feel sad. She loved everything about her. The dark hair. Thick bangs and silver hoop earrings. Those eyes.

"Yes," Bea says.

"She must have had it hard," says Mona. "Being the only girl with all those guys. Think about it. There were no girl bands back then."

"You've just finished telling me what it's like working with women. Besides, I worked with mostly guys. It wasn't terrible."

"Do you think she was happy?"

Bea remembers the book club lounge at the back of the cubicles. She remembers Joe. How he taught her to help people get along even when they were like angry wolves. How Joe would walk up to her and tell her it was time to go home, and she would walk out into the dark parking lot that was now night and feel dazed, having lost all sense of time because she was deep into a project.

She turns the blanket over and begins a new row.

"I think she was happy when she was singing," says Bea.

She looks over at Mona who has drifted away.

· · ·

When Bea went up to Montreal for that first Christmas, Janet and Antoine were still in their honeymoon stage, so she and Mona left the apartment as much as they could.

Winter was bad in Vermont, but Montreal was worse. The wind blasted through the streets and slammed their bodies up against brick walls. They held their hoods down with their heads tilted into the wind.

In the bar, Bea ordered the Kir Royale that Mona wanted but drank the ginger ale that the waiter set down in front of Mona. Nobody seemed to care that a fifteen-year-old was having a small glass of wine. Bea sorted through the bowl of nuts on the table. She picked out each macadamia and examined it before slipping it into her mouth. Mona sipped artfully. She seemed to be practicing how to hold the glass and sit at the same time.

"When I am your age I am going to drink wine and champagne every day," said Mona.

She wanted to know why Bea didn't drink alcohol. Normally, when people asked, Bea just let them assume she'd joined AA, but cozy in the bar with Mona, she told her sister the truth. That time Janet made her do a shot of whiskey when she got her first period and was having bad cramps, she threw up. Ever since, she just couldn't go near it.

"Even wine?" asked Mona.

"Don't want any of it."

"Well, that was a horrible thing to do," said Mona.

"No, she was being sweet. She didn't know it would make me sick."

Janet came back in with a hot water bottle wrapped in a flannel pillowcase. Bea was starting to get up.

Where are you going?

I gotta get dressed for school.

You don't have to go to school.

Pure relief washed over her. She crawled back into bed. So grateful. Her mother utterly dismissive of school.

Honey, you just do your best to be comfortable. Put this on your belly.

Janet stacked up her favorite books, Lulu, her sketchbook, pencil case. All next to the bed. With some ginger ale, crackers and chocolate.

Okay, I gotta head out. I'll be back before dark. You gonna make it?

Bea nodded shining, not even on Christmas did she feel such a gift. The whole day in bed? With her sketchbook and Lulu and chocolate and her mom's permission? Heaven. The first experience of what hours and hours and hours in bed felt like, always her reset. True nurturance, that sinking into nothingness. Even the pain of the cramps were okay in contrast to the pleasure of this freedom to just be.

Mona, back in the bar, said "I can't believe Janet did that."

"She was trying to help," explained Bea. "Didn't she offer you whiskey?"

"Please," Mona laughed. "I had my period for months before she even asked if I needed anything and I said no, I was managing fine on my own."

• • •

Bea leaves Mona's room. The night air on her face is what she needs. Bea opens the door onto the porch and folds herself into the wicker sofa. The dogs hop up to snuggle in with her, Luka across her belly, Little Bear at her feet. She pets Luka's head and watches the sky. Stars out. Moon out. Clouds pulling together and apart. Stars gone. Moon gone. That moment of complete darkness, not a single sound, when it feels like the whole world has emptied into a deep exhale and then, the first bird starts up and morning inhales. Sun begins to rim the clouds. Birds send and answer calls. Sky fills red pink gold. So much yellow. So much gold. Back to here. Where just moments before it felt like she was in another world entirely.

Giusita taps her arm. "How are you doing?"

It's morning. Her neck aches. Giusita opens the door to let the dogs in. Bea touches each plant in greeting, the ferns, the succulents, the orchids, the seedlings at the window above the sink. This is her kitchen. No curtains on the windows. Open shelves with jars of farro, oats and lentils. Just the way she always dreamed it would be except now, it isn't hers anymore. It belongs to Giusita and Diogo.

She wants to answer Giusita's question, but she is just too tired to try and find the words. And, on a deeper level, she knows there isn't a word to answer it. She lets silence grow in response to the question.

Giusita runs water into the kettle and sets it on the burner. When it boils, she pours hot water over the silver mesh ball filled with herbs and tea. Adds honey. She puts a mug down in front of Bea. It looks like Giusita might want to say something, but she doesn't. Giusita picks up the blue jeans she has been working on. Bea has shown her what Mrs. Tamamoto taught her.

On the mended kneecap of her jeans Giusita has created a small square with pretty little straight stitches. So many tiny white crosses in a field of blue.

more lies

I cannot believe all the things I didn't eat.

Janet's wedding cake when she married Marcus. It was devil's food with chocolate ganache, fresh raspberries and whipped cream. Craziest? I was the one who ordered it from that patisserie in the West Village and had it delivered all the hell the way out to Little Wherever the Hell not Newport and I didn't even take a bite. Not even a teaspoon of whipped cream. *Nul, je suis nul.* I said no to pancakes and french toast. Great thick fluffy pancakes in a stack, butter flecked with sea salt. No. Pasta loaded with sauce and sprinkled with parmesan cheese, no. Pizza, my most favorite food in the world, no. Once a week, if I'd been really good, I would go to the grocer off Columbus and walk the aisles. Tins of imported olives, artichoke hearts, an entire row of cookies and chocolates from England, Belgium and France. The scent of fresh bread filled the store as it was partnered with an artisanal bakery. I would go up to the counter and buy three of the breadsticks they sold like pretzel rods from a glass cannister with a chrome lid.

Out on the street I would eat the first one slowly, nibbling off the sesame seeds, savoring the crisp sensation that never failed to satisfy. God, I loved toast.

"You want toast?" Bea is surprised.

"Yes. And waffles with lots of butter and maple syrup. And pancakes."

She looks concerned.

"Just do it."

"Honey, that'll make you sick. You know that."

"I am sick. *Putain*!"

"Okay, okay." Bea straightens the sheets where I kicked them off.

"Lemme ask around who has a waffle maker."

The dogs jump up and follow her out. How does she do that? She didn't even look at them or whistle or anything and they just go where she goes. Everything always comes so easy to her. She never even has to try. And it's wasted on her. She's never cared about fitting in or if people like her.

· · ·

"What are you doing?" Mom was watching me.

I had unwrapped the sandwich so the wax paper was a pocket. I was eating it carefully from the edge where the sandwich was exposed. I had seen Marcy Bellingham do this. Marcy was the nice one in the group of girls that didn't want me. She wore blue barrettes in her hair and her body was the one everyone talked about. I got Janet to buy me the exact same jeans as Marcy, but they didn't look as good on me. When Marcy ate her sandwich, nothing dropped out making a mess. It stayed neat right down to the corner. Then, she would wad the paper into a ball and toss it into the can. Everyone watched as she walked over to the corner where the trash cans were and then back to her seat at the table with the other beautiful girls.

"I'm practicing," I told Janet.

Janet rolled her eyes to the ceiling then tapped her cigarette before drawing on it deeply. She went back to filling in the newspaper crossword puzzle.

. . .

"Does smoking make you thin?" I asked Auntie Annie. We were in the upstairs of her apartment. Downstairs was just one room big enough for her bed which was where she slept. Upstairs had the kitchen, bathroom and living room, where I slept.

"I don't know." She shrugged. "Keeps my hands busy. Can't feed my face if I've got a cigarette going."

"I don't want to smoke."

"That's a good thing. It's godawful expensive. I have to get my clothes dry-cleaned every week."

"But I want to be thin."

"You want to be thin and eat all the chocolate."

"Yes."

"Nobody gets to do that. Just so you know. Those girls eating chocolate in the magazine? They throw it up afterward."

"That's gross."

"Well, it's what they do."

"I hate throwing up."

"Monaboo, everybody hates throwing up."

· · ·

"It's okay, it's okay." Bea is helping Bryan clean me up.

I'm so embarrassed. It's the middle of the day. Sunshine is pouring in and I've thrown up everywhere. Across the sheets, on the floor, into the pillow, all over me. There's no hiding from it. It's so disgusting. My insides are cramping. It hurts all across my chest. I can't stop the diarrhea. It smells so bad. All I can do is cry because everything hurts and it's so humiliating. And they keep being so nice to me. Bryan is smiling and telling me about Clem. How she got sick on clam chowder in the back of the car once when they were stuck in traffic. He's trying to make me laugh but the bile has burned my throat and it's all I can taste. I just close my eyes and give over to it. Bryan lifts me up and I feel like I weigh nothing at all. He is so strong. I want to ask him about his aftershave. It's probably something cheap from a CVS but I love it. He smells so good. He carries me into the bathroom where Bea is waiting with a tub full of hot water. As he settles me in, god he is so gentle, I see I don't have a nightgown on. I am totally naked. I look down at my body and it is the saddest thing I've ever seen. Like one of those kids in the photos that go around at Christmas time to get you to send money. Knobby knees, thigh bones, everything emaciated except for the Santa belly. The water feels so good.

"My beautiful, beautiful girl." Bea strokes a facecloth across my forehead, down my cheek, my neck then comes back up to my mouth. I don't have the energy to tell her she is insane. There must be something around my mouth because she has to rub harder. I don't care. My eyes are closed. I sink into the warmth of the water and let it hold me.

. . .

We didn't take baths growing up. Janet always had us take showers. It was when I arrived at Auntie Annie's that I had the first bath I ever remember.

I was pretty shattered. Janet wanted to stay a couple of days and help me settle in. Maybe she just wanted some fun with Auntie Annie in New York, who knows, but I sent her back to Montreal. Auntie Annie's apartment was too small for three of us and I didn't want to share a bed with Janet. After she left, I missed her like crazy and I wanted her to come back, but I couldn't say anything since I was the one who insisted she leave. So I just sobbed on the sofa. Wanting my mom. Not talking. Feeling stupid. Useless. As always.

Auntie Annie took me by the hand and said, "Okay poppet, here we go. I've drawn you a bath."

She led me into the bathroom which had an old clawfoot tub filled with hot water and bubbles.

At first I resisted. I didn't want to take off my clothes. I didn't want a bath.

"Trust me," she kept saying as she helped me undress. She turned her back as I climbed in but then came over and kneeled next to me. She put a terrycloth pillow behind my head and encouraged me to lean back into it. I couldn't believe how my body relaxed. The water was so deep and the heat just melted me.

"Isn't that nice?" Auntie Annie smiled. She knew how I was feeling.

I nodded. It was too good. How did I never know about hot baths?

I took so many baths in the months I stayed with Auntie Annie. Somedays, especially when the weather was cold, I took two a day. Nothing else helped as much. When I remembered how things had ended with Marie-Thérèse, the pain would rush in and all the skin up the insides of my arms and across my chest and up my throat to my ears would flood with that terrible, prickly, rashy feeling, and I would just go straight into the bathroom, drop my clothes and get into the tub before it had even filled. That tub was my sanctuary.

"You know my water bill this month is gonna have us eating cat food," said Auntie Annie as I came out wrapped in her robe, wearing her slippers. She was sitting at the kitchen table.

I stopped. I hadn't thought about that.

"I'm sorry. I'll pay for it."

"I'm kidding." But she wasn't. I needed to get a job.

That's how I started getting better. Hot baths and getting a job with Luce & Mathilde Interiors.

I didn't know it then, but working with Tilly and Max was the best job I ever had. Their shop wasn't that old. Maybe they'd been doing it about nine or ten years when I joined them. They had met at Pratt. Tilly was a textile artist who wanted to work for a big company like Robert Kaufman or Marimekko, but Max wanted to have her own interior decorating shop and convinced Tilly to join her. They were lovers, I could tell.

Before the sign was turned to open, the three of us would sit at the little cafe table in the back room. Drinking coffee and eating doughnuts or banana bread that was still warm because Tilly had made it that morning. I could tell. Little glances between them. The way their knees touched. How Tilly wiped powdered sugar off Max's cheek with her pinky finger. But we never talked much about personal things. There was never time for that. Even when we were hanging out, it was always about the business. What's next. New client. Monster client. Asshole client. Waiting on checks. Late payments on deliveries. There was a lot of stress. Always. Tilly seemed to hold the stress. Max never seemed to worry.

"Things always work out," she would say.

If I wasn't on the subway down to 39th street, I was answering the phone, or grabbing a cab to deliver the books or the swatches or the tile samples that Tilly had forgotten for the client meeting on the Upper East Side. It was full. It was busy. It was fun.

Tilly was super disorganized but she was a genuine artist which made it somehow forgivable. She had this way of being that entranced me. She was original. Everything she did, how she did it, even in blue jeans and a white t-shirt, was utterly fresh. Sometimes she left me scribbled notes that were nothing more than an address or a shopping list but there was something so artful about them. I tucked them into my purse and added them to my box of treasures which was mostly magazine clippings and silly things.

Max was good enough to get into art school but she wasn't gifted like Tilly. Though, if persuasion were an art form, Max was a master. I once watched as she talked a man into buying a set of ridiculously expensive dishtowels with parrots on them all the while he told her about his abiding fear of birds. She was the kind of person who could always work the angles of anything, a conversation, an argument, a purchase order, how to get their landlord to put a new sink into the bathroom without having to pay for it.

Auntie Annie had pulled me in that first day. I didn't realize until later she had had this as a plan all along. Holding me with her arm tucked into mine, she pushed open the door to Luce & Mathilde and proceeded to chat up Max.

"I live a few blocks from here. On 84th," Auntie Annie said. "This is my niece, Monique. She has just moved here from Montreal."

And that's how it began.

And then, it was over in a blink.

I couldn't live on what they could afford to pay me. We all knew it. Max helped me get into NYU because they were both insistent I had to get a bachelor's degree, which meant I needed even more money.

Eleven months and eight days with L&M. Twenty-two days shy of one full year. But nobody's gonna put up with me blubbering about how much I didn't want to leave them since L&M parlayed into Pressley Common which, of course, was bigger, grayer, located in midtown and no fun at all, but they offered tuition reimbursement. My diploma arrived in the mail in the middle of August and I stuffed it into the box under my bed that held sweaters and winter tops. I ground that degree out in less than three years and don't remember any of it. Janet made some kind of mewling about wanting to have a party and I waved her off. Please. Night school. City College. What's the point.

Besides, I'd already had the best party of my life. Tilly and Max gave me a party on my last day of work. Nothing could ever top it. Tilly lit candles and strung fairy lights. There were tiny white olives for the martinis. The buffet was loaded with breads, olives and the most amazing antipasti with anchovy fillets from Costa Brava. They had music going and the people who were dancing made a circle around me when *We Are Family* played. I was the center of attention. They made me feel like a queen.

For dessert, Tilly had made her meringues and served them with lemon curd and fresh strawberries because she knew I loved when she made meringues. There had to be forty people in the room. Incredibly dressed, cool, hip, fabulous people who gave me hugs and wished me well. Max made a toast. Tilly tucked a gift into my hands from both of them, but I knew she had chosen and wrapped it. I had never felt so happy or so sad.

Well, no. Scratch that. The saddest was a week before when I went to get some clothes for job interviews and realized I had gained nearly twenty pounds since I started at L&M. Add my midnight grabbing a slice of pizza in order to be able to keep studying with those late afternoon stops for a cafe eclair or a pain chocolat on top of the way I ate with Tilly and Max. Really, don't know how I could be surprised. But I was. Shocked. Probably because I had begun wearing leggings and boots and skirts like Tilly did. Loose dresses. Stretchy mini skirts.

Auntie Annie walked in just as I stepped off the scale. How could I have possibly gained seventeen pounds in less than a year?

"Well, if you're gonna hang out with lesbians, you're gonna get fat," she said.

The next morning I shook my head, no thanks, when Tilly held out the plate of gingerbread stars.

"Need to watch it," I said, drinking my coffee black. "I'm getting fat."

"You are not fat," said Tilly. She was almost insulted, angry. "Who told you that?"

I didn't answer. I was not going to make her not like Auntie Annie.

When I came into the apartment after work, Auntie Annie was always there. She must have gone out during the day because there were groceries in the fridge, fruit in a wooden bowl on the counter. We didn't run out of toilet paper. It was just so different from Janet who was almost never home at night.

"Oh god," says Auntie Annie, stretching her legs and moving them so they were next to mine. We would sit like that on the living room couch. Her on one end, me on the other, ankles in the middle.

"Who can afford to go out every night? Who would want to?" She looked at me. "I mean, you should. You're young. Why aren't you out at the clubs?"

I liked sitting on the couch in our jammies, drinking Diet Coke, eating popcorn with salt, no butter and talking. I wouldn't even know where to go. The idea of getting dressed up and doing my hair and makeup sounded like work. But I didn't tell her that. I shrugged.

"When I was your age, Jesus. Let's say I'm lucky to be alive."

"You make it sound like it was dangerous."

"Well, if you go looking for trouble, you can find it."

"Why were you looking for trouble?"

"Because I thought it would be fun."

Auntie Annie told me things she and my mom would do. How when they were still in high school Janet would climb out of her room at night to drive around with boys. What her dad did when he found out.

"If she was his favorite, why was he so mean?"

Auntie Annie didn't have an answer for all my questions, but she did have stories about everyone. Janet, Nana, my real aunts Ruby and Rose. She knew Bea's father. His name was Jim. A music professor at the college they had gone to. Janet would drag Annie with her to listen to him play in jazz clubs. Turns out he had a wife who lived in Chicago.

I don't know if she told me everything. On Sundays, when my mom would telephone, I wanted to ask her about the things Auntie Annie told me, but I never did. Janet was totally unreliable. I couldn't believe anything she would tell me. Maybe it was true, maybe it wasn't. More often than not, she would shrug and say *oh honey, I don't remember*. I definitely wasn't going to ask her about Jim.

"Were they in love?"

"Sugarcake," said Auntie Annie. As she picked up the red plastic bowl that had only a gritty scrabble of salt and old maids in the bottom and carried it to the sink. "I don't know much about love. But I can tell you they were as much in love as any two people I've ever seen."

. . .

I watch Bea as she pours water into the black plastic trays by the window from a small can with a long, thin spout. How would she feel if she knew she looks like him? Should I tell her what I know? I was going to that weekend she came into the city. I had it all planned out so that if she wanted to go see him, I knew where he was playing both nights. But everything blew up instead.

How was I to know she was going to bring that damn dog? I mean, I knew she was bringing a dog, but the only dogs I ever saw were fluffy little things that were the size of rabbits that women held in one arm as they sailed into Saks, or carried in oversized pocketbooks, little faces peering out. When I opened the door, her dog barrelled in. This was a dog. Big. He ran right in and was wagging everywhere. He knocked over my bonsai. Dirt went all over the carpet.

"Henry's just excited. There was a lot of traffic. We've been in the car for hours. He needs a walk."

We argued like Eddie and Janet. Cruel and sharp.

"You treat that dog like it's a child."

"You said I could bring him."

"I didn't mean loose. I thought you would have a cage or something."

So she left. Before she'd even taken off her coat. Before I could tell her what I had been planning for months to share.

She smiles over at me. The light coming through the window behind her.

"You okay?"

If I tell her now, will she hate me for knowing and never telling her? Will she hate Janet more? Oh god, my chest is getting that hard knot. I don't know what the right thing to do is.

"Auntie Annie wants to come see you." Bea sits in the chair next to me.

Oh god, then it will all come out. And Bea will hate me. I can't fix this.

"No," I say. "Tell her no."

"Honey, she wants to see you."

"I told you that's why I'm here. No visitors."

"But your friends came up. Remember how much you liked that?"

"Jesus Christ, Bea. For the last time, they are not my friends. Fucking colleagues. And I don't care, plus that was days ago. I can't see anyone now. I'm too far gone. There's no cleaning me up."

"She's not gonna care about any of that."

"Are you not listening? I care."

I turn my head away from her. Now I'm being a bitch and I can't stop it. How did I become this horrible person? Was I always like this? Wasn't I fun and bright and got along with people? Maybe not when I was stressed out at work, but other times like in Paris with Patrick. That was me. I was so easy and light. I wasn't spitting and cursing and being ugly. We danced. Oh my god, we danced.

Putain. Tears.

"Please. Can you just leave me alone?"

. . .

The morning after the first night with Patrick, I woke up early and threw back the covers. Sumptuous. I stretched like a cat. Most gorgeous linens. I had the sweetest pajamas on. Boy style with piping and a pocket on the top, elastic waistband bottoms. Made from white lawn cotton with a pattern of tiny violets. I loved those pajamas. They were short sleeve and not really appropriate for November, but I didn't care. The window had a balcony. I unhooked the iron latch and pushed the shutters back and stepped out, barefoot into the quiet silver air. This was the first day of the rest of my life.

Looking out, on the morning rain, I used to feel so uninspired. I was singing. I couldn't go back to bed. Couldn't sit. Couldn't wait to see him again. He said he'd come by around 10 a.m. God that was hours from now.

I wanted to wear the exact same outfit as yesterday. Everything about it was so right. The ballet flats because I knew I'd be walking a ton and wanted to be comfortable, but who knew I'd dance in them until my toes were red and shiny? Deep pockets on that cotton skirt so I wouldn't need a purse, just a lipstick and coin purse for cash. Left my key at the front desk. I hugged my knees in at how it was so perfect and all of it such wild synchronicity. I'd worn that skirt so many times I almost didn't even pack it, but threw it into my suitcase at the last minute in case there was time in Brussels to do an early morning photo walk.

My hair was in a ponytail. The only effort to acknowledge I was in the most stylish city in the world was that I pulled on a pink cashmere sweater I'd picked up in London, but really, it was almost like wearing a sweatshirt. I didn't care, I'd been dressed to the nines for days. It was Thursday but felt like a Saturday. And, nobody was gonna notice me anyway with this many beautiful people everywhere you looked.

But he did notice me. He had dark hair that fell across his forehead, almost into his dark brown eyes, but didn't. I couldn't believe how easy it was to talk with him. I wasn't nervous. In the brasserie, they gave us a table by the window. I ordered *poulet roti*, he did the same and they both came with frites. So many frites and we ate them all. One by one. We must have been there for hours. He told me about summers at his grandparents' house in Michigan. I told him about working with Tilly and Max.

When we left, he put my arm through his. It was the most natural way of walking, ever. We were walking to a cafe he knew in the 5th for a *digestif*, but we both stopped cold when we heard the music coming from a *boite*.

He looked at me with a *yes?*

Yes, I nodded. And, just like that, we entered a whole nother world. The music was coming from downstairs. Steamy. Smoky. So warm from all the bodies in the small space.

We got to the bottom stair just as the band slipped into *In the Mood*. I took off my sweater and tied it around my waist. Patrick took my camera and gave it to the bartender to tuck behind the bar. Then, he offered his hand. It was strong and warm. He spun me in a soft twirl before pulling me in close. We were right in the middle of the dance floor. The music an ocean around us. He was smooth. Experienced. A gentle lead. His confidence made it so easy for me. I didn't have to think. I just followed where he led. I began to feel playful and turned my chin on the beat, from one shoulder to the other, as I'd seen Janet do a hundred times. From that moment on, I channeled Janet's loose and flirtatious style. When the band cut loose with *Sing, Sing, Sing*, the floor fell away and there was no one but us. We held nothing back. We responded to each other in lightning harmony as if we had one brain. We played little games with each other. Watching. Faking. Anticipating. Matching. Quick stepping. Almost like playing dare. It was as if I had never understood the word before. This was dancing. This playful, non-verbal communication. His touch on my back, the light tug on one hand, switch and then the other. His smell. I felt his fingers, his eyes, his lips. I watched our feet. My pale pink Italian flats. Perfect for dancing. I never knew how hours of dancing together dropped you into an intimate, intuitive place. When a guy tried to cut in, Patrick shrugged him off.

Oh, was the feeling when that happened. *Oh*.

During set breaks, we sat at the bar with his knees grazing mine. His mom had taught him how to dance at their place up on Torch Lake. There was nothing else to do at night except play bridge or dominoes. He made a face as if it were the most boring place in the world, but we both knew the truth of nights like that. When he laughed, his chin went up and I could see the shape of his throat.

"I love how you smile the whole time you dance," he said to me.

"I do?" Am I blushing?

He nodded.

"I guess I can't remember it ever being so much fun."

"But you've obviously danced a lot."

I told him how Janet loved to go swing dancing in Montreal. Antoine was passable. Janet always searched out the best dancer, so I danced with Antoine mostly. Growing up, I danced with Eddie in the living room and sometimes at country club parties but Janet mostly wanted to dance with him because he was the best dancer.

Pause.

"You're better," I said then took a sip of my kir. I couldn't believe I just said that. He was going to know. He was going to know I was falling for him so hard.

He smiled deeply and leaned in to take my fingertips to his lips.

One of the last songs of the night was *String of Pearls*. My sweater was somewhere lost on the floor under the barstool. I didn't care. All that was between us was the thin cotton of my t-shirt and his shirt that was warm with sweat. This was the real thing. I knew it to my core.

When we came up to the street the cold was sharp. Suddenly we were both shy. I busied myself by pulling on my sweater and looping the camera strap over my neck.

"Where are you staying?" he asked.

Patrick hailed a cab and we climbed into the back seat. He put his arm around me. I leaned my cheek to his collarbone. I listened as he asked the driver to take us down along the Seine, turn at Pont Royal and come up rue du Bac to Raspail. He wanted me to see all the lights. I had seen them before but never like this.

Nobody could put this into a movie, is what I was thinking. Not even a photograph could touch on this feeling. Everything but this was a shadow.

And then we kissed.

Friday he was in the lobby waiting for me. He'd just showered and smelled of vanilla and sandalwood. I wore short black boots, black tights with a Sonia Rykiel sweater dress and Jean-Paul Gaultier jean jacket. We shared a plate of eggs benedict at a tiny place on Monsieur-le-Prince that made real American breakfast.

We looked like one of those fabulous French couples I had seen. The handsome guy with a great haircut and a scarf expertly looped at his throat with a girl he can't take his eyes off of. How could this be me? How could I be that girl?

We walked and walked. Wandered into the Musée Luxembourg for an exhibit on the story of Pont d'Aven, maybe one of the most poetic shows I'd ever experienced. A blending of art, community and the sacred power of unconditional generosity.

When we came out, the wind had picked up and it was already getting dark. The best time of day for a cafe. We pushed our way into one that was heaving with people, *garçons* in their long white aprons expertly winding around the tightly packed room to set down a demitasse of espresso with a bit of lemon peel on the saucer, a large cup of hot chocolate topped with chantilly.

"What did you think?" he leaned in close so I could hear him.

"It was extraordinary. Did you know about it?"

He shook his head, *no*.

"I just love how they took them all in, you know? They were poor and grungy and probably smelled awful, and yet here is this town of people that values art. The artist."

I stopped talking. I sounded stupid. I was going to bore him. But the exhibit cracked something inside of me. The idea of people opening their homes, allowing artists to sleep in their barns, to feed them, to model for them instead of chasing them out of town.

"I was thinking it's kinda sad that this one town is such an anomaly," he said. "Why isn't it the norm?"

He was in Paris studying urban development. He had just come back from a year in Kyoto. His parents still lived in Ann Arbor. Patrick's younger brother was studying down in Aix.

"Do you have brothers or sisters?"

I nodded. "A sister."

"Where's she?"

"Vermont."

Chouette.

It doesn't seem possible that we never separated the whole day into the night, but it's true. Patrick had a favorite restaurant in the Marais where we ate in a burgundy velvet banquette. He ordered wine with authority and it was delicious but it could have been tap water and I would still have been floating.

"You like Ska?"

I don't really know what that is. Is it punk? I don't want him to think I'm *nul*.

"I'm game," I said.

We grabbed the metro to République. When we came up from the station onto the street, it felt very sketchy, not at all like the night before. Patrick could tell I was nervous and he took my hand.

The club was dirty, loud, smelled like beer and the people dressed like they were all homeless. The dancing was some kind of goofy looping thing.

"This is ska?" I said.

He laughed and pulled me onto the dance floor. I picked it up pretty quickly following Patrick's lead and watching the people around me. It was silly, totally silly.

I loved it.

There was a song playing. It wasn't new. I had heard it before. Patrick knew all the words.

Every story has to be about something, I suppose.

He sang parts of it to me as we danced.

At the doors of my heart again

I can feel love thump

Boom-boom, boom-boom

Each time the chorus said *boom-boom* he knocked his fist into his chest.

Saturday morning we were out walking before the shops opened. The sidewalks were wet. Trucks rolled by perfuming the air with diesel. A parade of school children in navy peacoats clutching a satchel in one hand and gripping the adult's hand with the other chattered nonstop to the perfectly dressed parent, sometimes the dad, sometimes the mom who accompanied them to school.

"Half day," Patrick explained.

The trees in Luxembourg gardens glistened. Chestnuts scattered across the ground. We kicked at them. There was a hushed quality as if rich in promise of what lay ahead. The excited kids bouncing at the promise of a pain chocolat for good behavior. The trucks making their deliveries.

Patrick held me as we walked, his arm wrapped around my neck so I was pressed in as close as possible, my arm around his waist. Nothing in my life had ever felt so right. On rue Bonaparte, I stopped at a display in the vitrine of a small shop and nearly hit my nose on the window. The styling was charming, naif, Provencal.

Block print tablecloths, santons and painted tin pitchers. A stack of dessert plates, set of eight, captured me. Not at all my style, but somehow I felt they would be perfect for summer dinners on the porch with Patrick and our children. I could see it all so clearly. At the lake house, ours would be down just a little bit from his grandparents. His parents would look at each other and nod, silently agreeing on what a good choice Patrick had made in choosing me. Our children, in little outfits from Petit Bateau on the green lawn that rolled down to the water. Patrick would be so proud of how I made such a beautiful home for them. How I still looked sexy even after two babies. I would be dressed Audrey Hepburn casual, white jeans, navy shirt, gold studs. As I brought out dessert—meringues I had made, served with lemon curd and fresh strawberries—his mother would examine the plates and exclaim *how darling* and we would laugh and Patrick would tell the story of how we found them the weekend we met. That crazy wild most romantic storybook right out of the movies weekend in Paris when we fell in love.

The shop didn't open for another hour but the woman let us in anyway. Patrick pressed next to me as I stood at the counter to buy the plates, his arm across my shoulders.

"Do you ship?" I asked.

The woman nodded and I dropped my business card onto the counter for the name and address.

"Swanky," said Patrick.

"Just keeping up appearances," I replied.

Sunday morning Patrick had made a plan for us to go out to Chartres. He was shocked to learn I had never been.

"You haven't lived til you see it. We must go."

I practically skipped down the steps of the hotel. His car at the curb. The doorman opened the passenger side for me. I settled in and Patrick gave me a long kiss before putting the car into gear.

"You look pretty."

"Pretty good for exactly zero sleep."

"Pretty because of zero sleep?"

"Behave." I hated that I blushed.

I leaned back into the seat. It was raining lightly. The wipers made things smeary but I didn't mind.

"Hey," he said. "We need to hit the Gare du Lyon before we can get on the road. That okay?"

"Sure."

"Great. I totally forgot my mom is coming in and asked me to pick her up. It won't set us back much. We just need to drop her *chez ma tante* which is in the 14th so we won't be too far off route."

"Sure." My stomach cramps. His mother?

"Won't she want to see you?" I asked. "We don't have to go to Chartres today. You can drop me here. I'll see you later so you two can hang out."

"Are you kidding?" He looked over with a smile. "I'll see her all next week. She always comes into Paris in November. It's when she gets her Christmas shopping done. She was down visiting my brother in Aix. And, catching some rays no doubt. She hates the Michigan winters."

The ball in my throat was growing. If I could put on sunglasses, I would, but it was crazy foggy and that would be ridiculous.

"You okay?"

"Yeah, fine."

"You've gone all quiet."

"I'm not quiet."

"Listen, I'm sorry I messed up. I just totally forgot and this is her car. Well, it's my car because she's never here, but it's one of the things I do when she comes into town, you know?"

"Patrick, it's fine. It's your mom. Of course you are gonna pick her up."

"I'm kind of glad she's gonna get to meet you." He looked over and smiled again. "Didn't plan it, but lucky timing if you think about it."

"Yeah," I nodded. "Lucky."

I waited in the car while he ran into the station. When they came out, I knew it was over. His mother was petite, dark-haired and I had met her a thousand times before. She was just like Janet's Westmount ladies. The vintage Burberry coat, the pashmina, the Louis Vuitton bag, the perfect salon hair. Everything rich in that understated way only old money can do. I looked at her shoes and felt the heat of shame begin to suffocate me. I was in her seat. In her car. With her son.

"Bonjour, Monique," she said.

"Bonjour." I stepped out and held the passenger door open for her.

"Ah *non, non*. I'm just a quick ride over to my sister's. Stay where you were."

"No, I insist," I slipped into the backseat and pulled the door shut.

Merci. She slid into the seat that I had kept warm for her.

Je vous en prie.

They chatted about her visit with Julien, his brother. His mother's family was from Aix. Julien lived with his uncle near the university. Patrick's grandmother was coming up to Paris next week.

Vous restez jusqu'a quand? She made a quarter turn in the seat to direct the politesse.

Je pars demain.

"Monique lives in Manhattan," Patricks said, changing the conversation to English. Why would he do that? Does he not want her to hear my québecoise accent?

"*Ah bon*? It's not too hectic for you?"

What do I say? What's the right answer? If I say no, will she think I'm a crazy New Yorker? If I say, yes, it's hectic, exhausting, unrelenting, won't she think I'm just another stupid, greedy, crass American?

"Sometimes," I said.

I was cold and clammy the way you get right before you come down with the flu. It was all over. It had been a dream. What was I thinking? It was only a matter of time before she found out I'm a fraud. No family. My mother made money giving manicures and scrounging through rich women's closets and selling their clothes at second-hand shops. She was on her third marriage. I was not from Montreal. We were squatters in my mother's boyfriend's parents' apartment for a couple of years. I was from nowhere. I was nobody. She knew I didn't deserve her son. Even if Patrick fought for me and we married, she would never accept me and he would be torn between us. Soon enough he would realize I was not the person he thought I was and that his mother was right and then he'll have an affair and we'll divorce and I'll be alone anyway so why not avoid all the misery?

Ça va? Patrick looked at me in the rearview mirror.

I nodded and tried to smile. My throat was closed tight.

Patrick pulled up in front of a Haussmann building with ironwork trellises at each window. On another day I would have found it enchanting. In this moment, all I saw was metal and cement. Forbidding. *Interdit.*

Tu peux m'aider, cheri? She wanted him to carry her bag in.

Patrick went to the hatch and pulled out her bag. She turned to me.

Amusez-vous bien à Chartres.

Merci.

She got out. I took her place in the front. Her perfume was Cabochard.

I watched as they walked up together to the carved wooden double door. They stood and talked for a minute. Then, quick *bisous*.

He jogged down the steps and climbed back into the car. Eager. Excited.

On y va, he said.

He looked over at me. He saw something was wrong.

"I need to get back to the hotel. I'm so sorry. Such a good idea to go out to Chartres but it might have been a bit ambitious for me. I had a helluva week last week and I'm realizing I'm not feeling so great. I think I need to go lie down. I'm sorry."

"Oh, okay. Sure."

He drove. We didn't talk. It only took a few minutes to get me back to the Lutetia. He put the gear into park and shut off the engine.

"Are you okay? Should I have picked up my mom first and then come get you?"

"No—no. It's not that. Everything's fine. I'm just. I just got hit with—I just don't feel 100%. That's all."

"Okay," he touched my cheek. "You look so pale. Go take *un grand dodo*."

He was being adorable. So tender. So understanding.

"Thank you. I'll feel better after I lie down."

"Okay, great. So—dinner?"

"Sure!" I was outside the car now.

"I'll come by around 7?" He leaned across to look up at me, the seatbelt cutting across his chest.

"Wonderful—thank you, yes. That'll be great. I'm sorry for cancelling."

"Not a problem. Chartres has been there for seven hundred years. It can wait."

I nodded. Shut the door. Gave a wave and then worked my way up the stairs to where the doorman was holding the door open for me.

The moment I was in the lobby I rushed to the elevator. When I got to my room I threw the key to the bed and raced to the bathroom. Oh my god, I was so sick. I avoided looking in the mirror. I pulled on the most comfortable clothes I could find, then sat on the edge of the bed and dialed the front desk. I felt like I was committing a crime. What was it Valmont said again and again? *It's out of my control.*

When the bellhop knocked, I opened the door and watched as he put my bag on the golden trolley. I stepped into the elevator and it descended like a glacier.

I left a note for Patrick with the concierge.

My cab was waiting, luggage already stowed. I dropped into the backseat. The doorman tapped the roof and the cabbie pulled away from the curb.

"Charles de Gaulle?"

"Yes."

I put my sunglasses on and didn't take them off until I was in JFK.

• • •

"What are you doing here?" Clary drawled when I walked into the office Monday morning. She stopped turning the spoon in her mug of coffee. Her antennae were up. She knew something had happened.

"I thought you were taking some time off."

"Caught an early flight."

I headed into my office and closed the door behind me. There wasn't anything that needed my immediate attention but I threw myself into every project I could find. Even doing preliminary research on client work that wasn't due until March.

"Congrats," said Luke, my boss. "We landed the Portugal account and you're the lead. Hope you weren't planning on going anywhere for Christmas."

I wasn't. I spent every hour I could at the office and I planned on keeping it that way until I could breathe again.

Then, just when I had begun to find my rhythm, ignoring calls from Auntie Annie who wanted to do our annual high tea at the Carlyle, calls from Janet wanting to make plans for the holidays, when I least expected it, the blue slip in my mailbox. There was a package for me at the desk. I had no idea when I went to see what it was, imagining it was something from Bea, a homemade wreath, a jar of honey, squares of peppermint soap she found at some craft fair. But it wasn't from Bea.

It was the box of plates.

As the elevator carried me up to my apartment, I held it in my arms.

What was I going to do with it? I couldn't leave it somewhere. I couldn't drop it at Goodwill. I couldn't open it. In the end, I stuffed it into the bottom of a closet and crawled onto the sofa where I stayed until the next morning. Calling in to the office to say I would be late. Dragging myself to the shower. Pulling on clothes. Wearing my hair scraped back into a chignon low on my neck so I didn't have to deal with it.

But from that moment on, I felt like I was always on alert. I could never know what would trigger the creature, all teeth and screeching like the beast in *Alien*, to land on my chest and rip out my heart by the mouthful.

Once, in a taxi on the way to JFK, months and months after November, Diana Ross came on the radio singing *Someday We'll Be Together*. At first, I tried to sink into the song and find pleasure in the pain, but the pain was unmanageable and I had to shout at the driver to turn it off, but it was too late. Even with the radio off and the traffic sounds all around me, the song was now playing in my head and nothing could drown it out.

There were days when I would think, he could find me. The woman in the shop had my card. He could go back, get the card, blast into my life with rage and seeking an explanation and I would drop to my knees. Penitent. *I'm sorry. I'll make it all better. I'll fix everything if you can forgive me.* For a while I could play out that story over and over but, eventually, it faded. Why would he? What if I reached out? I know his name, his address. But what would I say? *Hey, remember me? You still up for impressing me with that best in the world cinnamon toast you learned how to make in Japan? How about we get together? I know I walked out on you, but—*

I kept thinking I would. So many drafts of that letter did I write, but as the days slipped past and then weeks became months, the fantasy became impossible to feed.

Joan Armatrading singing *Down to Zero* was the only song I could listen to. That, and *Bring on the Night*, on repeat.

. . .

Someone is pulling up the shades and opening the window. It's Ellen.

"Good morning," she says.

Why is Ellen here?

"Where's Bea?"

Ellen pours water into a glass for me and helps me drink it. One of the nurse people who are always bickering comes in to clean me up. She tries to be pleasant even though I know she can't stand me.

Ellen sits back in her chair, pulls out a half-eaten pack of red licorice from her pocket and tugs off a rope of it. I remember red licorice. I loved gnawing on it at the Fireman's Fair.

"Nice breakfast," I say.

"I'd offer you some, but you probably can't have any."

"I can have it, but I'm so sick of getting sick, I'll pass."

She nods and rocks in the chair.

I like that about Ellen. She isn't looking for anything from me. She isn't offering me anything. She's just sitting there. And I'm just here, dying.

. . .

Ellen has already left when Bea walks in. Her cheeks are flushed. She is so healthy, god. She must have been out in the woods or fields or wherever the hell she goes. Everything about her in this moment is vibrant, radiant.

Bea's hands are cool. They hold my forehead. Press on my cheeks.

"Bea?"

"Yeah, baby."

My eyelids feel wrecked—like they have been on fire.

"One time I asked Mom who she loved more—you or me."

"You asked Janet about love?"

"It was in California. We were walking down the street. She was holding my hand and we had to stop at the crosswalk and I just asked her."

"Did she have an answer?"

"Yeah. She said it doesn't work like that."

Bea sits in the rocking chair. She tips it back and forth in a small, steady motion. The dogs settle as near as they can without getting too close to the runners.

"Well," she says eventually. "That's true."

"You don't love your dogs all the same?"

"Nope."

"So then you love one more than the other."

"No."

This is so typical. I'm trying to have a conversation with her and she shuts me out. I don't have the energy to get her to tell me what she is thinking. I turn my head away from her and gaze at the painting above the battered green bureau. I wonder where she got it. It's really good, but I'm done talking to her. I'm not asking her anything.

Bea stills the rocker.

"You want me to explain love?"

I shake my head. Maybe that's what I wanted, but I don't care anymore. No wonder she never married. Who could put up with her?

"They killed the mother," she says.

I look over. Her eyes are wide, sad. Her chin slightly tipped up. She cups her elbows in each hand.

"Humans come into the world, naked and alone. The plan was for them to land in the mother's love. They would grow in that pure stream of love. And because they were loved, wholly, their heart always stayed open, trusting, knowing love, believing in love. They get older and romantic love is crowned with the orgasm, ecstasy. The ecstatic experience awakens their heart and all they want to do is be dazzled by how beautiful and magical this world is and live from there of love into love into love.

But it got all fucked up. They killed the mother. They made her believe she was evil and hideous. They crushed her spirit, which is how the mother's love got diseased. So when the new human arrives, it is bathed in poison. The river is toxic. The new human doesn't get that drenching, heart opening love and so here we are. In this mess. All because of the hatred toward women, which is hatred toward the earth. The shackling, raping and destruction of women is exactly what we do to the trees, the meadows, the bugs, the lichen, the woods, the sheep, the elephant, the tiger, the vole. Dolphins, tortoises, frogs. Nobody cares. When they killed her, they killed us all."

"Jesus. That's what you think about love?"

She doesn't answer me, of course. Did she really think I was going agree with her version of the apocalypse? Christ on a stick.

"Well, gosh, Bea. Thanks for that. What a comfort. I can rest easy now, knowing you have such dark and soul-crushing beliefs."

Bryan raps at the door.

"Hey there *mademoiselle*," he says. "I brought the pictures you asked for."

Bryan sets a few photos onto my lap. I pick them up, one at a time.

He and Clem playing badminton in their backyard. Clem at soccer practice.

Should I tell Bea that I want her to marry Bryan?

Bea helps Bryan turn me onto my side, change the sheets, put on clean clothes. Even if it is a tee shirt and cotton gym shorts, at least it's not a nightgown in the middle of the day. I like that I still have standards in this hell. I've made it clear to Bea how I want things to go right up to the end.

Bryan carries the bundle of sheets out, then returns to the rocker. The meds have kicked in. A bath and clean clothes keeps the edge off the misery. The sores in my mouth are epic and the numbing stuff they rub on them does nothing but make my tongue thick and heavy. I can feel myself start to doze.

I look over at my sister. Has she never been in love? Is that why she lives with such an ugly nightmare of the world?

I gesture to her to put the bed into full recline. She comes over and presses the button. The motor hums. I sink back into the pillow as it lowers me down. Even if it was only three days, I knew love. I breathed in every bit of him and never in my life, before or since, have I ever felt so alive. It was love.

the day of the morphine does not go as planned

They say that a mother bat can hear her baby and identify it among thousands of other baby bats squeaking in a darkened cave.

Bea learned about the amazingness of bats from Mrs. Stewart who kept the guano in a special metal can in the garage. Bat poop! Bea could imagine Janet's reaction if she had ever told her how preciously Mrs. Stewart guarded this fertilizer, but she didn't want to be mocked by Janet or, for her mother to ridicule Mrs. Stewart either.

Bats were marvelous, Mrs. Stewart explained as they kneeled side by side planting tulips. First, they made a series of precisely measured holes in the ground then, they would set the bulb, with its papery skin, its body a cross between a small onion and a large chestnut, into the hole with the pointy side up.

"Not only is it the one mammal in the world that can fly," Mrs. Stewart's words puffed out as she patted the dirt down, "but the mother bat has to fly around to get food while her baby hangs on to her by its claws and teeth until it can go off on its own which can be as long as six months."

"Ow," said Bea reflexively.

Mrs. Stewart smiled at Bea's response as if they shared a little joke.

"Bats are raised in harems," she continued. "If something happens to the mother, she explained, "then the pup will be adopted by another female bat."

The fact that lodged most deeply with Bea was that baby bats weigh around one-third of the mother's weight. She could never shake the image of what it would be like for a 150-pound woman to give birth to a 50-pound baby.

. . .

Bea steels herself against the sound of Janet's voice. There is no other sound in the world that causes everything within her to spin and ache. She listens as Janet explains that she is calling from a hotel in Lucknow. Bea is shocked by how clear the connection is. It's as if Janet is in the next room, not seven thousand miles away.

"You can't believe how beautiful everything is. The people. Why did we never know about this place? I wish you could see what I'm seeing, darling. The colors. It's like there is a magic. I wasn't even shocked to get your telegram. When we were in Kathmandu there was a ceremony. It lasted for days and days and I had a whole vision thinking of my girls. How proud I am of you both. My daughters. You have made it in this world on your own. Without a man. Each of you have carved out the lives you wanted to live as I always hoped you would. Independent. Strong."

Bea stands in the dark hallway, breathing in the medicinal stench of Mona's room as Janet's sunny commentary buzzes in her ear.

"I'm not the one you need to talk to right now."

Bea takes the receiver away from her ear and pushes the door open. She carries the telephone over to the bed and sets it up so that Mona doesn't have to struggle to hold the receiver. As she walks to the door, Bea can hear Janet's voice tinny and small because of the space between Mona's ear and the receiver, but she knows for Mona, the sound is rich and, that the sound of her mother's voice will rip her wide open.

Mona makes a small yelp. The whimper of recognition.

"Mommy." And then, she crumbles. "Mommy… Mommy, I'm sick. I'm so sick."

Bea shuts the door and battles with the desire to go down the hall and pick up the extension to listen. She has never read anyone's mail. She would never eavesdrop, and yet it takes all her inner willpower not to pick it up and listen in. What will Janet say? Will she distract Mona with stories of their hiking through Kathmandu? Will she promise Mona a Buddhist altar with a circle of bodhisattvas to chant in her honor? Or maybe Janet will surprise her. There has never been a time when Janet didn't surprise her. Maybe Mona will ask Janet a question she's never asked before and Janet, robed in her recently acquired mantle of enlightenment, will tell the truth.

Bea goes out to the porch and sits on her hands. She remembers the fight they had the night before Janet married Marcus.

September 1984. She and Henry were living in a tent by the construction site at the sugarbush. There was a utility sink with running water in the first building they'd begun to renovate, but that was only good for face splashing and teeth brushing. She figured swimming in the cold clear water of the lake constituted a shower, but then when the weather turned, she began stopping in on Ellen to take a hot shower once or twice a week. All of this felt wonderful. Sleeping outdoors, watching the progress day by day as the foundation was dug and the sill laid down to meet it. She had never felt so awake and connected to a place.

If she could have skipped the wedding, she would have. There was nothing she wanted to do less than get in the truck and drive five hours to some ridiculous hotel on a beach in Rhode Island, but her mother insisted she and Mona be in the wedding ceremony which was the most excruciating bit of all.

"At least I don't have to worry about what to wear," she said to Henry as she threw his dog bed and her duffle bag into the back of the truck. Her mom and Mona had picked out the dresses and the shoes. All she had to do was show up.

They pulled into Little Compton late Thursday afternoon. Traffic coming through Boston had been thick and Bea felt the congestion of humans with each mile she put between her and the sugarbush. She had planned to stay in the background, but her mother seemed insistent that she engage. At the dinner that night, hosted by the groom's brother, there was no assigned seating but Janet maneuvered it so that both Mona and Bea sat at the center of the trestle table. It was one of those glorious late September days when, after the previous week's chilly temperatures, warmth and humidity return like a final farewell kiss from summer not to forget her in the long months ahead.

The brother had a brown-shingled house with the windows trimmed in white. It sat on a bed of green grass and had views across the ocean to Cuttyhunk and the Elizabethan Islands. Bea thought it was just the striking contrast to her current living situation, a tent in a field amidst a job site, that made the house seem beyond luxurious, but even the jaded New Yorker was impressed.

"This is spectacular," breathed Mona.

The dinner was intended for the families to meet and get to know one another. The brother had a wife, and a son who was a couple years older than Bea. Marcus' parents were in their eighties. Auntie Annie was there, but not Janet's real sisters Ruby and Rose. There were some cousins and family friends. The whole group was less than thirty people. Henry seemed to be her ambassador since the only people not smitten with him were Mona and Janet. The brother's wife was super sweet to him, offering treats straight off the buffet table and talking to him in a dazzawuzza voice; the little cousins encouraged Henry to chase them around the lawn. Marcus rubbed Henry's head affectionately when he came by to say hello to the group sitting in white Adirondack chairs.

"Great dog," said the brother's son. Bea never knew what to say when people made comments like that, or when they'd say how handsome he was. She couldn't say thank you, it's not like she had anything to do with it. So, she just nodded and smiled.

After dinner, everyone walked down to the beach where a bonfire had been lit. The sand was cold and damp under her legs. Henry snuggled in and gave her warmth. That night, as they settled into the guest room above the garage where they had been assigned, Bea lay in bed with Henry snoring beside her and decided she would not be a brat. Tomorrow and Saturday, right up to the moment she and Henry climbed back into the truck on Sunday after the post-wedding brunch they were required to attend, she would be kind, helpful, supportive. Then, she'd get back to their hideaway that was tucked in an old sugarbush on a hill off a country road in Vermont and she would never think about any of this again.

But that's not what happened.

They were in Janet's hotel suite. Everybody in their dresses, uncomfortable shoes, wearing lipstick. Auntie Annie was making kir royales for the three of them.

"Sure you don't want?" She held one up to Bea. Bea shook her head, no.

Over the course of the day, Bea had continued to swallow down her annoyance at her mother's behavior, wanting to adhere to the commitment she'd made to herself the night before. Marcus' family was nice. They'd been very warm and welcoming to her. They'd been so sweet with Henry. But ignoring Janet without being able to leave the room was beginning to feel impossible. She was such a child. And she lied. She embellished, effaced, exaggerated. Her account of anything could not be trusted.

Auntie Annie and Mona left the room and headed down to join the guests gathering for the rehearsal dinner. Bea stayed slumped in one of the upholstered chairs, shoes off, her legs draped over the arm.

"Time to get a move on," Janet said, with a last glance in the mirror to admire herself.

"Don't you ever get sick of all the lies?" The words popped out like a fat toad.

"What are you talking about?" Janet was still in her bubble, completely disconnected from where Bea was calling from.

"Burying men as you leave them behind you? My father is dead.

Except, he's not. He lives at the same address where you left him. Maybe he was thinking you'll come back some day and he wants you to be able to find him. Mona's father wasn't a photojournalist who went missing in Vietnam. Raymond Bastarache has an art gallery in Sydney, Australia, mostly photography but paintings, too. Oh, and by the way, his parents are also still alive and so is his brother. Didn't think about that, did you?"

The bubble had been popped. Janet checked that the door was closed. She marched over to look down at Bea, who had not changed her position.

"What do you want me to say? What could I say that would change anything?"

Bea finally had her attention. She knew exactly what she wanted.

"I think an apology could be—"

"An apology!"

Janet's face filled with the blackest storm Bea had ever experienced. Maybe she knew it was in there but it had never been turned on her before. And yet, Janet knew to keep her voice down. She knew that she did not want one single person to overhear them, so she stepped even closer and threw Bea's feet to the ground, causing her to sit up properly.

"You rotten, ungrateful child. You have no idea. Do you know I couldn't get my own bank account? Did you? That I couldn't buy a house, or sign a lease to rent an apartment. That a divorcé with two kids isn't welcome anywhere? Do you know how much I can earn without a college degree? What kind of jobs I can get? I did my best by you girls. I gave you every opportunity I never had and you want an apology? You don't want lies? Fine. I was 19 when I got pregnant with you. 19. Unmarried. Do you have any idea the death sentence that was? Do you? And I found a way out. Jim's sister lived in Los Angeles and she took me in. For as long as she could. She had her own family to keep alive, but she gave me a room that I shared with her twelve-year-old daughter. I slept on a twin mattress getting up every two hours to go pee, stepping over her twelve-year-old daughter who slept on a mattress on the floor because I was in her bed. Let's just hope that's all the birth control that girl ever needed. Bessie let me stay there until it was time to go to the hospital and have you. Which, let me tell you Miss Needs An Apology, was a fucking nightmare. I'd rather have been eaten by sharks. And Bessie kept helping me through those first months which I don't even remember so when you were always asking for stories about what you were like when you were a baby, it's not that I'm lying. I don't remember anything. It's just a big blur of no sleep, worrying about how I'm going to get money, nipples stuck to my bra because of dried blood—get mastitis sometime see what that circle of hell is all about—clothes that don't fit, no money to get new ones, crying in laundromats and trying not to leave you on the steps of some orphanage so I could go kill myself."

"Oh please. You would never kill yourself."

"That's right. That's right. I made it through. I fought it out. And what is it you would prefer? Which of your little made up stories have you living some beautiful life that you think everyone else is having, everyone but you?"

Janet paused, shaken by her own intensity. They had both entered into an altered state. The air seemed to be holding them. No one else in the world existed except her and her mother. They were the only two people alive, in this hotel room where they had never been before and they would never be again. On the second floor with views out to the sea and red geraniums in a silver pot on the bureau. Bea watched the thoughts and memories crossing her mother's face. The chin slightly tilted up, eyes vacant, seeing something, watching some movie playing out from some long ago life. Her mother's reverie ended abruptly. She walked over to the vanity and shook out a cigarette from the pack. She lit it and put out the match with her exhale. She seemed exceedingly calm, too calm. She walked over to sit on the edge of the sofa that faced Bea. There was a brass ashtray on the small table between them.

"I met Ray at a blues club. Bessie knew someone who worked there and that's how I got a job hostessing, wearing a dress that would hide my belly that still hadn't gone down from having you. The guys were nice and the money was better than working at Woolworths. Plus you were sleeping when I left and when I got home."

She took a last drag and then crushed the butt into the brass dish. Somehow stronger from the nicotine. She lifted her chin as if daring Bea to judge her.

"I liked it. I liked dropping into that world where all the struggles of the day fell away and people laughed and got all dressed up. And then I met Ray. He let me come to his place, with you. He was doing okay. He had money. He was working for Paramount as an on-set photographer. Doing stills for the movies. And it was good. For a really long time. It was good. It might have been, looking back, that might have been," Janet's voice phlegms up and she coughs.

"And then, I got pregnant. I had done everything not to, but Ray said he was happy. He was always so good with you and I believed him so we got married because that was what you do. But then the four of us were too much for his place so we moved out to that apartment off Crenshaw Boulevard. It's what we could afford and I thought things were good and then, he went off on a shoot. And never came back."

Janet walked across the room to get another cigarette. She lit it, then spun around hard to look at Bea.

"Do you think I went asking him for an apology? No, I asked him for a divorce."

"Only once you had met Eddie and needed one." Bea has resumed her sprawl on the chair, determined not to let Janet's version change anything. Her bare feet hanging limp over the arm of the chair as if she could care less about anything Janet has just told her.

Janet sat back on the sofa and leaned over to exhale smoke directly into Bea's face. There was a dangerous look in her eyes. Cold. Her voice a twisted, low growl.

"Oh, aren't we clever. Little Miss Watchful writing up her comic book versions where she is always the hero. Just the facts? Is that it? Tell me, how did you like that fancy high school you went to? All your tennis lessons and pretty clothes. Oh, and the very expensive liberal arts college you went to? Paid for by Eddie. It was part of our divorce settlement. Something I had to fight for. But of course, Little Miss Head in the Clouds doesn't know anything about how she gets to float through life. His mother had made him get married and I was the patsy so I told him that unless he wanted me to tell everyone what was really going on, he would pay for your college. And you want me to apologize? Get out."

Janet jumped to her feet and kicked Bea's feet to the ground.

"Get out. And don't come back until you apologize to me."

Black Irish fury. Just like her grandfather. Bea remembered the crashing argument between Janet and her grandfather and realized it felt, through the floorboards, just like this.

Janet headed to the door. Bea sent a parting shot.

"Mona should know she has a father and that he is alive."

"Mona," her mother answered coolly, the words riding on a straight stream of smoke, "has never asked." The door clicked shut behind her.

Game. Set. Match.

• • •

When she hears no more sounds, Bea pushes the door open slowly, ready to pull back if they are still talking, but Mona is on her side, the phone receiver tucked against her chest, its base held in place by her swollen belly.

Everything go okay with the call with Janet? She wants to ask but the words refuse to budge from where they sit in a confused clump at the edge of her tongue.

• • •

Mona had made the plan before she ever called Bea to come and get her. This was what she wanted; the least Bea could do is let

Mona be in charge about how she would leave this world since her diagnosis was without hope and Mona had no interest in any treatment. Mona wanted to make this all go away as fast as she could. She chose the day she would stop eating. The last thing she asked for was chocolate cake with whipped cream and fresh raspberries. Then, they were not to give her anything. No food, no water. Nothing. Bea imagined Mona's fierce heart saw this as the final test of her willpower and took some kind of satisfaction in having control, doing it her way even if that meant every hour was worse than the last. Bea knew that underneath the flippant attitude and sharp words, Mona was ashamed to be so sick, to have failed in such an epic, ungainly way.

· · ·

"Oh my god," Mona says, not even shaping all the syllables but letting the sounds all bleed together in pain. "I'm so thirsty."

She looks up at Bea, her face filmed with sweat, her eyes fevered.

"I keep dreaming that I'm at work walking toward the soda machine, but I never get there. Please tell me I am not going to the office when I die."

"No baby," says Bea, wishing she could feed a chip of ice into Mona's mouth. "Never again. I promise."

"My head. Like quitting coffee but a thousand times worse."

"I know, baby. It's the blood sugar going down. I'm so sorry. I'm so sorry."

Mona had postponed the next morphine as long as she could, trusting that if she got it at her weakest, then she would slip away once and for all. But that was a plan, an intellectual idea. Actually doing it was excruciating.

"What was the point?" Mona's voice is hard to understand. Her lips are cracked and swollen. Her every breath is labored. Bea wants to stroke her but she knows the touch will cause even more pain.

"The point of what, sweetie?"

"Me." Her eyes are hollow, tormented. "You." Her voice makes whistling sounds as it falls and breaks over the words.

"I was such—and we," her mouth has gone dry. Mona begins to cough. The coughing gets worse before it quiets again.

"We could have been friends." Mona looks at Bea, an invitation.

Bea's head floods with too many things at once. She wants to say exactly what Mona wants to hear. The exact right words. What is the best thing she could say to Mona right now? But she doesn't get a chance. Ellen raps at the door. It's time.

Bea gets up and sees everybody is in the hallway as she had asked.

• • •

That morning, she had found out Bryan would not be here today and she couldn't tell Mona. Mona had made her promise that Bryan would be the one to administer the morphine. Bryan always talked about his little girl, Clem. Clementine was ten years old and, if you believed Bryan, the brightest light to ever land on the planet. Instead of triggering jealousy, Mona sank deeply into the stories of what Clem ate for breakfast, what she said to the school assembly, how she named her stuffed turtle Moses and how she knew all the words to *I Wanna Dance With Somebody*.

Mostly though, Mona sank into how much Bryan loved his little girl. She wrapped it around her like a shawl.

But Clem has an overnight field trip to Ticonderoga and Bryan is a chaperone.

Ellen found Bea in the kitchen scrubbing the sink. The sink hadn't been dirty to begin with but now it was immaculate. Bea rubbed the porcelain dry.

"What the fuck?" said Bea, whipping the dishtowel against the countertop.

Ellen pointed toward Mona's room to say, *careful, she will hear you.*

"How could he do that to her?" Bea whispered angrily. "How could he just decide to make some excuse about his kid's school?"

"Well," said Ellen, "Have you considered the possibility that he has gotten very close to you both and he is just not able to do this? It's different and he knows it?"

"It's his job," Bea hissed.

"Maybe in this case he's developed some strong feelings and he can't do it."

Bea crumpled into the corner. Ellen was right. It was better that it wasn't him, but Bea had promised Mona.

"I can't tell her," whispered Bea.

"So, don't." Ellen snapped the refrigerator door open and pulled out the jar of pickled cauliflower. She ate one of the florets slowly.

"Distract her. Give her something else to think about."

"Like what?" asked Bea.

· · ·

Bea went out and told Giusita and Diogo what was happening. Ellen went home to get the cassette and boombox. Bea pulled Ginny and Paulette out to the side porch.

"I don't care if you burn each other's house down tonight, I will personally give you each a gallon of fucking gasoline to do it, but for six minutes you are gonna stop thinking about how much you hate each other, go in there, think about my sister, generate happy energy and dance your asses off."

· · ·

Bea stands by the doorway and begins to flick the light on and off. Mona looks up as everyone crowds into the room.

"What—," she croaks.

Ellen clears the bureau and sets the boombox down on top of the dresser scarf. She presses play and the first beats fill the air.

Mona tries to assert control. This is unexpected. She did not plan for this.

Her voice is swallowed into the sounds building up to Sister Sledge singing *We Are Family* and all the bodies begin dancing. Mona's wary confusion relaxes. She understands. Mona points to Bea to step away from flashing the light. *Dance*, her finger commands. Bea dances.

The song ends with a slow fade out and Ellen helps it along by lowering the volume. Giusita and Diogo exit the room. Bea turns and sees a man, maybe in his late 30s, standing in the doorway with a medical bag in his hands.

Ellen snaps off the box and hoists it onto her shoulder after blowing a kiss to Mona. She steps past the man in the doorway. Paulette and Ginny, working from opposite sides of the bed, fluff and smooth the bedding and help Mona back into a full recline. They press Mona's hands before they leave.

And then, it is just Bea, Mona and the stranger.

The room is quiet but still reverberates with energy. Bea pushes Mona's hair back from her brow. Somehow her cheeks are pink and flushed as if she had been dancing, too. Mona gazes up at the man seated next to her bed. He is clean shaven and wears a navy button-down shirt with soft ecru chinos.

"Patrick?" Her chin so small against the pillow, her eyes luminous.

The man looks across to Bea who wills him, with all the power she can summon, to not crush it.

"I'm right here, honey," he says without missing a beat. Bea presses a fist against her mouth. She doesn't want to make a sound and have Mona turn to see her crying.

He lifts Mona's wrist and holds it in the gentle curve of his fingers.

"Oh Patrick, I'm so sorry I left." Her chest makes sharp, staccato movements. "Patrick I'm so sorry. I'm so sorry. I'm so sorry I left. So sorry. So sorry—"

He continues smiling and then, god bless, him, this man who had only walked into the room two minutes before, says, "it's okay honey, I'm here with you now."

At this, Mona's tears stop and Bea's explode as if a volcano she didn't even know was inside of her begins to pour forth snot and sobs that heave up and over her back to crash through across her face, chest, belly.

"Wait," Mona coughs. Her head doesn't turn all the way but she is talking to Bea.

"One more." Her lips are yellow and cracked, a white mucus in the corners.

Bea grips her knees to help her shaking breath find the steadiest voice that she can through her sobs.

"Once upon a time, on a sunny day in January, a tiny baby, came into the world. She had a sister. A kind of weird sister—"

Mona's chin inches left to right, *no*.

"—sometimes—they would play together in the grass—pretend to be witches—making potions. Gathering up weeds and dandelions and making crowns. Lying back on the grass and looking up at the trees, to the sky."

"Stories," Mona says on a scratch of breath.

"The sister would tell stories. Made up stories about a girl who became a butterfly and went on adventures."

ELIZABETH DUVIVIER

Mona's eyes close, but not all the way. Patrick slips the needle out from under her skin and holds Mona with one hand on her shoulder, one on the wrist.

Bea presses her face into the space next to Mona's body where it is cool and dry. Maybe she could stay here, just like this, forever.

a forever home

Like the very day she and Setsuko had pledged to be best friends forever, she came home to find her mother pulling out suitcases because she was getting married and they were moving across the country to Massachusetts. Like the time she arrived at the abandoned lot that was filled with wildflowers only to find someone had mowed it all down. Like the time she came home to the phone ringing, having just signed the papers selling the sugarbush to Giusita and Diogo, and Mona needed to be picked up immediately and taken somewhere private and beautiful because she only had a couple of weeks to live.

Like that. Life doesn't care about your plans.

Mona didn't say, bring me home. She couldn't. They didn't have a home.

Such a strange concept, home. Bea slows her rocking to a stop.

There has been no relief from the low-pressure, the thick humid air that makes the mosquitoes more intense, that flattens any volition she might have had to do anything. The dogs have dug under the porch for shelter from the heat, laying their bellies onto the cool earth. She can hear them panting. The radio had said thunderstorms were coming, as if any idiot couldn't feel that tension building in the air. The question was, when.

She thinks about Eddie's house that was always cool, even on hot days, the house he grew up in. Every single morning he drove out route 16 to jump onto the Mass Pike and head into his office in Boston. Summers meant Route 6 to Hyannis for the ferry to Nantucket. Those were his three roads. He never lived anywhere else and never would.

If you never leave, does that make it home?

Cage, Janet would say.

Where's your home, dear? Asked Sally's grandfather.

Once, when she was living in Cupertino, Bea went back to where she grew up. It was a three day holiday. Office closed. Everyone spending the weekend having backyard barbeques or heading into San Francisco with a group of friends.

She woke up Friday morning feeling lost. The day stretched out blankly. Usually she loved a whole day open, but for some reason it felt odd, like she was supposed to be somewhere having fun. Even Mrs. Cooper was surprised to find her in the kitchen making coffee.

"Aren't you doing something for the weekend?" she asked Bea.

Why didn't she have friends, she wondered as she pushed herself back and forth on the loveseat glider that was in the backyard of the house. Guys had asked her out at work, but they weren't looking to be friends. She had reached out to the Tamamotos but they were spending the long weekend in Mendocino.

She thought about Setsuko. That was the best friend she had ever had. How long did they get to be together? They met in kindergarten and Janet had taken Bea away to Wellesley the summer before she turned fourteen. So, eight years. Definitely the longest she had ever been friends with anyone. Their connection was so easy, so light. Whoever got a new Lulu didn't read it until they could read it together. Bea's favorite issue had Lulu on the cover wearing a papoose on her back made from a baby doll carriage. She still had it, one of the few things that she had hung on to all these years. And they both loved Pippi Longstocking.

For Halloween, Setsuko's mother drew three dots on each of their cheeks for freckles and then braided their hair so it would stick out on both sides. Bea's braids were really good, Setsuko's hair was a little too slick and heavy, but they were both Pippi. Knocking on doors, collecting candy. Holding hands before crossing the street.

"Going somewhere?" the woman asked as Bea made a thermos of lemonade and stacked two sandwiches and an apple into her beach bag.

"Yeah," said Bea. "Gonna head down to L.A. I grew up there."

The woman said good luck in a rather discouraging way, which Bea didn't understand until she began driving down the freeway.

It took way more hours than she had planned. Long weekend meant heavy traffic. Her plan was to get a hotel nearby and spend the night. Walk over to the elementary school, visit the little lunch counter where Janet sometimes took them on Saturdays for tortillas and beans where the man with the beautiful brown eyes would call her Rosalita, but she never got out of the car.

She had remembered dandelions growing through the cracks in the sidewalks and roses tangled with honeysuckle. Girls with barrettes in their hair. The greengrocer with boxes of avocados and strawberries by the door.

But not this. They lived here? She kept checking and double checking the street signs. This was where they lived? She pulled over across from where Setsuko's house had been. That small backyard with the white pebbles that they would stack and count and lay into rings. And all the houses that had been next to it. The entire block was now one large complex of condos or apartments or whatever they were called. Living units. Built from the cheapest materials they could get away with. Everything was run down. It looked like a war zone.

She sat, her wrists limp in her lap. Her mouth dry. Her memories erased.

She took the 10 out thinking she would pick up the 1 to head north, but instead, she pulled over not far from the Santa Monica Pier. Unable to see the road. Finding it hard to breathe. She sat in the car with the engine off, until it became too hot even with the windows down. She got out and walked down to the beach. Smoggy sky.

Sand was gray and gritty with bits of trash mixed in. A city beach.

The ocean valiantly washing in and out, but there would be no resurrection today.

She sat until the hot feeling was gone. An emptiness ballooned in its wake. Her chest felt cavernous. Like when her mother threw the stones out the kitchen door.

A couple twists of cigarette butts were within reach. Bea scooped them up and tucked them in her pocket to throw away later. She watched the tide inch closer. A slow, steady, inevitable progression up to where she was sitting. Two steps forward, one step back. She watched it eat away at the squat cylinder of sand some kid left behind. Empty of imagination. Dumped out from a pail shaped like a turret. A plastic pail produced by the thousands with the same indentations molded into each one. When the turret was nothing more than a wet lump, Bea walked back to the car.

. . .

She gets up from the rocker. The dogs wriggle out from under the porch and hurry to catch up with her as she walks up to sit under the great matriarch of the sugarbush. The magnificent maple tree that she actually named. She couldn't help it.

This much beauty and endurance deserved recognition, giving it a name, somehow, says I see you, I love you. She puts her hand onto one of its strong roots that winds up and down through the earth. The bark has pushed up from under the ground and forced the moss to split. Her hand pops off the root as if she had touched a hot stove. It reminds her, suddenly, of that day outside the co-op.

It was his sneakers. They were dirty with a big split. He had wrapped packing tape over the top of one toe but the tape was filthy, worn-out, and curled back to show the hole underneath. His teeth mossy. She hadn't even recognized him. Not even his voice.

"Carrot Girl, as I live and breathe."

She had just come out from the co-op with her farmshare pick up, the tote bag heavy on one shoulder. She looked at the drug-ravaged face. Stringy hair combed long behind his ears. Bea didn't know who it was. Was it the guy at the comic store she had shown her drawings to? Who would know *Carrot Girl*? But then, with a punch, she knew who it was. Ricky Stewart. He smiled and did a little move, twitching his shoulders, stroking a hand over his head, as if nothing had changed and he was flirting with her on the third floor. She couldn't speak. There was a stink about him like rotting meat. The woman with him looked older, harder.

"Let's go," the woman said to Ricky.

"I'll be right there," he said to her. "This is my friend."

The woman wore boots with sharp heels and a short jacket that didn't close all the way across her chest.

"Hurry up," she said. She walked ahead a few paces and then stopped at the corner to wait for him.

Bea looked over to her truck where Henry sat in the passenger seat watching her, his head tilted to one side. That was her real life, the truck, Henry. What was this happening in front of her? The weight of the bag was too much and she had to shift it to the other shoulder but instead it dropped to the ground with the loops in both hands.

This was Ricky Stewart?

His words rambled, his eyes darted. His body unable to be still.

"What are you doing here anyway? You live here? I have a place near here. Big piece of land, beautiful. You should come see it sometime. Well, not today. I won't be up there today. I uh, actually," he laughed, again trying to swagger like he was telling Bea about a drop in the stock market that he could easily shrug off.

"I had to sell most of it, well, let's be honest, we were always about truth, right? Had to let it all go. For now, for now — "

"Richard," the woman barked from the corner.

"Gotta go — " he jogged up to the woman, his sneaker flapping. Bea had not moved. She watched as the woman held him by the elbow and they huddled. She was trying to get him to do something. He broke away from her and shuffled back to where Bea stood, the canvas bag of vegetables between her feet.

"Hey, listen," he said. Bea had to take a step back. His smell. His ickiness. He didn't seem to notice.

"My friend and I are late for work and need to catch a bus but she forgot her bus pass," he shrugged.

Was he asking her for money?

"Just, you know, five bucks. Three bucks. Just so we can get to work. I'll totally get it back to you. Just a loan."

Bea looked over at the woman who was watching them. She let the handles of the tote bag drop to the ground and dug out her wallet. She took all the bills she had and held them out to him.

He grabbed them with the bite of a hungry dog.

"Great," he said. He loped back up the sidewalk to where the woman stood, her fists in the pockets of her jacket.

"Just a loaner. I'll get it back to you," he called out with a wave.

Bea watched as the woman tried to pull on his arm but he skittered to the right. The woman followed close on his heels and they disappeared around the corner.

A man in a down vest came out of the co-op and began picking up the potatoes and onions that had rolled out of her bag. He lifted the bag and handed it to Bea. She pulled it into her chest, holding it like a baby.

"You okay?" the man asked.

"Thank you," Bea said. "Thank you."

She crossed the street over to her truck and climbed in, the bag on her lap. Henry thumped his tail and licked her cheek. She felt the terrible heat rolling up. She pushed the bag to the floor and flung open the door just in time to vomit onto the curb. She was panting, sweat on her brow. She wiped at her mouth, her forehead. She tipped her head back onto the headrest and tried to breathe.

That night she walked around the house with an old pillowcase, like a burglar, but instead of stealing her pearl necklace or silverware, she dug through every drawer, every old journal, every box of stuff to gather up every bit of anything she had that might remind her of Ricky Stewart.

The pillowcase was tossed onto a brushpile and squirted with lighter fluid before she threw a match on it. She sat with the fire until it was low enough to pull the hose over and sprayed water onto the embers which hissed before, eventually, it went silent, dead.

In the morning, she followed the dogs as they walked by the charred wood, they paid no interest to it. She felt lighter, purged.

No hard feelings, she said to the pile of blackened bits. And she meant it.

She followed the dogs up the hill for their walk that would carry them into the woods and out to the stream. She looked across the hills, the sky, this beautiful life. Would she have made these choices if not for Ricky Stewart? She whistled for the dogs and of course, Henry was the first one to come bounding, reaching her side before the others. What a good boy. What a love. This life. Henry. She was nothing but happy that day, deeply happy.

. . .

Mosquitoes are swarming, but she doesn't care. Her clothes and baseball cap have so much of Giusita's repellent soaked into them she doesn't even need to reapply. She reeks of eucalyptus, thyme and cinnamon and whatever else is in there. The dogs find a spot in the shade. They like sitting up here. The view is so lovely, even on sweltering, hazy days. Or, maybe they know Henry is here. Bea doesn't pretend to understand how dogs think, but she knows Little Bear went into a deep depression after Henry was gone. It wasn't her imagination.

They sat with her then, although it was anything but hot. November was bitter, but the ground hadn't yet frozen, so she could bury him here. And this was where she sat when it rained, when flurries blew through.

She had dragged the old tent she and Henry had lived in and set it up under Mabel, for the dogs. She put down thick bedding and left the flap partially up so they could look out. Sometimes, when her bones were so stiff she could hardly unbend her legs, she would crawl in and pull the sleeping bag up over her to get some relief from the cold, but mostly, she didn't care. She let the wind whip her as hard as it liked.

She couldn't leave the mound where Henry lay curled underneath the soft dirt with big slabs of stones to keep him safe from animals digging him up. He was wrapped in the softest green wool blanket she had. She'd put a dog bed underneath him. Around his head she had placed flowers, dried lavender, his favorite biscuits, and the small purple towel that was in his crate when she carried him out of Randi's shelter. The towel was ragged, stained, nearly gray.

She couldn't leave the mound because her sense of what was real was spinning. She could not believe he was gone. It had happened. And, it wasn't possible.

On those long, slow, sweet days driving together across the country as they left California behind, she realized there was nowhere to return to, nowhere she called home. The tiniest bit of connection to that sense of place was her grandparents' house but she would never go there now. It would destroy the glimmer she could still touch on.

So as Bea and Henry passed through each state, she looked around. Maybe here? She felt like the mother in *Make Way for Ducklings*. Each time it just wasn't right. Colorado seemed good, but then the hippies made her uncomfortable; they were too unhinged. The flatness of Iowa wasn't terrible but the people felt foreign to her, as if she didn't speak their language. She almost stayed in Ohio. The farmland and Amish Hex signs a warm memory of driving to Nana's, but some dudes in a white van caused her to get Henry back in the truck and get out of the campground so fast that she left her shorts and t-shirt on the clothesline she'd rigged up.

She didn't stop again until they had reached Albany. By then, she was so close to Vermont she figured she might as well, since that was the original plan. Plus, upstate New York had that same bad, dank energy as San Francisco. What was that about? She didn't know. And she never told anyone so she didn't know if she was the only one who felt things like that. She didn't really care, it was just a sort of vague wondering. Do other people feel what she feels? But she definitely felt a certain relief, some kind of validation that she was not crazy when they crossed into the green mountains and everything felt better.

For days after Henry was killed, Bea didn't so much walk across the fields as pace. She was unable to sit. Unable to be near anyone. She moved one foot in front of the other out to the perimeter and then back again. Luka and Little Bear stayed vigilant with her.

When she finally could sit by him, it took more days. Sitting. Under the maple. Sorting through it all. Hundreds upon thousands of thoughts like seeds in a terrible mess. All mixed together. Lentils, rice, corn, millet, peas. The miller's daughter had an angry little man to make it all go away, but Bea had no one to help her. She had to sort it all out herself.

Hunters wear neon orange. They look for things to kill. They are allowed to do this. Laws say yes. You can go shoot something alive, breathing, finding food for its family, helping its pups learn how to find water. Something beautiful and good. Hunters want to kill it. This is their pleasure. People like death. They like killing. The library overflowing with murder mysteries. It's not just hunters. This is their entertainment, their pleasure. They want to read about killing. Again and again.

"Are you sitting shiva?" It was Ellen in boots, snowpants, winter jacket, hat, scarf, gloves. She put a blanket under her and sat. She had a thermos with her.

Shiva? Shivering? Was this Vermont talk? Bea's eyes were clouded.

"Sitting shiva," Ellen explained as she unscrewed the thermos and poured hot tea into a cup for Bea. The steam wavered weakly against the bitter cold. "It's what Jews do when someone dies. You sit for a week. You share stories. Remember things they did."

Bea sipped at the cup.

"It's not coffee."

"No," said Ellen. "I figured you probably don't need to be kept awake."

"I can't sleep," said Bea.

"You could do this inside, you know. It'd probably be better for you."

Bea could feel her jaw slack, her tongue unable to shape words. She shook her head, no.

"This helps. My head. I can't get my thoughts. It's all—It's all—"

Ellen nods and rocks a bit as the wind kicks up.

"Listen, Bea—how about we go inside for a little while. The tent is not really enough for them."

Bea looked over at Luka and Little Bear curled into each other as the wind shook the side of the tent. They were cold. Her eyes filled with tears.

"I'm so sorry, I'm so sorry."

"It's okay. They're fine. Let's just go see if we can get a fire going, okay?"

Her legs stumbled and struggled down the hill. Ellen held her by one arm. She was the scarecrow. Knees buckling. Stuffing knocked out of her.

Inside, she sat on the sofa where she and Henry had snuggled and the pain shot through her. She jumped up.

"I can't. I can't sit here."

Ellen looked up from where she had gotten the wood stove going and shut the grate.

"You can't sit outside. Look, the dogs are getting warmer. See? This is good for them. I'm going to bring in a rocking chair from the porch, okay? Just stay put for one minute."

• • •

The rocking chair she had been sitting in all morning. Bea gazes across the field to where it sits on the porch, where, from here, it looks like a piece of dollhouse furniture. She looks over at the dogs now panting in the heat. They had been so cold that day.

• • •

Ellen got her to sit in the rocking chair by the wood stove. Ellen coaxed her to talk, but even Bea knew it was a jumble of words, like puzzle pieces dumped onto a table. Nothing fitting together. Was this insanity? Is this what happens? All the things that never made sense, that no one could ever explain, come rushing in all at once and break your brain?

Joan of Arc got burned alive for trying to stop a war. But the wars never stop, isn't that what Janet told her? They climb into boats and find new places to hunt and kill. And massacre. At Middlebury she learned about the Wabenaki, the Seneca. Eddie's house in Nantucket? That belonged to the Wampanoag who had helped the English people survive. They had helped them and then the English annihilated them. All those names around Wellesley? Massachusetts, Natick. That house of Marcus' brother in Rhode Island looking out to the sea? And people have champagne and cut down trees for more view and eat lobster. Can no one feel it?

How do you sit shiva for a holocaust? Martin Luther King, Jr. trying to get people to see the truth. Shot. Dead. He wasn't carrying a gun. He was trying to talk sense into people. Setsuko's parents and the internment they would never talk about. That was in California. People she knew. Massacre is everywhere. Cambodia, South Africa. Right now, Bosnia. The hunters are everywhere.

"It's just, it's just—" Bea tried to explain to Ellen. "I don't know how I can stay alive anymore. How are we supposed to be able to stay alive? I thought coming up here would be—I thought I could make a place. But there is no place."

The Romans would mutilate and destroy, eating grapes, while animals were in agony, people being slaughtered. Blood dripping into sand. Cheering. Cruelty and Killing. Entertainment. The pleasure in killing. It's never going to end.

"I don't want to be here anymore."

"You don't have to stay," said Ellen. "You don't have to stay, it's okay."

"At all. Like be here, at all."

"I know what you meant and that's okay."

Ellen opened the grate and jammed in two big logs before wrenching the handle to make sure the woodstove was shut tight. She stood and slapped wood grit from her pants.

"How about we just get the dogs some food? We'll just get them something to eat, okay?"

. . .

That's how she did it, Bea sees this now. Ellen let her be jumbled, heartbroken, without hope. She never tried to get Bea to think differently or see differently. She just got Bea to focus on Luka and Little Bear and the wood that needed to get stacked and the potatoes that needed to be peeled. And help Giusita and Diogo with the pigs. And make sure the chickens were warm enough and that their water didn't freeze.

In late December, the month after Henry was shot, Bea was slumped against the passenger side door of Ellen's VW as they headed back to the sugarbush. It was late on a Saturday afternoon. And it would be dark in another hour. Ellen had shown up early that morning and wrangled Bea into her car. They spent the morning gathering up donations of blankets, paper towels and dog food from people's homes, the country store and the local elementary school that was having a holiday craft fair and had set up a crate for donations to the Humane Society. With the back of Ellen's car stuffed to the roof, they drove up to Burlington and pulled into a parking lot that was nearly full.

Bea held out her arms and let Ellen load them up just as they had done earlier in the week with stacks of wood. Inside the Humane Society, Bea could hear the barking from the cages and saw a kind of bucket line had been set up to get the arriving donations organized and set into place. It didn't take long, maybe an hour or so. There were a number of kids in the mix. All helping out. On a Saturday. When they were through, the staff gave them a big thanks. There was hot cocoa with tiny marshmallows and candy canes. The barking never stopped.

"I want to bring them all home with me," Bea said to Ellen who had pushed the plastic down on her candy cane and was sucking on it so the bottom became a thin point.

"Damn," said Ellen as the point broke off in her mouth. "Almost beat my own record." She crunched the candy. It made her a bit drooly.

"You want to bring them all home with you?"

"But I can't."

"Still, a good sign," Ellen said.

And it was. She wasn't better. She wasn't fixed, but she had felt the pulse of that room. She felt part of something bigger, something good. The ride home was beautiful. December had such shades of purple in its sky. Her heart began to ache again. Was this how it was going to be? Moments of ease where you think you might be okay followed by the grip of talons piercing the softest part of you.

"The hell?" Bea sat up as Ellen pulled her car to a stop next to a Toyota SUV. She looked over at Ellen. Whose car was in Bea's driveway? "Who is it?"

When Ellen shrugged, Bea knew that she knew. Ellen was a terrible liar.

The porch lights were on. The door opened and Luka and Little Bear came barreling out to greet her. Stepping out behind them were Janet and Marcus. On her porch.

"You called my mother?"

Ellen put the engine into reverse.

"Get out," she said to Bea. "I'll see you later. Thanks for the help today."

If Bea had felt that her sense of reality had finally begun to settle into place, having Janet and Marcus on her porch was a snow-globe turned upside down and shaken, hard.

"Quite a place you've got here," Marcus said as they sat in the kitchen eating the spaghetti he had made. He was impressed.

"No dining room," Bea countered. She hadn't thought about what it would be like to have people over for meals. It wasn't in her mind as she shaped the space. The kitchen was big enough for four people, but only just.

"Who needs a dining room?" Janet scoffed. She offered the basket of garlic bread to Bea. "I wouldn't change a thing."

Bea let them tell her about life in Providence. She watched as Marcus rubbed Little Bear's head but didn't give her any food from the table. Janet was taking classes at URI. Literature, Art History, Comparative Religion.

"Have you ever thought about becoming a Buddhist?" she asked Bea.

Bea had to laugh. She had struggled to eat the pasta. Eating and sleeping had become arduous in the past weeks, but as they sat with the dogs under the table, in the small kitchen, with the good smells—and her mom. Her mother right here in her kitchen as if it was the most normal thing in the world. And there was Marcus with his big bear energy. He was strong, easy, helpful. Something so comforting about him.

She couldn't believe she could feel a laugh, but there it was.

Only her mother, who moved through the world putting on lifestyles like an actress in a new play, would pose a question like that in absolute seriousness.

"Why are you laughing? I'm serious. I think it would really suit you."

"That's why I'm laughing."

Marcus insisted on doing the cleanup and sent them out to the living room.

"No coffee?" her mother asked.

"I haven't been sleeping great," said Bea, tipping back and forth in the rocker.

"I brought something for that." Janet set out a bottle with three rocks glasses. She cracked the bottle open and poured an inch into each of the tumblers.

"Take it," she held one out to Bea.

"My stomach already hurts, this will make things worse."

"Take it," Her mother set the glass into Bea's hand.

Marcus joined Janet on the sofa. They clinked glasses.

"To a great dog," Marcus said. "Who was taken from this world cruelly and wrongly, but when he was here, he was loved. He had a wonderful life. And I just want to say, here's to Henry. There will never be another one like him. One in a million."

Bea reached her glass across to tap on his glass. The tears were pouring down. She couldn't hold it back. She took a sip hoping it might help. It did. The burning flamed down her throat, up into her nose. She sipped again, liking how it stopped her from crying.

"Is this scotch?"

"Glenfiddich," said Marcus.

"Mom! Do you—" Bea didn't even get the whole question out.

"Of course I remember! Oh my god—you stole Eddie's father's scotch."

"I didn't steal it—I was going to replace it—"

"Until you found out it was a gift from Eddie's father to him when he graduated college. A ten-year old scotch when he got it in 1947, but of course by the time it went missing—"

Bea explained to Marcus. "A friend asked for a bottle of liquor and I took one I thought no one would notice cause it was way in the back and looked old."

"A friend who was running away to Canada to avoid the draft," adds Janet.

"Sounds like a noble cause," said Marcus, with a slow smile that started in his eyes and then stretched out across his lips.

"1937 Glenfiddich," Janet crowed, pouring herself another inch. She held out the bottle to Bea who accepted another inch, too. She could feel the medicine of the scotch. There was heat in her neck and in her chest. She realized she was so glad that she was not alone, that Janet and Marcus were here with her. Her toes tipped the chair back and forth. She admired the clean lines of her living room and the snapping flames behind the glass of the woodstove. And what a kind thing Marcus had said. He didn't have to do that. She hadn't expected that. So kind.

"His father died young," said Janet, looking pretty warm herself. "No doubt because of that battle-axe he married."

"Mom!"

"Oh please, you cannot sit there and tell me one good thing about that woman."

Janet's head was tilted back. Her cheeks were flushed. She was laughing, happy. They were laughing together.

"I liked her dog."

"Her dog didn't even like her. Didn't you ever notice how she was constantly trying to escape?"

"The plaid coat she made Miss Flossy wear for the holidays."

"That matched her holiday apron."

Janet and Bea were howling now, both seeing the same memory.

"Finish the story," Marcus interrupted their laughter. "What happened when the bottle was found missing?"

Janet sobered up a bit, wiping at her eyes. Big exhale.

"Oh, some great brouhaha, I'm sure." Not quite as light as before.

"Mom covered for me," said Bea. "She said she'd taken it to a bridge club. And Eddie went ballistic. He didn't talk to her for a week."

Marcus put his arm around Janet and she tucked her head into his chest.

"It was very sentimental to him," Janet said. "Anyway, who cares? Here's to surviving what you think can't be survived."

Bea sipped. She had totally forgotten that. Janet had stepped right into the line of fire and protected Bea from Eddie's anger.

"Did I ever thank you for that?" asked Bea.

"I'm sure you did," said Janet. "You always had very nice manners."

"I guess somebody raised me right."

They lifted glasses to each other, then sipped. Letting the snap of the fire and the snoring dogs be the only sound for a while.

It took Bea an entire day and night to recover from drinking alcohol. She had never felt so sick in her life as she did the morning she woke up after drinking scotch with Janet and Marcus. The rest of their visit consisted of Bea lying in bed with Janet coming in once in a while to check on her. When they drove out Monday afternoon, Bea was able to stand in the driveway to wave them off.

Her pajama pants tucked into her boots, a parka over the sweatshirt she had been sleeping in. As she walked back into the house, she looked up the hill to the mound. Her heart still ached, but she was able to look at where he was buried. She felt exhausted, her head tinny from the hangover that seemed to never end, but it had ended. A whistle brought the dogs running and she held the door open for them and then kept it open with one foot as she maneuvered an armful of firewood into the house.

Oatmeal, she thought. *I'm going to make a bowl of oatmeal with maple syrup.*

As she ate the oatmeal that also had cinnamon sprinkled on it, she could feel Nana. She pushed back her chair and went to get the beads from where she kept them in her bureau. She set them next to the oatmeal and continued eating. For the past few weeks, she hadn't been able to touch them. She didn't think she would ever be able to touch them again.

Her spoon sat in the half-eaten bowl of oatmeal. Thoughts were still drifting, still puzzling but not like before. It was as if she were waiting for the water to settle so she could see down to the bottom. A ripple of memory. Parvati's bakery. Some flower power people talking big ideas. A woman with long hair parted straight down the middle wearing heavy earrings that pulled her earlobes low. She had said, *nothing is added, nothing is taken away*. And that felt true to Bea. All the elements are still in the ether. We come from stardust. They pulverize our bones, and the elements are still in the earth. The beauty and goodness of the gentle, fierce wisdom of the ancients, will surface again. She doesn't understand how or when, but the feeling of peace fills her and she reaches for the beads.

. . .

Bea looks down to the porch where Paulette is waving a dishtowel. It's the sign that Mona is awake.

Before she goes into the house, Bea stops by the shed, pulls off her baseball cap and runs water from the hose over her head and neck. She walks into Mona's room, toweling off her hair. She ties it up quickly into a topknot. A small fan blows on Mona. Her body is on top of the sheets. Bryan has been putting cold cloths on Mona's feet, wrists, across her forehead. Somehow, Mona doesn't seem to be minding the humidity as much as everyone else. Bea joins Bryan, pulling cloths out of bowls with melted ice, wringing them out then replacing the now warm ones with fresh cool cloths.

Bea remembers calling Mona that spring of her senior year. She wanted to tell her she was going to head west with some guy to San Francisco, but she never got the chance.

"How are things on Planet Chaos?"

"All is calm. Antoine is taking her to some gallery opening or something."

Mona did not like to be alone like Bea did. Being left alone on a Saturday night was sad for her. Lonely. She was fifteen.

"Are you going out tonight?" Mona asked.

"No chance. My exciting Saturday night is studying in a crappy lounge that smells like spilled beer and—"

"You know we'll be there for graduation."

This surprised Bea. She had never imagined. Janet grabbed the phone from Mona.

"Of course," her mother said, all breathy. "How could you think we wouldn't be there for your big day? Of course we will be there."

And they were. In the surging clumps of bodies moving across the lawn, the white nylon gowns unzipped and flapping to reveal crisply pleated chinos or skirts grazing bare legs, the fabric expensive and floral, the legs tanned from tennis or long hours sunbathing on the quad.

Bea stumbled along in a daze of pleasure she had no idea had been waiting for her. Antoine looked handsome and rather European with his cream linen suit, pale blue shirt, collar open, hair slicked back, clean shaven, a moderate amount of good cologne. He seemed wise to the momentariness of his role that he really didn't belong in the family photos and so insisted on being the one to snap Janet with Bea, Bea with Mona and then the three of them together.

As they made their way to the parking lot, her diploma in its navy leather folder in one hand, Bea could see how she looked to others. This was her family. And after years crossing these same lawns in thick snow, late nights and rainy afternoons, always feeling so alone, being part of this little unit that she hadn't even realized she belonged to made her smile and wave to the other graduates in white gowns who, for the moment, were just like her. The experience of belonging, of being part of something bigger than herself swept her up in its comfort, and she had to keep checking in because the feeling was so utterly unknown to her and like nothing she had ever imagined.

Janet looked young and vibrant in comparison to the other mothers. She got lots of looks. Her wrap dress both appropriate for a gathering of WASPS, but also setting her apart as the kind of woman you notice for her style.

Mona, wearing a blue and white sheath that had a very tight fit and narrow skirt, had trouble walking across the lawn because her knees were held close by the dress fabric but also because she was wearing shoes with heels that plunged into the grass with every step. She didn't seem to mind. She was the party hostess for the day. She had planned everything. Janet had let her and Bea was startled by how it made her feel to have such a focus on her, to be so clearly seen and understood, to have anyone take pains to make plans, luncheon, place for a walk and picnic, gifts, so much thought. So much love.

. . .

"I can smell it," says Mona, delighted that a part of her is still working. Bea has gathered a posy of lily of the valley for her. She sets it into a glass of water next to the bed. The bright green stalks, the simple perfection of the cascading white bonnets. Mona absorbs every bit of their beauty.

Les muguets, she says.

Bryan gets up and takes his break in the kitchen.

Bea strokes the cool cloths over Mona's feet, up her calves, down her shins.

"Ellen told me," says Mona.

Bea looks up. "Told you what?"

"That's why your realtor is around. You sold this place."

Bea strokes cool cloths over Mona's wrists, up to her shoulder, down along the inside of her elbow.

"Why didn't you tell me? Is it money? You need money? I have money. You are gonna get all my money. Is it because of money?"

Tears are slipping down Mona's cheeks. Bea presses the button for the head of the bed to lift up so Mona is more upright. She helps Mona blow her nose.

"I lied to you," says Mona.

Bea looks up, pauses. Unsure what the reveal is about to be.

"I did want to come here. I knew you would take care of me. I wanted you to take care of me. I knew you could make me feel safe."

"In a junk shop by the side of the road?"

"I was an idiot. I want to live here. I want the dogs and the pigs and Ginny and Paulette fighting in the kitchen and people going crazy in Waco and Linda Ronstadt singing and flowers from the garden that smell so good. I want it all. You can't let it go. Tell them you changed your mind."

Bea walks over to the window and touches the seedlings that won't be planted by her.

"I'm not cut out for this," she tells Mona. "I thought I was. I wanted to be, but it's hard. It takes a different kind of person. Plus, I was on my own. It's too much for one person."

"Hire someone—"

"I did. I brought Giusita and Diogo on to help me, but it turns out they are the right ones for this. They are gonna be able to make it all I wasn't able to—"

"But you could stay if they're here."

"I can always come back and visit. It's not like Janet leaving," says Bea.

"But you built it. You have a home and friends. How can you leave this?"

"It's not what it looks like. It's time for me to go."

"Where will you go? What are you going to do?"

"I'm not sure."

"What do you mean you don't know?"

"I haven't figured it out yet."

"Stop it. Stop it." Not having a plan causes Mona's tears to shift into sobs.

The sky suddenly goes black.

"It's getting dark," Mona cries out. "Everything is getting so dark. Am I dying?"

"No sweetie," Bea says. "Look out the window. We've got a storm."

Bea goes to close the windows that are wide open, the long white curtains swelling wildly in and out like a wave of surf. Mona stops her.

"No, please. Leave them open."

"The rain will come in."

"I don't care. This is amazing. Isn't this amazing?" The energy of the storm has stopped her tears.

The curtains begin whipping and twisting. Water splatters on window sills, the floor. Spray is carried on the wind. Bea watches as Mona lifts her face to it, eyes open. Lightning snaps, causing Mona to jump.

"You okay?" Bea asks.

Mona nods. The thunder rolls and cracks. It is violent and right to the edge of scary, but Mona doesn't look frightened at all. If she could lift her arms over her head and squeal like she was on a rollercoaster, she would.

The eye of the storm is on them now. Hard thunder is tremendous and skull splitting, cracking right on top of their heads. The sun has been obliterated from view. Tree branches are wrenched up and down and swung about.

"Does it hurt them?"

"No," says Bea. "Remember when the physical therapist lifted your legs for you and moved them about to open up the joints and soften you up? I think of it like that."

Mona pulls her gaze from the window for one full moment to look at Bea.

She is so weird.

Then she is back to letting the storm crash through the window. Branches getting their joints rotated and massaged. Mona was always scared of storms. She would never have actively sought one out, but in this moment she looks like a delighted child. Mouth open, squealing and cringing, pulling the edge of her sheet to her mouth when it cracks, settling her hands back to her swollen abdomen waiting for the next one. Enchanted, frightened and loving it.

Bea sends a silent thank you to the heavens that it is more like a summer storm, not too violent, not too harsh, just to the edge enough to give her some shivers but nothing too awful and then, as fast as it arrived, it is gone.

The wind drops. The sky begins to clear. Birds call out with chatter and evening song. Thunder is in the distance now, a muffled thumping from far away.

Mona sinks back onto her pillow. Radiant.

"What bird is making that sound?" she asks.

"A robin."

"Really? It's so pretty. I thought robins were ordinary."

"I love robins," says Bea. She rubs a towel in circles across the floor with her foot to soak up some of the water. With another dry towel, she wipes down the bureau.

"The color of their breast. It's an orange gold that defies description. Their independence. You know they won't eat from feeders. I love their posture. The blue of their eggs. That shade of blue—"

Mona isn't listening. She is drifting. Her face is still wet from the storm. The thin skin stretched taut against the bones of her forehead, cheekbones, nose, transparent like the rice paper wraps of a fresh spring roll that let you see through to the lettuce, rice noodles and julienned carrot underneath. Bea is immediately embarrassed by thinking such a thing and reaches out with a soft facecloth to wipe Mona's face dry, but Mona stops her.

"Don't. I want to keep feeling it."

Bea sits next to the bed, hands in her lap.

"Wasn't that amazing?" Mona is still looking out the window. "How have I never experienced a storm before?"

Bea watches her lying in bed, her knees loose, her wrists relaxed. Her small chin pointed toward the curtains now gently puffing in and out. Outside the window, the sky is four shades of blue and filled with white clouds whose curves are outlined in pink and gold.

"Look," says Mona. "Isn't it beautiful?" Her voice softens, "It's so beautiful."

Bea nods.

Her eyes not on the window but on her sister's face that is beaming, wet, tender.

> *"The unread story is not a story;*
> *it is little black marks on wood pulp.*
> *The reader, reading it, makes it alive:*
> *a live thing, a story."*
>
> —Ursula Le Guin

Acknowledgments

I am most beholden to the following people for all their love and support as I wrote this book.

First up, the Baronesses who walked alongside of me every step of the way and whose friendship is the world to me: **Karen Stevens, Jeanne Bernardin** and **Samantha May Lamb**.

My Silver Cloud Sister, **Autumn Fussell**, who just gets me—and god, does that feel good, but who is also the best partner in absolute silliness, big ideas, small moments, and finding the way through this crazy world with light and artistry.

Luigi Boccia and **Jared Flood**, *hermanos*. Two of the most heart-centered, wonderful men in this world who have scaled mountains with me and, who show me what a life lived with integrity, originality and courage looks like. I am so grateful that we get to be in this lifetime together.

The biggest shout out to all the makers, dancers, poets, painters and wild hearts of the Squam community whose active collaboration in the creation of Squam Art Workshops has been one of the greatest joys of my life and what gave me the confidence to find my voice. In particular, I want to thank my spirit guide and mentor, sister from another planet and all around sacred witch of the woods, **Terri Dautcher**. And, biggest love and gratitude to the graceful woodland fairy, queen of the willow, **Meg Fussell** who said YES to it all (because she is a warrior like that).

Squam sisters who have nurtured me with friendship, loyalty, love and kindness: **Mindy Tsonas, Susannah Conway, Tory Williams, Tracey Gatlin, Giusita Michelle Vitale, Donna Wynn, Colleen Attara, Anne-Marie Gallant, Gerri Smalley, Terri Simonds, Amy Gretchen Maher, Tracey Williams, Asya Palatova, Harriet Goodall, Joy Fairclough, Em Falconbridge** and **Page Sargisson.**

To **Dave MacCrellish,** a grateful heart for walking the road less traveled with me. Forever gratitude to my sister-in-law **Evelyn Duvivier** and my brother **Marc,** who so generously kickstarted the life change that got me on this path.

À **Dominique Fortin,** qui est si douée, gentille et généreuse! Je vous dois la lune. Merci mille fois. Merci à **Ondine** for the little note between sisters and to **Kylie Maxie** for her copyediting mojo.

To each of the intrepid spirits who have joined me for the Magic of Myth and Into the Mystic offerings, you have no idea how much your presence in my life has meant or how grateful I am to each of you for all that you have taught me and for taking that journey with me.

To **Tara Murphy,** my best friend of thirty-one years and counting—girlfriend, it might have taken a while but never doubt the power of wishes made in the Lorelei lounge!

Douce, Jack, Oliver, Henry, Daisy and **Remy.** Angels, all. If I believe in magic, and I do, it's because each of you came into my life.

Lastly, a note to my nieces **Lauren Elizabeth Olaksen** and **Katherine Duvivier Olaksen.** Kate and Lolo, when you came into this world, you saved my life. It's that simple. I am so glad we get to be friends. *love always, Auntie Beth*

Elizabeth Duvivier
Squam Lake, September 2013

photo credit: Tory Williams